I0780755

The Viscount Needs a Wife

ALL FOR LOVE
BOOK 2

WREN ST. CLAIRE

© Copyright 2025 by Wren St. Claire
Text by Wren St. Claire
Cover by The Swoonies – theswoonies.com

Dragonblade Publishing, Inc. is an imprint of Kathryn Le Veque Novels, Inc.
P.O. Box 23
Moreno Valley, CA 92556
ceo@dragonbladepublishing.com

Produced in the United States of America

First Edition October 2025
Trade Paperback Edition

Reproduction of any kind except where it pertains to short quotes in relation to advertising or promotion is strictly prohibited.

All Rights Reserved.

The characters and events portrayed in this book are fictitious. Any similarity to real persons, living or dead, is purely coincidental and not intended by the author.

AI Statement: No AI or ghostwriting was used in the creation of this story, or any story, published by Dragonblade Publishing. All text, structure, content, ideas, and concept are 100% human generated solely by the author whose name appears on the cover. It is prohibited to use this material, or any copyrighted material, for AI engine training.

ARE YOU SIGNED UP FOR DRAGONBLADE'S BLOG?

You'll get the latest news and information on exclusive giveaways, exclusive excerpts, coming releases, sales, free books, cover reveals and more.

Check out our complete list of authors, too!

No spam, no junk. That's a promise!

Sign Up Here

www.dragonbladepublishing.com

Dearest Reader;

Thank you for your support of a small press. At Dragonblade Publishing, we strive to bring you the highest quality Historical Romance from some of the best authors in the business. Without your support, there is no 'us', so we sincerely hope you adore these stories and find some new favorite authors along the way.

Happy Reading!

CEO, Dragonblade Publishing

ADDITIONAL DRAGONBLADE BOOKS BY
AUTHOR WREN ST. CLAIRE

All for Love Series
An Inconvenient Marriage (Book 1)
The Viscount Needs a Wife (Book 2)

Dedication

This one is for my dad, the wisest, kindest, most patient and gentle, yet strong man I have ever known.

Donald Leonard Simpson
22nd December 1918 – 13th January 2021

Prologue

14th May 1790

My name is Nicolas Benedict Redmayne, and I have lost ten months of my life.

I was thrown from my phaeton, apparently as I was returning to my father's country seat in Lincolnshire on the 12th of March 1790, presumably to attend my mother's funeral. I say apparently and presumably because I can recall nothing of my purpose or intention prior to this event, as I sustained a severe head injury in the accident and was insensible for some time. Fortunately for me, I was near enough to my ancestral home to be recognized, and I was transported there to recover my senses.

Unfortunately, I have not been able to recall a single damned thing about my life from the ten months prior to the accident. The last thing I remember from May 1789, is leaving my London residence in Ryder Street, with what intention I do not know. I remember distinctly mounting my phaeton to the driver's seat, dressed for a journey in an overcoat and tricorn. My luggage was affixed to the boot of the vehicle, and I was traveling alone. It seemed that for this journey, I was taking neither groom nor valet with me. Where I was bound I cannot for the life of me recall, and it was the last that any of my staff or my family saw of me until I apparently reappeared on the 12th of March just outside of Spalding, lying on the side of the road beside my vehicle.

I am keeping this diary on the advice of my physician, in

the hope that by writing things down, my mind might be persuaded to return my missing memories to me.

Chapter One

8th of August 1818

E MRYS FITZGERALD, VISCOUNT Ashford, surveyed his three
offspring with misgiving.

"We are not going another step until you tell us where we are
bound, Papa!" Miss Lizzie, the eldest at eight years old, was the
instigator of this mini rebellion, and she was regarding her sire
with a minatory eye, her arms akimbo and her feet planted firmly
apart.

He contemplated picking her up and placing her in the carriage, but decided such high-handed tactics would result in
repercussions down the road that he didn't wish to deal with.

"Yes, Papa," agreed Charlotte, or rather Charlie, his second
daughter, crossing her arms and assuming a stubborn expression
in imitation of her sister. Charlie was six and was a miniature of
her mother with strawberry-blonde curls and deep-green eyes, a
resemblance which caused him no small degree of pain. Everyone
predicted she would be the beauty of the family.

Little Ewen regarded his older sisters with bewilderment and
stuck a thumb in his mouth. Ewen was three.

Lizzie and Ewen resembled him more closely, which was a
shame for Lizzie, since he knew he was not handsome, and a
female version of him was unlikely to become a beauty. Not that
such a thing could diminish his love for her one whit, of course.

All three of them had such firm hold of his heart that he would gladly die for them in a blink.

"It is supposed to be a surprise," he protested.

"We don't like surprises," said Lizzie firmly. "Tell us!"

"Very well," he said with an exaggerated sigh. "We are going to The Castle and the Watsons will be there."

Lizzie looked at her sister with a burgeoning smile and whooped. "Yay! Zibby and Emanuel!"

Charlie grinned and said breathlessly, "Japheth and Zeke!" Charlie flung her arms round Emrys's legs and hugged him. He patted her curly head as she looked up at him and said, "Thank you, Papa!"

Unable to resist, he bent down and picked her up. "You're welcome, poppet." He looked at the other two. "Now will you get into the carriage?"

Lizzie nodded enthusiastically and, grabbing Ewen's hand, clambered into the carriage dragging Ewen with her. Hastily Emrys set Charlotte down and picked up Ewen, depositing him on the seat, and helped Charlotte up the steps. With a wave to his coachman, Jacob, he climbed up after the children, and they were at last underway.

They had left his grandmother's house in Bath two days ago, and the girls had pestered him for their destination all the way, speculating on it as they stared out the window and tried to guess their location and direction of travel. That is, until this morning's little rebellion.

Ah, well.

At least the weather was excellent, if hot. It was late July, and the roads were in fine shape. They were making good time, and he expected to reach their destination in Leicestershire by mid-afternoon, the principal seat of his friend the Duke of Troubridge, dubbed The Castle. Though it wasn't actually a castle, as the name was only a romantic carryover from its origins as a Norman keep. Nothing of the original building was left except a few tumbledown walls and a scattering of stones in the grounds.

The Watsons in question were the younger siblings of the duke's new wife, Sarah, who was the eldest of the Vicar of Littledon's brood of eight children. The children had all become acquainted on the occasion of the duke's wedding some four months earlier and had become fast friends. As the carriage rocked its way along the road, Emrys watched his offspring playing a guessing game, trying to identify objects they could see out the window, and was glad for the first bit of joy in what felt like a long time. Though it had truly only been four months since his world fell apart.

He had gone from being—so he'd mistakenly thought—a happily married man, to a cuckold and then a widower in the space of three weeks, and the experience had torn the heart from his chest and left him a wreck of his former self. It was really only his children that had kept him from unravelling.

The last time he left The Castle, after the wedding, it had been only himself and Caro in this carriage. The children had ridden in the second one, a hired vehicle, with the servants. And Caro had been furious with him. Seated opposite to him, the anger had come off her in waves as she stared out the window and refused to look at him, her hands clenched tightly in her lap.

"For God's sake, Caro, you cannot believe there is anything in it!" he'd protested.

"If there was nothing in it, why did the duke feel compelled to give you a black eye?" she'd asked, throwing a scorching glance in his direction.

He'd put up a hand to the swollen purple extrusion forcing his left eye almost shut. It was still giving him a thumping headache.

"Because he's a bloody jealous blackguard, and he overreacted!"

"Language, Ashford!" she'd admonished him, using his title rather than his given name, which she always did when she was annoyed with him.

He'd sighed and closed his other eye, leaning his aching head back against the squabs of the carriage seat.

"And what, pray tell, was he *overreacting* to?" she'd asked sweetly.

"That Sarah gave me a hug," he'd said sullenly.

"Sarah! On mighty intimate terms with the new duchess, are you not?"

"Caro, you know damned well you have been on first name terms with Robert for years. It was made clear we were to address her as Sarah."

"And why was the duchess compelled to hug you?"

"I was upset."

She sniffed. "What could you possibly have to be upset about?"

His self-control snapped at that point, and he'd leaned forward. "Because I found your blasted lover's letter!"

She'd blanched. "I don't know what you're talking about!" But then she'd flushed guiltily, as red as she had been pale moments before.

He'd watched this display of disingenuity with a sick feeling. "How long have you had that letter, and why the bloody hell did you feel compelled to bring it with you on this trip?"

She'd opened and then closed her mouth, her hands wringing in her lap. He didn't miss the tears starting to her eyes, and his heart turned over.

"It's from Greathouse isn't it? I recognized his writing."

She'd swallowed visibly and nodded.

His hand had clenched on his knee. "The prick! He has the gall to pretend to be my friend, and all the while he is sending my wife love letters!"

"He *is* your friend!" she'd protested. "He feels most uncomfortable about it, really!"

"Really?" His sarcastic tone could have cut glass.

"He didn't say anything for a very long time. I had no idea he felt—" She'd stopped then, swallowing and searching in her reticule for a handkerchief, wiping her eyes.

"You should have shown me that damned letter the moment you received it!" he'd said, trying to ignore the effect her tears were having on him. He never could abide it when she cried.

"I know!" she'd said, sobbing freely by then. "You're right. I should have. I'm sorry, Emrys."

"Caro!" He rose and moved to the seat beside her, putting an arm round her and drawing her against his chest. "Don't cry, love. If it's just a letter, I can overlook it. When did he send it?"

"S-six months ago!" she'd said haltingly. A cold feeling settled into the pit of his stomach.

"And you're still carrying it around with you? Why?" He had drawn back.

She covered her face with her hand, sobbing hard. "I'm sorry Emrys! I t-tried! I r-really did! I t-tried to resist . . . but I love him . . . I'm so sorry . . ." she whispered at the last.

He'd closed his eyes as her words hit him like hail, stinging pings against his skin. Unreal and shocking. A numbness spread through his chest where his heart should be. He felt ill.

He had moved back to the other side of the carriage and stared blindly out the window. They said not one word further to each other beyond the necessary and the mundane for the rest of that interminable journey back to London.

Three days later she had moved out of their home in Cavendish Square and three weeks after that she was dead, the result of a carriage accident in France, whence the lovers had fled. Caroline had been thrown clear of the carriage. She'd hit her head on a stone and never regained consciousness. Greathouse had been uninjured beyond a broken wrist. But now he had to live with her death for the rest of his life.

Emrys shook his head to clear it of its melancholy thoughts and drew out the book he had been reading and opened to the page he was up to.

Chapter Two

MISS ANNIS PRINGLE sat up, jerked out of her dream, her skin bathed in a cold sweat, her heart thudding. The tendrils of terror still clung to her like spiders' webs, sending tremors through her slender frame. The images were fading quickly, like will-o-the-wisps, as hard to grasp as water running through her fingers.

She took a deep, shuddering breath. *Why was she having the nightmares again?* She hadn't had them for years now, and suddenly, in the last few months, they were back. *It all started when she began having this notion someone was watching her . . .*

Annis shoved back the bedclothes. It was a warm night. The moonlight coming through the window lit up part of her room, sending the rest into shadow. She shivered, her skin clammy. Her nightgown was damp and clung to her. She rose and went to the jug of cold water on her dresser, poured some into the bowl. Loosening her nightgown, she gave herself a quick sponge down and dried off with the towel. It was the middle of the night—she ought to return to bed, yet the notion sat ill with her. Instead, she lit a candle and curled up in the chair by the empty fireplace with her book until her head was nodding, only then returning to her bed to sleep until dawn. It was becoming a pattern.

Several hours later, rising with a slightly heavy head due to interrupted sleep, Annis was glad of the coffee brought by the maid with her breakfast of toast and eggs. With the house full of guests, the majority of whom were small fry, the responsibility for entertaining them had fallen once more on Annis's shoulders. She ought to complain. She was a governess, not a nanny. Yet she couldn't resist the opportunity to devise educational experiences for them that would also be fun. She had planned a visit to the medieval ruins in the grounds for the afternoon. It would be a good opportunity to combine an outing with a history and literature lesson for all the children. This morning, the younger ones were in the nursery, amusing themselves with the Layne toy collection, which was considerable, overseen by Miss Mary Watson, the eldest of them.

Annis's primary charges were the duke's youngest sisters, Lady Heather, who was sixteen, and Lady Ingrid, thirteen. Lady Ava, the eldest Layne daughter, was out now and no longer under her purview. Though that didn't stop her dropping by the schoolroom to see her former governess, which was gratifying.

Sailing into the schoolroom, Ava wore an elegant and very becoming gown of jonquil muslin dotted with embroidered green leaves, and her hair was very fashionably dressed. The difference one season had made was clear to see. Ava had always been a lively young lady, almost a romp, leading her younger sisters into all manner of cheerful scrapes. She was now poised and elegant. But her eyes still glittered with mischief as she entered the room and embraced her sisters, who left their lessons immediately to pelt her with a dozen questions. Ava and their mother had arrived late last night from London after the girls had gone to bed.

"Ava, tell us about your beaux!" said Ingrid pertly. "Is it true you have had six proposals?"

"Ingrid!" said gentle Heather. "Where did you hear that?"

"Robert told Sarah over breakfast the other morning, I heard him."

"Yes, it's perfectly true," said Ava. "In fact, I have received eight all told. And refused them all!"

"Are they old and ugly?" asked Ingrid frowning.

"No, not all of them, but I haven't met one gentleman I wish to marry yet. Mama is most put out with me. She favors Lord Tavistock, for he is young and handsome and an earl to boot. But I think he has shifty eyes, and I do not trust him."

"Then you should not marry him," said Heather firmly.

"I don't plan to. Robert will not compel me. He says I may have my pick—within reason of course. Though I think he would have his say if my choice fell upon someone wholly ineligible. But I don't mean to disoblige him or Mama. There is no hurry, however. I am only eighteen after all, and I am having by far too much fun." Ava grinned as she smoothed her skirts, and she perched in one of the schoolroom chairs. Her attitude gave the impression, Annis reflected, that she could at any moment dart up and fly about the room like a fairy.

"Have you danced the waltz?" asked Heather.

"Dozens of times! You cannot imagine how wonderful it is to be taken in a man's arms and move gracefully across a ballroom as one."

Annis cleared her throat in warning and Ava colored faintly, but a little smile curved her lips and she said lightly, "Then again, when one's partner is portly and spins you about upon his waistcoat, it is not at all pleasant. So, one must take the good with the bad."

This made the girls giggle, and the noise attracted the attention of Miss Mary Watson, who came to the interconnecting door between the schoolroom and the nursery and gushed, "Lady Ava! How wonderful to see you!"

This prompted a rush from the other children, who all crowded the door for a glimpse of glamorous, pretty Ava. Little Ewen perched on his eldest sister's hip.

Annis allowed the ensuing cacophony for precisely five minutes before calling a halt with a brisk, "That is enough, children!" accompanied by a loud clap of her hands to make sure she was heard over the din.

"Morning tea will be served momentarily. Miss Watson, please see that all hands are washed prior to eating."

"Yes, Miss Pringle," said Mary, blushing with pleasure to be addressed as Miss Watson instead of Miss Mary. Annis was fully alive to Mary's desire to be treated like a young lady. She was the same age as Heather, though somewhat lacking in social poise, due no doubt to her less sophisticated upbringing, as the Watson children were raised in a simple country vicarage. The opulence of the Duke of Troubridge's residence had rather gone to Mary's romantic head. Her older sisters, Ruth and Deborah, had not accompanied them on this trip, so Mary was gallantly assuming the position of leader of the Watson tribe.

Morning tea was served shortly and all eight of the visiting children, five Watsons and three Fitzgeralds, lined up to have their hands inspected by Miss Pringle before falling on the feast of buttered bread, cakes, cheese, and fruit, laid out for them by the servants.

Heather, Ingrid and Ava joined their ranks, none too proud to share in the treat. Annis even allowed herself one small slice of cake and a piece of fruit.

When there was nothing left but orange rinds and crumbs, the children filed back into the nursery, Ava went in search of more adult entertainments, and Annis resumed the morning lesson in mathematics. The duke held liberal views on the education of women, and all his sisters were to receive a thorough grounding in the sciences as well as the arts.

"Do we have to?" whined Ingrid, slumping down in her seat, her blonde curls a wild tangle round her still-round face.

"Yes, we do," said Annis calmly. "This is your list of problems to solve, Ingrid. I expect them done before luncheon," she said, pointing to the list of equations on the righthand side of the chalk board.

"I hate mathematics!" muttered Ingrid. "What use is it anyway?"

"When you are required to manage a household, you will

find it extremely useful. Would you wish unscrupulous persons to dupe you?"

Ingrid's mouth gaped and she flushed. "I would not!"

"Well then, learn mathematics and you will always have the upper hand."

Ingrid bent over her book with a sigh. Heather, who was quietly applying herself to her own list, glanced at Annis with a sympathetic smile. If only all her charges were as sweet and biddable as Heather. With the darkest hair of the three Layne sisters and less spectacular in looks than her elder sister, she had a tendency to fade into the background in company, her shy, retiring nature making her quite self-effacing.

Annis persevered until lunchtime when the midday meal was served in the schoolroom for all the children. Plates were almost empty when the schoolroom door opened, and a shaggy head appeared round it. Viscount Ashford. His eyes roamed the room and found Annis looking at him with a raised eyebrow. He smiled which made his somewhat uneven features light up. Coming into the room, he closed the door with a backward flick of the hand.

He was dressed with extreme casualness, possibly in deference to the heat, in shirtsleeves, an unbuttoned waistcoat, a pair of buff-colored breeches, and scuffed boots. His hair was too long to be fashionable and looked like it needed a comb. He had eschewed a neckcloth altogether, and his shirt was open at the neck. *And a fine neck it was, too!* A solid column with just the hint of hair at the base. Annis flushed faintly at this nakedness, an unexpected wave of awareness of his masculinity hitting her in the solar plexus. His dress was bordering on improper, but he seemed blissfully unaware of it.

"Miss Pringle, I understand you have an outing planned for this afternoon?"

"I do, my lord," she said, rising from her place at the trestle table and attempting to cover her momentary discomposure, slightly shocked at her own visceral reaction. "I am taking the children to see the ruins."

"Then you will require an escort. Can't send you out with a whole detachment of infantry and no accompanying officer," he said with a grin.

She smiled back at his military analogy. Really, he might dress like a shag rug, but he was charming when he wanted to be. And it was kind of him to offer to help. Suddenly this afternoon's outing seemed more fun and less of a chore. Not that she minded looking after the children, of course. "Thank you, yes. That would be welcome."

"Good. I'll see you downstairs in half an hour, shall I?"

"Papa!" Little Charlotte tugged at her father's sleeve.

"Yes, poppet?" he said crouching down to her level.

"Look!" she held out a drawing. "This is for you!"

"Thank you, sweetheart." His face softened as his eyes took in the stick figures in the picture.

"It's a family portrait," said Charlotte seriously. "See? You,"—she pointed to the biggest figure—"Mama,"—a figure with long red hair—"and Lizzie, me, and Ewen." Three smaller figures. The viscount's face twisted, and he kissed the little girl on her reddish-blonde curls. "Thank you, darling, I'll put it up in my room." She smiled and gave him a hug.

He hugged her back with one arm while he held the drawing in his other hand, then straightened and watched her climb back into her chair to resume her dinner. Lizzie waved at him as she stuffed something in her mouth and Ewen watched him with big eyes as he chewed on a piece of cheese. He waved back at Lizzie with a lopsided grin and stroked Ewen's untidy mop of brown curls.

The viscount cleared his throat and made an attempt to hide his obvious emotion. Annis's heart contracted for the poor man.

She had met him on many occasions, as he was a frequent visitor to The Castle, but they'd had little opportunity to actually speak of anything beyond the commonplace. Her position had kept her mostly confined to the schoolroom over the last several years, and it was only now, as the girls were older, that she and they had been invited to attend evening meals with the family and their guests. It was only during the recent wedding festivities that they'd had occasion to converse a little, and all of that had been related to his offspring, whose charge had fallen on her shoulders at the time.

He was not precisely a handsome man, although he was well proportioned, being just under six feet in height and broad through the shoulders. She had remembered him being a trifle stout on previous occasions, but he seemed to have shed those extra pounds more recently, and he wore an air of lean hunger about him that was strangely compelling. There was a weariness to his eyes also that spoke of the suffering he had endured in the past few months. No one at The Castle could remain in ignorance of the tragedy that had befallen him. Annis's soft heart was wrung by the cruelty of fate. To lose a beloved wife in such a way.

"I will see you shortly, Miss Pringle," he said with a nod and left the room, the drawing still clutched in one hand.

After the meal, Annis assembled her noisy troops downstairs in the entrance hall. The viscount ambled slowly down the stairs while she was counting heads. Despite his earlier emotion, he appeared cheerful enough now, as he smiled at her lazily and immediately took charge of his son, who was too young to walk to the ruins under his own power.

"Miss Pringle, are all the troops assembled?" he asked.

"They are, my lord."

"Excellent. Company, right foot forward, out the door in pairs, please," he instructed. "And wait for myself and Miss Pringle by the fountain, understood?"

"Yes sir," responded the children in unison.

Annis glanced at her regular pupils who were smiling at this display of orderliness from their guests. Heather and Ingrid stood at the back of the line. At the front were the two youngest Watson boys, Japheth and Ezekiel, behind them came the Fitzgerald girls, Elizabeth and Charlotte, then the Watson twins, Hepzibah and Emanuel, then bringing up the rear, Mary, Ingrid and Heather. Ingrid inched forward to walk with Hepzibah who was closer to her in age, and Mary and Heather naturally fell in together.

Annis adjusted her bonnet and followed the viscount down the front steps and across the gravel driveway to the large fountain forming a roundabout in the center of the approach to the house.

"I think we should lead from the front, don't you, Miss Pringle?" asked the viscount.

She nodded. "As you wish, my lord."

He waved at Heather and Mary. "Girls, alert us if anyone is having trouble keeping up!"

Heather acknowledged the instruction, and the cavalcade set off for the ruins which were situated to the right of the current building beyond the front lawn, flanking the eastern wing of the house.

It was a fine, sunny day, warm as the previous several days had been, with a light breeze to temper the worst of the heat. Two servants had also been instructed to follow in an hour with refreshments and blankets for the company when they reached their destination. It promised to be a completely enjoyable afternoon.

"What other delights have you planned for the children's entertainment during this visit, Miss Pringle?" asked the viscount juggling his son up onto his shoulders.

"A mock battle on the south lawn, a treasure hunt in the woods, a game of hide-and-seek in the rose garden, and a picnic by the lake. That will at least keep them busy until the end of the week. And will give me time to come up with some more ideas." She picked her way across the gravel, feeling it even through the soles of her kid boots.

"You have an ingenious imagination, Miss Pringle. I could wish I were a boy again to enjoy your entertainments," he said, putting out a hand to help her down a shallow set of steps. The touch of his hand was warm and somehow comforting. The governess was seldom the recipient of the courtesies shown automatically to a lady of birth.

"You're very welcome to participate, my lord, there is nothing children enjoy more than having their adults spend time with them on their adventures."

"Very true, Miss Pringle. As a boy I loved it when my father made the time to play soldiers with me." The viscount waved away an insect.

"You are fortunate, my lord. Not many men of the upper classes deign to spend time with their children." She glanced at his profile and decided that it might be his best angle. He had a rather elegant nose.

"No. That is why I try to spend as much time as I can with mine. It's a precious period and doesn't last long."

"Papa!" interrupted Ewen, his little hands grasping his father's hair and tugging to get his attention. "Look, the roons!"

"So, it is Ewen," said his lordship, wincing and extracting locks of hair from his offspring's fists.

The "roons," or ruins, were the remains of the Norman and medieval keep from which The Castle took its name. There was a crumbling wall and tumbledown tower that showed a stone staircase, just over six feet in height, on one exposed side. Plus, a collection of half-submerged moss and creeper-covered stones—obviously parts of the original structure that had fallen and remained where they lay—were scattered about. The approach dipped and then rose in a half circle before the structure—the remnant of a filled in moat, Annis surmised, based on her reading of the hopelessly out of proportion sketch of the original building plan that she had found in the duke's library. The viscount again offered his hand to Annis to assist her in negotiating the uneven ground. She was glad of her stout kid boots as well as his hand.

"Thank you, my lord," she said as they gained even ground again.

The children ran at the dip, racing down one side and up the other with a whoop of delight. Heather and Mary, mindful of their dignity, traversed it at a slower pace. When they were all assembled, Annis commenced her history lesson, conscious of the viscount sitting casually on the wall with young Ewen beside him, listening attentively. She noticed he had given Ewen his fob watch to play with as a distraction. His daughters hung about him, little Charlotte leaning against his legs and Elizabeth holding his hand. Given what they had been through, losing their mother in such a tragic way, it was no wonder they stuck close to their father.

"Can anyone tell me what these stones represent?" she asked.

Hepzibah put her hand straight up. "They are the remains of the old castle," she said.

"That is right. Can anyone tell me how old they are?"

"As old as Stonehenge?" suggested Japheth.

"No, not that old."

"I know," said Ingrid wearily. "As old as the Conquest—1066. Our ancestor was given the land by William."

"Very good, Ingrid, I'm glad you were paying attention."

Annis went on to elaborate on the Norman Conquest and what it meant for the formation of England. For the girls she spoke of the Bayeaux Tapestry and its record of the events leading up to the Battle of Hastings, adding a few details of the battle for the benefit of the boys.

Emanuel interrupted at this point to say, "The duke told us about his ancestor who fought for William in the battle."

"When did you hear that?" asked Ingrid, inclined to be proprietorial about her brother's stories.

"When he brought Sarah home before the wedding," said Mary.

Annis went on with the lesson, talking about what it was like to live in a castle and why they were built.

"What did it look like? When it was new?" asked Mary.

"It had four towers, one on each corner. This is the only one left." Annis gestured behind her. "There were curtain walls between the towers enclosing a courtyard, and there would have been a big portcullis gate cut into one of the walls. And the whole structure was surrounded by a moat."

"What is a portcullis?" asked Ezekiel.

"An iron grid with spikes that could be dropped down to block the entrance and chop off the heads of the enemy!" said his elder brother, Emanuel, with bloodthirsty relish.

A collective *ooh* went up from the children and Annis judged that was enough history for one day. "You may take a look around, but stay in pairs and don't wander too far away. The servants will be here shortly with the refreshments."

"And no climbing the tower," said the viscount with a significant look at the Watson boys, who groaned at this curtailment of their fun.

"Why not?" said Japheth, inclined to argue.

"Because you may slip and fall and I've no mind to carry your broken body back to the house," said the viscount with brutal frankness. "The stones are old, and the masonry no longer sound. They may crumble at any moment—especially with young boys clambering all over them."

Mary unexpectedly entered the lists at this point and said, "Papa would say the same, you know he would." This seemed to exercise a powerful effect on the young Watson males, and they scampered off to explore the ruins at ground level. Elizabeth and Charlotte followed, linking up with their favorite Watsons.

"You have obviously done some research Miss Pringle," the viscount said, falling into step beside her as she walked in a slow circumnavigation of the ruins, his young master once more installed upon his shoulders.

She smiled up at him using her hand to shade the sun from her eyes, as the angle was wrong for her bonnet to stop it. "Yes, I found some early records in the duke's library."

"Have you uncovered any hoary legends about the place?"

"No, unfortunately. The children would love that."

"You could always make something up."

"I don't believe my imagination will stretch that far, my

lord."

"You read novels, surely?"

"I do," she admitted. "But I lack the skill to make stories out of nothing."

He waved at the tower and surrounds. "This is not nothing, Miss Pringle. There is history here, heartache, romance, tragedy . . . if these stones could only speak."

"I believe you're a romantic, my lord."

He smiled, a shade wistfully she thought. "I was once."

Guessing that he alluded to his loss, she laid a sympathetic hand on his arm. Her gaze caught and held his for a moment. His eyes were hazel green, she registered with a mild shock, a deep moss green at this moment. Their intensity stirred something in her, and she had the oddest sensation of heat rising in her chest.

"Papa!" said Elizabeth, appearing breathlessly in front of the viscount. "You must come and see! The boys have found something!" She tugged at his hand.

"Can Miss Pringle come, too?" he asked, casting a sideways look at Annis, a half-smile on his face.

"Yes, yes!" said Elizabeth rounding the tower wall and leading them toward a gnarled old tree leaning at a perilous angle, perched on top of a distinct mound covered in ground creeper, around which the children were clustered. She could see Emanuel, Japheth, and Ezekiel were down on their knees scraping at the earth with sticks.

"What have you found, boys?" asked the viscount, lifting Ewen from his shoulders and crouching down beside them. Ewen crept in, squatting next to him.

Emanuel glanced round, his face red with perspiration, a smudge of dirt on one cheek. He sat back on his heels so that the viscount could see, and Annis craned her neck for a view of what they had uncovered.

Some old, pitted stone was visible, partially exposed by their scraping the earth away from it. The part that was revealed had a curved edge and appeared to carry some markings, though she wasn't close enough to decipher what they were.

"What do you think it might be?" asked Emanuel.

The viscount looked up and beckoned Annis forward. "Miss Pringle?" he asked. Japheth and Ezekiel shuffled sideways to allow her better access, and she crouched down beside the viscount and put out a hand to touch the roughly pitted surface of the rock. It was cold and damp to the touch, a dull grey, coarse stone, but obviously carved.

"Hard to tell," she said slowly. "But perhaps part of a Celtic Cross? Or a gravestone marker? It was likely upright at some point and has fallen and been buried."

Emanuel's eyes lit up and he said, "Someone might be buried here?"

"It's possible," said Annis.

"Shall we uncover it?" he asked, addressing the viscount.

His lordship grinned. "Of course. The duke will want to know about this, I am sure. Here, let me help."

The viscount found a stout stick and set to helping the boys uncover the stone while the girls crowded round for a view of the buried treasure.

It took them ten minutes of industrious digging and scraping to reveal the whole of the stone. Annis was excited to see that her guess of a Celtic cross was correct. It was incomplete, being only the upper half of a cross. The lower extremity had clearly been broken with a diagonal crack sometime in its history, answering the question as to why it was lying flat on its back instead of standing upright.

As the viscount worked to clear the dirt from the markings, the intricate scrollwork was revealed and within it some clumsily marked letters, possibly in Latin.

"This must be late Roman, I think. I wish my Latin was better, I might be able to read it." she said in frustration. "My lord, can you read it?" she asked.

He bent over the inscription running his fingers over it. Some of the letters were very faint or missing altogether.

"I can't read the name, I think it has been partially erased, but this bit is *hic iacit*, which means 'lies here,' and this is *filis*—'son of.' Again the name has been damaged. So, this is the burial stone of some fellow, but I can't tell you who."

"Is the grave here then?" asked Emanuel.

The viscount shrugged. "It may be, but then this could have just been tossed here, given that the base has been lost."

"Can we dig and find out?" pressed Emanuel.

"Not today. We will need shovels, not sticks. And in any case, we will need the duke's permission to start digging up his grounds."

Emanuel looked disappointed but accepted the viscount's dictum.

The servants appeared just then, and they all left the interesting find to have refreshments and sit under the trees out of the sun.

Chapter Three

T HE FIND OF the Celtic cross formed a subject of conversation over dinner that night, Emrys raising it with the duke.

"The boys are keen to dig and see if there is a grave underneath it. It may predate the Keep by five hundred years or more according to Miss Pringle," he said, nodding to her down the table. "Are you amenable to digging it up, Robert?"

"I don't see why not. I'll write to Aberdeen of the Antiquities Council about it. If you've found something of note he'll want it recorded. You say you couldn't make out the names?"

"No, they appeared to have been damaged."

"*Damnatio memoriae,*" remarked the duke cutting into his beef.

"Yes, very likely. Wonder who he upset, poor fellow," said Emrys.

The conversation passed to other matters, and at the end of the meal the ladies withdrew, leaving himself and Robert to enjoy a port or two.

"How are you bearing up?" asked Robert when the servants finally left them alone.

Emrys shrugged, "Well enough." He toyed with his glass.

"If there is anything I can do . . ." said the duke awkwardly.

"Thank you, but there is nothing."

An uncomfortable silence fell, and Robert tried again. "Sarah says she may have found a nanny for you . . ."

"Yes, she mentioned. The woman is coming at the end of the week. I've tried several, but the girls haven't liked them."

"It must be difficult. How are they?"

"Up and down. They have good days and bad. It helps having playmates. It was a good notion to invite the Watson tribe." He sipped the port.

"You've lost weight—Sarah remarked on it."

Emrys smiled ruefully. "Well, that's one good thing to come out of this."

"I'm sorry, Emrys," said Robert quietly. "I can't imagine what you've been through."

Emrys shook his head. "I know. Sometimes it feels like a nightmare, and I'll wake up one morning and everything will be back the way it was. But then each day it becomes more and more obvious that it won't." He sighed and rubbed his face.

"Do you want to join the ladies?"

"Aye, why not?" He tossed off the rest of his port and rose, straightening his jacket. His damned neckcloth felt too tight. This wretched heat didn't agree with him.

He was still fiddling with it as the duke held the door for him as he stepped into the drawing room. There was no fire—the doors stood open to the gardens, letting a cool breeze into the room—and the ladies were scattered about the room on sofas. Lady Heather and Miss Mary Watson were bent over a book, Lady Ava paced restlessly before the open windows, Sarah, and dowager duchess talked quietly, and Miss Pringle, by herself, engaged in some needlework under the light of a candelabra on the table beside her.

She was dressed neatly in a plain, dark-blue muslin, with a white shawl draped round her shoulders. The gown had a modest neckline, and her only jewelry was a seed pearl brooch, fixed to the center of her bosom. The placement drew his eyes inexplicably to the swell of her breasts outlined by the plain navy ribbon running beneath them. He recalled the moment she had placed her hand upon his arm this afternoon in wordless sympathy and a sudden restless surge of heat disturbed his equilibrium.

He averted his eyes from her in confusion, hoping that the faint flush in his cheeks went unnoticed by the company.

Ava turned at their entrance and pounced on her brother. "Robert! Some entertainment please—country life is insupportable! I have become overly spoiled by my London season. What do you suggest we do?"

"We could play cards," suggested Sarah. "There are eight of us, two tables of Whist?"

The duke glanced at him. "You amenable, Emrys?"

"Why not?" he said with a shrug.

In a few minutes, tables and chairs were assembled, two decks of cards produced, and candelabra situated to give adequate light to the players. Emrys found himself paired with Miss Pringle against Lady Ava and the dowager duchess. Since both the duchess and Lady Ava were fiercely competitive, it became quickly obvious that he needed to pay attention. To his surprise, Miss Pringle proved an astute player, and he kept his gaze away from that disturbing brooch, or rather its disturbing location. Surprisingly, the game jerked him out of his fit of melancholy. It was impossible to remain melancholy in Lady Ava's presence he discovered. The young lady's vivacious spirits refused to allow it.

"Mama, what were you thinking? I was counting on you to trump Lord Ashford's wretched king!" she exclaimed in the last round.

"I'm sorry, my dear. I had nothing else to play!"

"You must allow us another game to be avenged upon you, Lord Ashford," said Ava gathering up the cards.

"What say you, Miss Pringle? Should we assay another game or quit while we're ahead?"

"One more game, then Heather and Ingrid must retire, and me with them," she said.

"Oh, you cannot leave before the tea tray comes!" exclaimed

Ava.

"Only if the duke permits," said Miss Pringle firmly.

They played one more hand and Ava and the dowager were victorious. The tea tray arrived on the heels of the game, and Miss Pringle and the girls stayed to partake of tea before she whisked them away to bed.

The dowager yawned and left them soon after, so that it was just himself, the Lady Ava, and the duke and duchess. Ava, still bubbling with energy, then demanded that her brother play while she sang. She had a lovely voice and the ballad she chose was stirring, a tale of a young maid's lost love. He found himself with a lump in his throat. He was altogether too vulnerable to melancholy at present.

The duke then put him to the blush by saying in heartening accents, "Ava, you play while Emrys treats us to his voice."

"Oh yes, please do, Lord Ashford," said Ava with a wide smile, taking her place at the instrument. He reluctantly joined her, and they found a tune they both knew. Ava smiled up at him and casually touched his hand with hers, which made him freeze in alarm. *Lady Ava could not be flirting with him, could she?* He straightened, acutely uncomfortable, and cleared his throat.

He sang the song but refused to be drawn into singing more and retired to a single chair as far away from Ava as possible. He just hoped Robert hadn't noticed. He would have his guts for garters if he suspected Emrys of any intentions in that direction, and he wouldn't blame him. Not that he *had* any intentions. Ava was a pretty girl and lively as a sparrow, but even if she hadn't been Robert's sister, he was emphatically not interested in pursuing any woman at present. He doubted very much if he would ever do so again. His heart was shattered, and his sense of trust broken.

He retired to bed soon after that and found his valet, Felton, in his room waiting for him. Felton was annoyed with him, which was nothing new, but the man was too well-trained to show it openly.

"Do you require a nightshirt, my lord?"

"No, thank you. It's too hot. You don't need to linger, Felton. I can undress myself."

Felton bowed precisely and said with offended dignity, "If you would allow me to have that waistcoat, my lord, it has an indelible stain."

"What stain?" Emrys looked down at his waistcoat. "Oh that. I hadn't noticed."

"No, my lord." Felton said with feeling and moved to take the waistcoat off him as Emrys undid the buttons. Sliding it off his shoulders he continued, "If your lordship permits, I will repurpose this garment as it is not fit to be worn. If I'd known you proposed to *wear* it—"

"It's my favorite waistcoat," protested Emrys.

"That's as maybe, my lord, but the ink stain won't come out. I have tried every weapon in my arsenal, and nothing will budge it."

Emrys sighed. "I'm a sore trial to you, aren't I? Why do you stay?"

Felton took the offending waistcoat, folding it carefully. "I live in hope, my lord."

"Of what? Me suddenly turning into a dandy?" Emrys grinned. "Not until hell freezes over, my friend." He loosened his neckcloth and ripped it off, heaving a sigh of relief.

"Not a dandy, my lord," said Felton, with all signs of revulsion.

"Of what then?" asked Emrys, pulling his shirt over his head.

"If my lord would just permit me to shine your boots occasionally?" begged Felton.

Emrys shrugged, unbuttoning his breeches. "If you insist, but it's not necessary."

"It is, my lord, very necessary," said Felton feelingly, taking each item of clothing Emrys carelessly tossed onto the floor and folding them up carefully into a pile.

Emrys turned to the water bowl and began to give himself a

quick wash. He ran his hand over his chin, encountering the scritch of bristles. He probably should have a shave in the morning.

"That really will be all. Thank you, Felton," he said with a smile, as the man gathered up the pile of clothing and gave him a correct little bow.

"Good night, my lord."

He left, and Emrys dried himself off and crawled beneath the sheets. It was too hot for much in the way of coverings, and he always slept naked anyway, which seemed to offend Felton's delicate sensibilities. He would insist on asking if Emrys wanted a night shirt, when the man knew he didn't wear them unless it was very cold or he was ill.

He tried to settle himself, but sleep eluded him, and he lay staring up at the large fourposter's canopy, vaguely visible in the still burning light of the bedside candle. He should get out his book if he couldn't sleep—it was better than letting the thoughts come. Surprisingly, however, his mind wandered to the day's events instead of the dark channels they had been occupying of late. It had been an interesting day and more enjoyable than he had expected.

When he had volunteered to help Miss Pringle, it was from a sense of obligation. The poor woman was saddled with all these children to look after, and it was partly his fault. The least he could do was bear her company with them. That her company had proven so pleasant was a bonus he hadn't looked for.

He recalled that strategically placed brooch in the center of her bosom and the unaccustomed flush of heat that had accompanied it. Embarrassment made his cheeks burn. He should not think of the governess like that. She was a lady and deserved his utmost respect. What ailed him? He hadn't entertained lewd thoughts of any woman since Caro had destroyed his world.

He sat up and reached for his book, determined to think no more disturbing thoughts about the governess—or any other woman, for that matter.

Chapter Four

10th July 1790

My headaches continue, I am tired and listless, and my concentration continues to be poor since the accident. My missing memories also continue to elude me. I think I dream them sometimes, but when I wake, the dreams evaporate like mist before I can capture them. It is very frustrating.

My father is pressuring me about an alliance with the Godfrey family. He has been friends with the Earl of Grenville since they were at school together and nothing would give him greater pleasure, so he tells me, than to see the two houses united.

Lady Damaris Godfrey is a well enough looking girl, she has nice manners, there is nothing in her appearance or demeanor to repel, and yet I cannot muster an inclination.

If I am honest, I do not care. I must marry someone, I suppose. I am eight and twenty. The earldom needs an heir if the name is to be carried on, for I have no brothers and am unlikely to at this late stage. My mother is gone, and father is showing no signs of wanting to replace her.

I know not the source of my reluctance, unless it is this damned lethargy that dogs me. I have no appetite for anything much these days. I am not myself. I wonder if I ever will be again.

I am forced to conclude that father is right. To continue in this fashion is unacceptable. I need to be getting on with my life. I shall offer for Lady Damaris. It will keep my father happy, if nothing else.

It is the least I can do for giving him such a fright. My disappearance was hard on him. It turns out that we had some difference of opinion prior to it, though my father refuses to discuss the subject of the disagreement. He says what is done is done, and he will not revisit it.

Chapter Five

EMRYS DESCENDED FROM the barouche and turned to hand his ladies down onto the pavement. First Lady Ava, then her sister Lady Heather, Miss Mary Watson, and lastly Miss Pringle. He had spent the carriage ride to the village with his knees virtually touching Miss Pringle's and trying to avoid looking at her. She was wearing that damned brooch again, and he was acutely aware of its situation in a most disturbing way. Today's dress was the same cut as yesterday's, just in a dark maroon. It ought to be plain and drab, in fact it was, but the bodice cupped her tempting breasts so neatly, he couldn't shake the flush of heat he felt just looking at them. Which forced him to look anywhere except at her.

"This way," said Ava, twirling her parasol and leading off. They were standing in the main street of Kegworth and were bent on a shopping expedition for lace and silk stockings, for which the village was famous. Sarah had volunteered to keep an eye on the children for the morning, ably assisted by the duke, to Emrys surprise, and to him had fallen the task of escorting the ladies.

"It is very kind of you to do this," murmured Miss Pringle. "I'm sure you will be horribly bored."

The viscount shrugged and patted the satchel he had slung

over one shoulder. "I brought a book, Miss Pringle. I plan to buy a tankard of ale from that inn over there and plant myself on that bench outside the shop and wait for you ladies to finish your business. I shall not be bored."

She smiled. "Very resourceful of you," she said and entered the shop behind the girls.

Emrys heaved a sigh of relief to be free of the embarrassment of her company, collected his ale, and settled himself with his book. The sun was warm, and he was soon removing his jacket and loosening his neckcloth. He had soon managed a chapter sipping at his ale and enjoying the sun and peaceful solitude. There were only a few people about and no one accosted him.

The shop bell tinkled as the door reopened and Miss Pringle reappeared. His eyes snagged on that brooch, and he swallowed a groan, dropping his book into his lap. *What is wrong with me?*

He raised his eyebrows. "All done? That was quick."

"Oh, the girls are not done yet, they will be another half an hour at least. But there is little point in me continuing to look, lovely as everything is. I fear the price of lace is rather beyond a governess, and it wouldn't be appropriate for me to wear it in any case." She took a seat beside him. "This is a very pleasant prospect," she said, settling herself while he put his book away.

"Do you care to take a stroll up the street and back?" he said abruptly, figuring if he was walking beside her, he couldn't stare at her breasts.

"Why not?" she smiled, and he rose and offered her his arm.

ANNIS TOOK THE viscount's arm and they set off up the street, but they hadn't taken more than three paces when she got that prickling feeling between her shoulder blades. She'd woken in a cold sweat again last night from the dream, and the prickling now set off a tingling, teasing panic down her spine and made her heart race.

"I'm sorry, what was that?" she said, turning to look up at the viscount, realizing he had addressed her, and she had not heard a word he'd said.

"I asked if you—" he broke off and frowned. "Miss Pringle, are you well? You have gone awfully pale."

"Yes, yes, I'm—" She swallowed and dropped her reticule. She stopped to pick it up, even as the viscount bent to do it for her, and she used the opportunity to glance over her shoulder. She saw nothing and no one suspicious, and she took her reticule from him with a gasp. "Thank you. How clumsy of me."

"Do you wish to sit down, Miss Pringle? Is the sun too much for you?"

"No, no, I am perfectly well," she said. The prickling feeling had stopped, and she felt like a perfect ninny for reacting in such a stupid way.

By the time they'd all returned to The Castle, she was quite recovered and had relegated her moment of silliness to the back of her mind. That afternoon's entertainment was a game of Princess in the Tower, a mock battle between two armies, one led by the duke and the other by the viscount. The objective for each army was to defend their own princess and capture their opponent's. The duke had offered up armor and blunted weapons for himself and Emrys from the armory, and the schoolroom produced toy swords and helmets for the children.

Lady Heather and Miss Watson played the respective princesses, and Miss Pringle, the duchess, and the dowager were the audience, with Ewen on Miss Pringle's lap.

THE SITE OF the battle was the south lawn, with the princesses both situated behind barricades of outdoor furniture, pressed into service as their towers, at each end of the field. Fortunately for the men, the day was cooler than the previous ones, with the sun remaining largely behind the clouds. That didn't stop it getting hot and sweaty inside the armor, but at least he wasn't in danger of cooking, reflected Emrys. The stuff was damned heavy, though.

His respect for medieval knights went up a degree or two as he charged down the field yelling his house motto in Latin, leading his troops behind him, all yelling at the tops of their lungs. Robert, bellowing the Laynes' motto, and tearing toward him with his rag tag bunch trailing him with equal enthusiasm, met him in the center of the field, and they hacked at each other with more theatricality than accuracy.

The small fry bounced around them hacking at each other with gay abandon. Emrys had the four girls and Robert the three boys. He was defending Lady Heather and attempting to capture Miss Watson, and Robert the reverse. Emrys was surprised at how well the girls were acquitting themselves in the fight. Ingrid and Hepzibah were fierce, and his Lizzie and Charlie were no less ferocious in their attacks.

Lizzie, dodging round Japheth, made a beeline for the tower holding Miss Watson, and began climbing the stacked chairs. He was so distracted by this that Robert got a blow into his shoulder that sent him staggering.

"Damn you, Rob," he said bringing his sword up and slashing with a bit more science.

The duke panted, huffing with laughter. "Haven't had this much fun since I was seven!" he said, dancing out of Emrys's range.

Lizzie had reached the top of the stack of chairs and stretched her hand in to help Princess Mary out of her tower. As the boys were still fully occupied with the other three girls, this was a major blow to Robert's team. At this point they were definitely losing. But Lizzie still had to get Princess Mary across the battlefield to safety in the other tower, so there was time for a reversal of fortune yet.

The duchess and the dowager were urging Robert's team on and Miss Pringle and Ewen were cheering for his team. So, between them and the yelling of the troops, there was a lot of noise and confusion.

Mary was free of her tower, both girls having clambered down the stacked chairs and landed on the lawn. Now they edged forward slowly, sticking to the edges of the lawn, Lizzie in front, protecting her princess.

At this point, Emanuel ducked round his twin, Hepzibah, and took off for Princess Heather's tower, determined to release her and get their team back in the game. But his sister wasn't letting him go easily, she gave chase and whacked him on the behind with her sword. Emrys lost sight of them then as they ran behind him, and Robert's renewed attack demanded his attention.

While all this was going on, Lizzie grabbed Princess Mary's hand and belted for Heather's tower. Suddenly Emanuel had two to fight, and Mary was able to climb the tower and drop inside the barricade with a whoop of victory!

"We won! We won!" yelled Lizzie throwing her sword up and bouncing around. The girls all squealed with delight and the boys looked defeated, dropping to the grass with groans.

Rob pointed his sword to the grass and shook Emrys hand, "Well done, old chap, some fierce little warriors you have there!"

Emrys ripped off his helmet and grinned. "I have indeed."

Miss Pringle came over and held out a medallion on a ribbon. "Would you care to do the honors? I think Miss Elizabeth wins the day for most valorous knight."

Emrys grinned and took the medallion, beckoning Lizzie over. "Kneel, Sir Knight, and receive your reward," he intoned in suitably portentous accents.

Lizzie, her face flushed and grinning from ear to ear, dropped to her knees, and he bent and slipped the ribbon down over her head and settled the medallion on her proud little chest.

"For intelligence and valor extraordinary in the field of battle, you are so rewarded, Sir Knight," he said solemnly.

Refreshments were then served, ale for the men, wine for the ladies, and lemonade for the children, and it was declared a vastly entertaining afternoon.

Ewen trotted over to Emrys, waving one of the wooden swords dropped by the other boys. "Will you teach me to fight too, Papa?" he asked plaintively.

Emrys squatted down and smiled at his son. "Yes, of course I will, Ewen."

Ewen grinned and swung the toy sword wildly, whacking Emrys in the legs, which made him wince. He would have a bruise from that! Then Ewen hurtled off to Miss Pringle, yelling, "Papa's going to teach me to fight, too!"

She received him, picking him up and deftly avoiding getting her eye poked out by the sword. Emrys strode over quickly and divested his son of the weapon. "Be careful, Ewen. You don't want to hurt Miss Pringle, do you?"

"No, Papa!" He flung his arms round her neck and hugged her, and she flushed with obvious pleasure. "I like Miss Pingle!" he said with a beatific smile.

Emrys heart melted as he reflected that he liked Miss Pingle, too, if she could make his little man smile like that. He resolutely kept his eyes away from her bosom but was physically conscious of her even so. A tingling in his breeches he hadn't felt in months provoked a blush that made him look away, lest she guess what he was thinking.

"Papa!" Lizzie came up holding her medallion in one hand and a piece of cake in the other.

"Papa!" Charlie attacked him from the other side, also with a piece of cake, but with fruit instead of a medallion in her other hand.

"Yes, girls?" he said crouching down to their level.

"Can we stay here forever?" asked Charlie. "It's so much fun!"

"Yes, can we pleeeease, Papa?" wheedled Lizzie.

"I'm afraid we can't do that, but"—he hastened to add as the pouting lips appeared—"we are not going home yet. And I believe Miss Pringle has more adventures in store, don't you, Miss Pringle?" He looked up at her, and she nodded.

"Yes, I do."

"Tell us!" demanded Lizzie.

"It's a surprise," Miss Pringle said with a smile.

Emrys waited for Lizzie to announce that she didn't like surprises, but she didn't. Instead, she stuffed the cake in her mouth and hared off toward Hepzibah, trailing Charlie behind her.

He rose to his feet, shaking his head. "I don't know how I'm going to turn them into young ladies. They are half feral, I fear."

Miss Pringle juggled Ewen on her hip and said, "Plenty of time. They are children still—let them enjoy it."

"Oh, I will. And I enjoy them immensely. I never know what they will say next."

Later that night, climbing into bed, Emrys settled back against the pillows with his book in hand, but his every attempt to concentrate on the written word was interrupted by snatches of the day. It had been both enchanting and disturbing. He couldn't shake the image of Miss Pringle's generous breasts encased discretely in the plain fabric of her gown. The brooch nestled in the center, the plain ribbon beneath, the way the fabric cupped them . . .

A sudden rush of hot desire assailed him, as his mind posed the question of what the soft, round globes of her breasts might look like beneath that prim and proper dress. And more to the point, what they might *feel* like?

The notion took so strong a hold that he couldn't dislodge it, and for the first time in months his cock grew stiff against his belly and his balls tightened uncomfortably. He uttered a soft groan as his hand groped for and seized his cock, stroking it almost without conscious thought. With blinding awareness, he knew his body needed release and would not be denied.

It had been months since he'd had any inclination for it, but he was suddenly ravenous. He spat upon his hand and stroked himself vigorously, trying to block any more lascivious thoughts of Miss Pringle. She was a lady and did not deserve to be the subject of his lechery, but those alluring breasts refused to be ignored, and he found his fevered brain wondering next what they might taste like, and how much of each one he could fit in his mouth. From there it was a simple slide to imaging what her reaction to such treatment might be, and in seconds flat he was spurting his seed all over his belly in a blissful, heated rush.

Getting his breath back, he lay spent while the tingles of desire slowly faded from his limbs, and he wondered why his fancy had led him to fantasize about the prim and proper governess over any other female of his acquaintance. It was a revelation to him that a pair of breasts could provoke such a reaction in him. Did he have a taste for well-endowed ladies then?

Given that he had been married since he was twenty-two, he actually had no idea what his taste was. He'd been hopelessly in love with his beautiful wife Caroline for the entirety of his marriage and never thought of another woman. He could see no parallels between Caro and Miss Pringle—no two women could be more different at a glance. Caro had been tiny, ethereal even, like a fairy princess. If there were any similarities to be found, a closer fit would be to Ava who was also small of stature, though more sturdy and shapely of build than Caro. But it wasn't Ava who had inspired his first stirrings of desire. It was unequivocally the governess.

He shrugged at the mystery of it and rolled onto his side, closing his eyes. As a youth and young man before his marriage, he'd had sudden urges and fantasies about random women, but it hadn't meant anything. No doubt this was the same.

Yet as he drifted into sleep it occurred to him that, enjoyable as it was to look upon her beautiful shape, it was Miss Pringle's undoubted mothering skills that he was truly drawn to. The picture of little Ewen's arms round her neck made him smile.

Chapter Six

ANNIS WOKE THE next morning to a knock on her door, which was unusual. She sat up, pushing her cap to the back of her head, and called out, "Come in."

The door opened, and Heather and Ingrid entered dressed only in their robes with their hands behind their backs.

"Happy birthday, Miss Pringle!" said Ingrid grinning from ear to ear. She rushed toward the bed with her hands now held out, holding a small, wrapped box. Heather, a little more sedate, followed her.

"Happy birthday," she said softly, also holding out a smaller package.

"Oh, girls!" Annis said with a smile, quite overcome.

Ingrid climbed onto the bed. "Go on—open it!"

Annis looked at the box in her lap as Heather sat down on the edge of the bed, one leg crooked up.

Undoing the ribbon, the cloth it was wrapped in fell away to reveal a small, carved wooden box.

"I bought it with my allowance, just for you!" said Ingrid. "Do you like it? It will hold your fripperies, ribbons, pins, and such."

"Oh, Ingrid, it's lovely! Thank you!" Annis hugged the girl, who grinned with delight and bounced on the bed.

"Now Heather's!" she insisted.

Annis took Heather's smaller package and unwrapped it to reveal a small square box. Opening the lid, she found an exquisite butterfly pin inside. The wings were done in a vivid turquoise enamel. "Heather, that is lovely!" she said, blinking back tears. She hugged Heather who blushed, pleased that her present was appreciated.

"Sarah has organized a luncheon on the south lawn for your birthday!" said Ingrid in a rush.

"Ingrid, that is supposed to be a secret!" admonished Heather.

"I don't believe in secrets," said Ingrid with a toss of her head. "It is much better to know about a treat beforehand and be able to anticipate it. That is *much* more fun!"

Annis smiled at Ingrid's point of view; she had something there. Annis preferred not to be surprised either, but mostly because for her, surprises were usually unpleasant.

"And," said Ingrid, "the best part is that Robert says there are to be no lessons today because it's your birthday and you shouldn't have to work on your birthday!" She bounced some more. "Yay, no mathematics today!"

Annis laughed and shooed the girls out so that she could dress. The Laynes always made a fuss of birthdays. It was one of the perquisites of working here. All the staff were recognized on their birthdays and given the day off.

Arriving downstairs for breakfast, she was met with a barrage of happy birthday wishes, from staff and family alike. Given the place of honor at the breakfast table and served by the duchess herself, Annis's cheeks flushed pink with embarrassment to be the center of attention. The viscount ambled in, in the middle of all this, looking his usual rumpled self. Apprised of the occasion, he kissed her hand with a flourish.

"Happy birthday, Miss Pringle, and may you have many, many more!" His green eyes twinkled at her, and the expression sent a warm wave through her chest. *Really, she liked the viscount far too much!* She wished he was less charming; it wasn't good for her pulse.

"We have organized a croquet match, followed by luncheon on the south lawn," announced the duke. "It is in your honor, Miss Pringle, and you are to do nothing but enjoy yourself."

"Yes, Your Grace," she said with a smile. "Thank you, Your Grace."

"You are very welcome, Miss Pringle. We value your contribution to the household. You must know that. How long have you been with us now? Six years?"

She nodded. "Yes, it will be six years in September," she said tucking into her eggs and ham.

Just then Ava burst through the door with a big bouquet of flowers. "Annis, these are for you! Smiggens sends his love!" Smiggens was the head gardener and had a soft spot for Annis, whom he treated like a daughter. She took the huge bouquet and was instantly enveloped in the heady scent of lilies and jasmine. "Ava, they are beautiful. I must thank Smiggens after breakfast."

The bouquet was borne off by a footman to be put into a vase, and breakfast resumed. The dowager wasn't joining them, as she preferred to breakfast in her room. More unusually, the children's breakfast was being supervised by one of the maids in the schoolroom. Annis was truly being given a day off.

After breakfast, she left the parlor to go in search of Smiggens to thank him for the bouquet. She had exited the drawing room via the French doors when she heard her name.

"Miss Pringle!" She glanced back and saw the viscount was coming toward her. She stopped, waiting for him to catch up with her.

"It's a fine day," he said, falling into step with her. "Where are you headed?"

"The orangery. According to Ava, that is where Smiggens is lurking. I must thank him for my flowers."

"Do you mind company?"

"Not at all." She smiled, a warm little tendril curling through her breast.

He strolled beside her, his hands in his pockets. "I wanted to thank you for yesterday's inspired adventure. My girls haven't stopped talking about it," he said. "And I admit the duke and I enjoyed it immensely, too," he added confidingly. "You have a genius for thinking up wonderful things for the children to do."

"I've had lots of practice, my lord. I've been a teacher since I was fifteen. I was raised in a seminary for young ladies, you know. My—aunt—was the manager." She stumbled over the word *aunt* and hoped he didn't notice. She'd only discovered that the woman who had raised her—the woman she had thought was her aunt—was actually her mother, on that lady's deathbed seven years ago. For a moment, her mind drifted back to that terrible day.

Aunt Janet's hands plucked agitatedly at the sheets, her breathing labored, her head moving restlessly on the pillow, her pallor showing starkly in the glow of the candlelight. She had been ill for a week now with the fever, and her lungs were battling to breathe. It hurt to listen to the gurgling noise they made with each breath.

Annis feared at any moment that the sound would cease. She felt helpless to do anything and anxiety chewed at her, bringing tears to her eyes as she watched this woman she loved like a mother fight for every breath she took.

Aunt Janet's brown hair was showing threads of gray in it now, though she wasn't an old woman—only forty-four. But her hands were worn with hard work and the lines on her face spoke of worry and burdens beyond her years.

Annis shifted in her chair, trying to get comfortable. She had been keeping vigil all through the night. She glanced at the clock; it was inching toward three o'clock. A log fell out of the fire behind her, and she got up to put it back and stoke the fire.

"Annis?" The breathy whisper brought her back to the bedside in an instant. "Yes, Aunt Janet?" she said, bending over the bed.

Janet grabbed her hand in hers and squeezed it weakly. "My little girl!" she said a hoarse whisper, tears leaking from her eyes.

"I'm here. Don't cry—you just need to rest, and you will be better soon," reassured Annis, recalling all the times her aunt had cared for her

during her childhood illnesses and the many girls that were in their care over the years.

"Fetch the box," she said, her breath catching and making her cough.

"Which box?" asked Annis bewildered.

"The wooden box . . . in the bottom drawer of my desk." Janet wheezed.

"All right," said Annis, reluctant to leave her, but the high color in Janet's cheeks and the martial light in her eye told her not to disobey. It was so like her usual self that Annis's heart lifted in hope that she was getting better.

Hurrying out of the bedroom, she ran down the stairs to the main office and, using the key she had on the chatelaine she had taken possession of when Janet fell ill, she opened the locked bottom drawer of the desk. Sure enough, inside was a plain wooden box. It also had a lock on it. Taking the box back upstairs, she half expected Janet to have lapsed back into a doze, but the moment Annis came back into the room, her eyes opened, and she smiled a weak smile.

"Help me sit up!" she demanded, her voice husky and fading in and out.

Annis lifted her up and stacked some pillows behind her. Janet sank back against them, her eyes closed for a moment, gathering her strength.

Annis hesitated, and then when Janet opened her eyes yet again and waved to her, she set the box on her knees. Janet reached for the chain round her neck and used the key on it to open the box. Annis had wondered all her life what that key opened. Now she knew.

Janet lifted the lid and Annis glimpsed some papers and knick-knacks inside. "Everything in here is for you," said Janet her voice hoarse and breathy. "But there is one thing especially that I want you to have."

She reached in and pulled out a man's gold ring, like a signet ring with a flat oval top.

Annis took it, puzzled as to its significance.

"He would have wanted you to have it—" Janet coughed.

"Who?" asked Annis bewildered.

"Your father," wheezed Janet through another paroxysm of coughing.

The words hardly registered as she watched Janet's lips turning blue. Her coughing getting worse.

Lifting the box off her lap. Annis eased her back against the pillows. Janet struggled for breath, exhausted by the coughing.

"Good girl . . ." she murmured tiredly. "You're my good girl, Annis. He would be proud of you." Her voice was a thread and Annis had to strain to hear the words. "Who'd have thought little Janet Pringle and a lord's son . . ." She sighed, her eyes closing. Her grip on Annis's hand loosened, and she sighed again. Her breathing shallow and stuttering.

Annis gripped her hand again, trying to find the meaning behind her words. Was she . . . "Mama?" Was that what her words meant?

"Yes, sweetheart . . ." murmured Janet. "So sorry . . ."

Annis gulped on a sob. "Why didn't you tell me?"

"So sorry . . ." repeated Janet tiredly. She roused with an effort, and gripping Annis hand weakly, she said with as much force as she could muster, "I did everything I could to keep you safe. You must tell no one! You understand? It's not safe. Tell no one! Promise me?"

Annis nodded slowly, a million questions on her tongue.

"Promise!" croaked Janet.

"I promise, Mama." Annis soothed. "Just rest, you will be better soon and can tell me the rest then."

Janet nodded, her body sagging back into the pillows. Her lips, still blue, moved in silent murmurs that Annis couldn't make out. Her eyes closed and she seemed to shrink, her breathing rattled.

She took another breath. And another. And stopped.

"Mama?" Annis wailed. "Mama?" She shook Janet's hand, and the woman's head lolled on the pillow. She was gone and the whole truth with her.

Chapter Seven

"**B**E CAREFUL!" SAID viscount, bringing her back to the present with a jolt, his hand grabbing her elbow to hold her upright, as she nearly tripped up the step to the orangery.

"Oh!" Annis clutched at his arm. "I'm so sorry. I must have caught the hem of my skirt!"

He smiled down at her. "I've got you."

"Thank you," she said, feeling herself flushing. When had she first noticed that the viscount was an attractive man? Not handsome, no, but there was a masculine presence to him that set her pulse fluttering in a most disconcerting manner. She shook herself mentally. *It is completely inappropriate for me to be thinking of him like this.*

The viscount held the door of the orangery open for her, and the warm moist air, filled with the sweet, tangy scent of oranges, surrounded her as she stepped over the threshold.

"Smiggens, are you here?" she called out.

An elderly man with a grizzled head popped up from a row of orange trees in pots, a pair of pruning shears in his hand.

"Miss Annis!" He said with a grin, crinkling his brown, weatherbeaten face. Seeing the viscount, he nodded his head. "Yer lordship."

"Good morning, Smiggens."

"Smiggens, I came to thank you for my lovely bouquet. I'm surprised there are any blooms left, it was so big!" said Annis, going toward him as he came out from behind the potted trees.

"Well, that was Lady Ava's fault. She kept selecting flowers until it was so big she could barely carry it. That girl has no sense of proportion, and she never did."

"True," concurred Annis. "Anyway, they are lovely, so thank you for cutting them for me."

"My pleasure. I hope you're also having a lovely day?"

"I am," Annis smiled at the old man, who was rather stooped but still strong as whipcord. "Will you be attending my birthday lunch?" she asked.

"Aye, the staff will all be there. Quite a buzz it's causing, too. Everyone enjoys an excuse for a good feed, and Mrs. O'Neal has been up since five preparing the victuals!"

"I am so spoiled!" Annis's heart leaped with gratitude toward her employers.

"Aye, well His Grace won't mind if I give ye one of these," said Smiggens with a wink, handing her an orange. She took the fragrant fruit and sniffed. "I shall enjoy that very much, thank you."

Annis and the viscount then left the orangery and headed back across the lawn. Down one end, the servants were already setting up trestle tables and chairs for the luncheon.

"It's such a fine day," said the viscount. "Do you care to take a stroll to the ruins and back? The duke asked me to check something on the cross we found the other day; he is writing to the Antiquities Board about it."

"What an excellent suggestion," she said with a smile, her heart lifting. They skirted the house and set off for the ruins. As they went, she peeled the orange and offered him a segment, which he took with thanks. She bit into a segment herself and the sweet juicy flavor exploded on her tongue. She barely stifled a groan at the taste.

"The duke will be pleased with this crop. They are delicious," he said, popping the rest of his piece into his mouth.

"Yes, they are." She offered him another one.

"Tell me, Miss Pringle, in your professional opinion, are my children behind in their lessons? They have been without supervision for several months now. I am concerned they are getting behind, but with the disruption of my wife's passing, I deemed it best to let them go wild for a bit. No," he corrected himself, "I confess it was more that I was at sea and not thinking very straight about anything."

"I don't believe that any irreparable damage has been done, but lessons should be resumed as soon as possible for the girls, especially Elizabeth. She has a lively mind that requires direction."

"She does," smiled her father with a hint of pride.

"It is customary to give the younger children a break from lessons in the summer months, in any case. They learn so much by being able to be out in the sun and doing things, that it is by far better for their health and development to be roaming free and exploring outdoors than stuck inside doing boring things like mathematics and grammar. You should hear Lady Ingrid on the topic!"

The viscount chuckled. "Yes, her brother says Ingrid is a handful. Worse than Ava."

"Lady Ingrid does have a mind of her own," said Annis diplomatically.

"Somewhat like Miss Hepzibah," noted the viscount. "I'm surprised Lizzie hasn't tried to tag after the older girls."

"She prefers Emanuel. And Charlotte has attached herself to Japheth. Ewen runs after Ezekiel."

"When he's not attached to you?" The viscount took the last segment and gave her a quizzical smile.

She flushed, looking down to watch her step. The ground was tussocky here and uneven. "I confess he does seem to have developed an attachment to me. And I to him," she admitted. "He is a sweet little boy."

"He is." The viscount cleared his throat. "The duke wanted me to record the letters on the cross," he said, taking a folded sheet of paper and a pencil out of his pocket as they skirted the ruined tower and headed toward the mound under the tree.

They climbed the mound, Annis lifting her skirts to avoid treading on them. Fashionable hemlines were rising, but Annis's gowns were a half decade old and out of fashion.

They reached the top of the mound, and Annis knelt to sweep away the leaves and debris that had gathered in the few days since they had uncovered the cross, while the viscount crouched beside her and copied the letters that were legible. She was conscious of a sense of contentment in his presence that made her feel very comfortable, safe even.

Safe wasn't a condition she had felt for a long time. It struck her with force that she had been living with a sense of fear and dread for so long that she didn't know what it would be like to be free of it. She had thought for a while, living with the Laynes, that she had shaken off the shadow that dogged her. But yesterday's sensation of being watched had rattled her badly. It had confirmed in her mind that the suspicions she had that she was being observed, suspicions she had been having for some weeks now, were indeed well-founded. And with that had come the nightmares and the constant worry.

But right in this moment, with the viscount, outside in the fresh air and sunshine, with the twitter of birds in the trees and the waft of floral scents on the light breeze, she felt a quiet sense of joy and contentment, a whisper of hope for her future. Perhaps good things might be coming to her? It was her birthday after all—maybe the start of a new chapter in her life? But she refused to probe further into what that might mean. She would take the feeling at face value and enjoy it. Such moments were to be savored, not questioned.

"There," said the viscount. "That should do it." He folded the paper up and put it and the pencil away. Rising to his feet, he offered her a hand up. Clasping her hand, he said with a smile,

"You are a most restful companion, Miss Pringle."

His words were so in accord with her own thoughts, her heart gave an odd jerk, and a warmth spread through her chest. She flushed faintly and said, "As are you, my lord."

He smiled, helping her down the incline of the mound. "Thank you. Yes, I've always thought myself an easy-going fellow. Not very interesting perhaps. But restful, yes." They reached level ground, and he added, "My wife was the lively one."

The shadow in his eyes as he said it made her heart ache for him, and she touched his arm in quick sympathy, quite forgetting—again—that such an intimacy between the governess and her employer's guest should be wholly inappropriate.

He smiled again, throwing off the dark look and, equally inappropriately, squeezed her hand where it rested on his arm, acknowledging her sympathy without a word.

The weather continued perfect, only a light breeze and sunshine that wasn't too hot. She wore a broad-brimmed hat to shade her face and one of her lighter cotton gowns with short sleeves that, hem length aside, was just right for the day's activities.

The game of croquet on the lawn was enormous fun. She didn't get to participate in such games as a rule, her role usually being referee and cheer-squad. But today she had been almost bullied by the duke into being captain of her own team, and she very boldly chose the viscount who naturally brought his girls with him as teams were being picked. The duchess, with real nobility, sat out and minded Ewen, who was too young to play. She also got Ava and Ingrid, and Heather joined the Watsons on the duke's team.

It was a nine-hoop game, with six pairs of balls for each team. With so many balls on the field and so many hoops to hit them through, it was a receipt for confusion and much hilarity, as when Emanuel was about to strike a ball through the farthest hoop and his twin sister screamed, "No Emanuel, that's Miss Pringle's team's ball!"

Or when the viscount hit a very neat putt that careened off the duke's ball and sent both balls through two hoops apiece. "Two points to each team," announced the duchess, when an appeal to the referee was made.

Her team won by a point in the end, though she rather suspected the duke threw the last shot wide to give her the win. However it happened, his team was most disappointed to lose. The Watsons, while not poor losers, were unaccustomed to it, and the boys in particular were much cast down.

The arrival of luncheon, however, was a welcome distraction, and Annis found herself seated beside the viscount. How that happened she didn't know, but she had no sooner taken her place in the middle of the long table on the adults' side and shaken out her napkin when his voice to her right made her look round. "Wine, Miss Pringle?"

He offered the bottle. The servants were all joining them for luncheon, and so once the food and drink was deposited on the table, everyone was helping themselves.

"Oh, thank you. Yes, please," she said with a smile.

He poured for her, himself, and Ava, seated on his right.

She took up the glass of sparkling wine, but before she could taste it, the duke was on his feet commanding everyone's attention.

"Today we honor one of our most valued employees, Miss Annis Pringle. Happy birthday, Miss Pringle, and may you have many more!" He held up his glass, and everyone murmured something in kind and raised their glasses and drank.

"Thank you, Your Grace," she said blushing. "Thank you, everyone, for a lovely meal. *Bon appétit!*" Then she brought her own glass to her lips and drank.

She caught the eye of Smiggens down the table, who winked at her. She tipped her glass to him with a smile.

"He's fond of you," remarked the viscount, offering her the dish of artichoke hearts in butter. Using the tongs, she took one with murmured thanks.

"Yes, and I confess I am fond of him. I never had a father," she admitted, helping herself to some of the sliced beef in gravy.

"Ah, that must be difficult. I was fortunate to have both my parents until I reached adulthood. Growing up without a parent—" He glanced across the table at his three, and she heard the tiny sigh that escaped his lips. "They need a mother. I shall have to do something about that." The words were uttered quietly, and she didn't think they were directed at her, so she said nothing.

After a moment or two, she said, "They are lovely children. You must be very proud of them."

"I am." He smiled.

"When you look to engage a new governess, can I suggest that you look for someone with a broad range of skills? Miss Elizabeth, in particular I feel, needs to be challenged. While Charlotte requires someone kind and patient."

"You know them well on such short acquaintance, Miss Pringle."

"It is my job to observe children closely and strive to understand them, my lord. You will recall I was raised in a seminary for young ladies. I have absorbed a great deal about education over the years, both overtly and I think to a certain extent unconsciously. I was so steeped in it."

"Tell me, why didn't you remain at the seminary after your aunt died?" he asked, reaching for his glass of wine.

She swallowed involuntarily and choked. She fell into a coughing fit, her eyes streaming, and it was some minutes before she was restored to equilibrium. The viscount, quite alarmed, rubbed her back very inappropriately, but no one seemed to mind. The duchess brought her water and when she was settled again and everyone had returned to their seats, she wiped her eyes and blew her nose, resuming her knife and fork.

"What were you saying, my lord? You asked me a question before that pea went down the wrong way."

"I asked what made you leave the seminary? Did your aunt not leave it to you?"

"Oh my—aunt—was the leasehold manager, but she didn't own the business. The owners let her do as she pleased with it, though, while she lived. But they sold it to new owners soon after my aunt passed, and they found they wanted to manage it themselves. Unfortunately, I came to understand that there was little use for me under the new regime." *It's mostly true*, she thought, *though the decision to leave was my own.*

After luncheon, the servants cleaned up and went back to their duties and the adults sat around enjoying the sun while the children played chasey round the lawn. She and the viscount pulled the hoops out of the lawn and gathered up the balls and mallets, narrowly avoiding getting themselves mowed down by children pelting past them at a rate easiest measured in knots. Squeals, shouts, and giggles, demonstrating that the game was reaching a crescendo.

"Oh, dear. I do hope there will be no tears," said Annis.

Just then a shriek followed by sobs rent the air.

Annis dropped her armful of mallets, the viscount dropped the bag of balls he was carrying, and both rushed toward the sounds of distress though the bushes to the side of the lawn.

It was Elizabeth. She had tripped and gone down in a heap on the grass.

Annis reached her first, closely followed by the viscount, who dropped to his knees beside Elizabeth, gathering her up into his arms. "What is it, sweetheart? Did you fall?"

The little girl gulped on a sob, "Stupid tree root! I tripped." She had her hands up, her fingers slightly curled, and Annis took them to inspect. Sure enough, she had put out her hands to save herself and scraped her palms. "Oh, sweetie," said Annis, "we'll fix those up in a flash."

Elizabeth nodded, choking on another sob. "My knee hurts, too!"

Annis moved aside her short shirt and revealed a scraped

knee, oozing blood. It wasn't too deep but would need to be cleaned and plastered. Annis looked at the viscount. "Bring her into the house, and I'll fix her up."

He scooped up his daughter in his arms. "Come on my brave knight. Miss Pringle will bandage you up!" He kissed her nose which made her giggle and stopped the sobs.

As they headed back across the lawn he said to Annis, "I gather you have experience with this sort of thing?"

"Lots," she said with smile for both him and Lizzie.

Charlotte raced up to them, alarm on her face. "Are you hurt, Lizzie?"

"Just a scrape," said Miss Elizabeth bravely.

"Oh, Lizzie!" said soft-hearted Charlotte, her face crumpling.

"It's all right, Charlie. Miss Pringle is going to patch her up all right and tight. Nothing to worry about," the viscount reassured her.

Charlotte tagged along with them to the house, refusing to leave her big sister's side.

"Put her on the couch," said Annis, as they entered the drawing room through the French windows. "I'll just fetch my wound kit."

"You have such a thing?" he asked surprised.

She nodded. "My—my aunt always had one at the seminary. I kept the habit. It comes in handy for this sort of thing. I'll be back in a moment."

She raced up to her room to find the hatbox she used to keep the kit in and brought it downstairs. Reentering the drawing room, she found the viscount sitting on the couch with Elizabeth's legs over his and Charlotte tucked into his other side.

"I rang for some water and cloths," he said as she entered.

"Oh, thank you. Yes, I should have said." Just then, one of the maids came in with a bowl of warm water, a towel, and some small cloths. Annis thanked her as she set it on the table and left.

"Right," said Annis sinking to her knees by the sofa and dunking one of the cloths in the water. "This might hurt a bit, sweetheart, but it will be over quickly," she said with a reassuring smile.

"It's all right. It only hurts a bit," said Elizabeth bravely. The viscount squeezed her arm.

"That's my brave knight."

Ten minutes later, Elizabeth's hands and knee had been cleaned, sprinkled with basilicum powder, and bandaged. "You will need to keep these on for a couple of days while the wounds heal. It is very important that they stay clean and don't get infected," said Annis. "I will change the bandages tomorrow."

Elizabeth nodded. "I suppose that means I can't play chasey anymore?"

"That's right," said the viscount scooping her up and planting another kiss on her nose. "You're going to sit with the grown-ups and help us eat Miss Pringle's birthday cake."

"Ooh, cake!" exclaimed both girls.

Annis joined them back out on the lawn when she had put her kit away and was put to the blush by the production around her birthday cake, which was served for afternoon tea with much palaver. *Really, I am having the loveliest birthday!*

The cake was very large, but there were a lot of mouths to feed, with hungry little hands reaching for their share of the treat.

The viscount fetched her a piece and a cup of tea, and then getting his own, sat back down beside her. In truth, he had barely left her side all day. *A woman could let such attention go to her head if she weren't the governess.*

"Thank you for your attentions to Lizzie. Those wounds could turn nasty if not properly treated."

"I know—that is why I have my kit. I'm confident that as long as I clean and change the bandages every day they will heal nicely. It only takes a couple of days to start the healing process. They should be safe enough in a few days to take the bandages off. She just needs to be careful not to reopen the wounds."

"You are very resourceful woman, Miss Pringle."

Annis blushed.

Much later, climbing into bed that night, Annis reviewed the day and reflected that it was possibly the best birthday she had ever had. For which, in no small part, she had to reluctantly admit, the viscount and his enchanting offspring were responsible. Though reminders of the past made Annis suddenly shiver, and she drew the covers up. The less she thought about those days the better.

Recalling the viscount's compliment as she lay in her bed, she flushed all over again and got a warm feeling in her breast. Yes, it had been a wonderful day, and the viscount had made it very memorable. She nestled into the pillows and sighed. *He really is a lovely gentleman.*

Chapter Eight

17th November 1792

I have a son! Lawrence Benedict. He is a fine, healthy babe, and Damaris has fared well through her labor; I cannot complain that my wife has not done her duty. My heart leaves my chest at the sight of him in his mother's arms, yet I am plagued with strange dreams these last few nights. Dreams that linger in the daylight. Dreams that disturb me.

I cannot shake the conviction that I have been through this experience before. Which is insane, yet the feelings persist. When I hold Lawrence in my arms, I am assailed by the sensation of familiarity.

There is another child. I'm sure of it. Yet how? How could I forget such a thing? It is lifechanging to hold one's child in one's arms. I cannot credit that I could lose the memory of such a thing.

Did the child die? Is that why I can't remember? The notion of losing Lawrence tears my heart out. I could not bear it.

19th November 1792

I pace the nursery with him when he cries. The nurse is shocked, but I will not leave him in distress. Only when he is quiet do I leave and sit in the library with a glass of whisky and try to recall.

My memories are coming back in fragments. There is a woman. There must be, of course, if there is a child.

When I first recalled her face, my skin became gooseflesh, and such joy filled my heart that I was reduced to tears. For I know that I love her, that she makes me happy. And such a longing to see her and our child consumes me that I sob uncontrollably even now at the thought.

I shall only call her J, here in this diary, for I must protect her identity. At least until I can find her. For I have left her alone to fend for herself all these months, and she knows not what happened to me.

My mind is a sieve, full of holes. I can see the house we lived in, yet know not the name of the place. From what I can recall, it must be a small village, certainly not the metropolis or even a large town. Somewhere small and bucolic. But that leaves thousands of villages anywhere in England.

I shall begin my search tomorrow.

24 November 1792

I have searched and searched, but I am no nearer to finding my J. I do have more memories, however. The child is a little girl. A sweet, beautiful babe, my little A. I ache to hold her in my arms again. I take some solace from Lawrence, but it is not enough. I have two girls who need me as much as he does, possibly more, and I am beside myself with worry for them. What could have happened to them in my absence?

I know now that I left my ring with her, the one father gave me when I reached my majority. I always meant to have it engraved and never got around to it. Father assumed someone robbed me of it when they found me without it in the accident. But J. has it. I am sure she will have kept it. How much I miss her!

Damaris thinks I have run mad, for I am barely home for more than a few hours' sleep before I am off again to search. She has no idea why I am doing this, what I am searching for. I must tell her the truth eventually, I suppose. But not until I have found my J. and A.

Chapter Nine

THE DAY OF the picnic dawned bright, clear, and sunny, bidding fair to be a hot day. The plan was to assemble out the front of the house at eleven o'clock. All the adults were coming to this event and Annis had spent some time with the housekeeper and the cook (with the duchess's permission) organizing the lunch hampers, blankets, and sunshades required for the comfort of the company.

The servants were sent in advance to set up the picnic site for their comfort, and the children were beside themselves with excitement, having been promised the opportunity to paddle in the lake, given the heat. Annis was vastly pleased with herself when they arrived at the site to see the blankets, tables, and chairs set out under the trees by the shore of the lake and the servants ready to serve wine for the adults and lemonade for the children.

The lake was an irregularly shaped, circular body of water, greenish in color, with rushes at the edges, and a particularly large-trunked tree with branches stretching over the water, standing like a guardian on the left side of the lake. There was a slight breeze across the lake to temper the heat, and the sun shone brilliantly on the surface of the water. Insects buzzed and the serenity of it was breathtaking. Until of course the shrieks of happy children shattered it.

The children splashed and played in the water, getting themselves thoroughly wet and muddy, but none of them ventured far from the edge on pain of the viscount's wrath. The adults lay about on the blankets or occupied chairs, eating cold chicken, fresh bread, cheese, and cake. The ladies held parasols to protect their complexions and wafted fans to keep themselves cool. The duke and viscount eschewed jackets and neckcloths and removed their boots.

A post luncheon somnolence came over the party in the dozy heat, and it was only a shriek followed by a splash that roused Annis to the knowledge of danger.

Sitting up, she saw to her horror little Ewen struggling in the water below the branches of the large tree.

Rising and kicking off her slippers, she ran straight at the lake and plunged into the chilly water. Catching her breath at the sudden change in temperature, she launched herself toward the child, thankful that she had learned to swim. Behind her, she heard the calls of distress from the ladies of the party and a bellow from the viscount, followed by a splashing behind her.

She didn't turn to look, all her concentration on young Ewen, whose head had just disappeared below the water. She struck out harder and reached the point at which he had vanished. Taking a breath, she dived and groped about, unable to see anything in the murky water. Her hands grasped an arm, and she tugged, kicking her feet to push herself to the surface. She broke the surface and, treading water, kept young Ewen's head above the waterline. In the next instant she was engulfed by the solid, hard heat of the viscount's body as he reached them and hauled them both toward him.

"He went under," she panted. "Go! Get him to the bank—I can manage."

"Thank you," he said shortly and set off, stroking strongly to the bank with one arm, his son in the other. She followed, emerging a few moments behind him, panting and spent, water pouring off her gown, which was filthy, streaked with green slime and weeds.

"Ewen?" The viscount was working over his son. The little boy suddenly coughed up a quantity of foul water and began to cry. "Ewen!" The viscount's voice cracked with relief as he held his son on his side while the paroxysm passed.

Sarah had rushed to wrap a blanket around Annis, and before she could say anything, the duke swept her up in his arms and set off after the viscount who was headed for the house with his tiny burden. Sarah and Ava began rounding up the children and reassuring them that Ewen was perfectly safe.

Annis, who was shivering with reaction more than any chill left over from the water, murmured, "I can walk, Your Grace."

"Nonsense," snapped the duke, striding purposefully toward the house. "You are a heroine, Miss Pringle. You just saved that boy's life!"

In short order she was deposited in her room to recover. After changing out of her wet clothes, Annis ventured to the children's rooms to find out how Ewen was. She found the little boy tucked up in bed with his father in attendance.

The viscount, seeing her, left Ewen and came toward the door. They stepped out into the anteroom off which the children's rooms all ran, and he said quietly, "He is sleeping for the moment. The doctor has been sent for. Are you well, Miss Pringle?"

"Yes, perfectly," she said.

"I cannot thank you enough for your quick action," he said, clasping her hands tightly. "If you hadn't—" He stopped, visibly overcome. "I blame myself for taking my eye off him. He should never have wandered off like that."

"We were all remiss!" she said quickly. "He must have climbed that tree and fallen in the water from there."

"Yes, I assumed as much." He swallowed hard and wiped his eyes. "Forgive my excessive emotion, Miss Pringle, but if I had lost him—"

"Please, do not apologize, my lord. Your emotions do you

credit," she said swiftly. "Indeed, I am so glad I reached him in time. I feel equally responsible, if not more so. Today's venture was my idea. If I had thought there was any danger to any of the children—"

"The responsibility is mine and mine alone, Miss Pringle. He is my son!" He spoke vehemently. "The truth is I have not been myself lately. Not paying sufficient attention—to anything. So damned self-absorbed I—" He stopped, closing his lips as if biting off whatever else he would have said. "They have lost their mother; they must not lose me as well."

"They have not lost you," she protested.

He grimaced. "I've been here in body, but my spirit has been somewhat absent."

"Papa?" A plaintive cry from the bedroom sent him back into the room, and she left.

Annis took supper in her room that night and retired to bed early.

LIZZIE AND CHARLIE came to say good night, and Emrys had to reassure them that Ewen would be well soon. They each gave him a kiss on his hot forehead and let Emrys take them to their beds and tuck them in. It was a reminder to him that they needed him, too.

Emrys had a truckle bed set up in his son's room, preparing to spend the night with him and was alarmed when it became clear at around nine o'clock that the little fellow was running a temperature. The doctor had warned him this might happen. The poor lad had been sick a couple of times from the foul water and the doctor had said he might have contracted something nasty from it. He had left a paregoric draught to administer in the event of fever and Emrys gave it to him, but it came up again almost immediately.

After that, Emrys spent his time sponging the hot little body down and feeding him small sips of water, trying to keep the covers on his shivering form and holding his hand when Ewen bleated "Papa?"

"I'm here, Ewen, and I will not leave you," he said steadily, trying to keep the fear out of his voice. "You will be better directly. The fever will pass." He hoped and prayed it would. He couldn't lose his son like this. It would, he thought, overset his reason.

It was after midnight when he heard a noise at the door of Ewen's room and turned to see a robed figure standing there. He blinked at this vision of a woman. Her hair was confined to a thick plait over her shoulder and her robe was tied about her waist, a plain white nightgown visible beneath. For a moment, past and present merged as he recalled another long, dark night, when Lizzie was sick of a terrible fever, and he and Caro had stood vigil by her side in the darkest hours before dawn.

But of course, this wasn't Caro, because she was gone, and in any case this figure was taller and more solid than Caro. It was Miss Pringle. She trod softly into the room and stood beside him, gazing down at the little boy, who tossed and turned and whimpered.

"Do you need to be relieved for a little?" she said. "I can sit with him."

"This is not your responsibility—" he began.

"By my calculation you have been with him for over eight hours straight," she interrupted. "I am accustomed to nursing children through illness. I grew up in a school for young ladies, I think I told you. I sat with many girls through fevers and tummy upsets in my years at the seminary. I assure you I can be trusted with him." She smiled sympathetically.

He swallowed and nodded. "Very well, thank you. I—I won't be long."

He took a few minutes to relieve himself and wash his face and hands, change his shirt, which had become drenched with sweat from his worry and the heat, and drink a long draught of water, suddenly realizing how thirsty he was.

He returned to the room and found her sitting on the narrow bed, holding Ewen's hand and singing to him softly. Her voice was sweet and the song soothing. It certainly seemed to be soothing Ewen, who lay still and quiet, no longer tossing and whimpering.

His heart swelled at the sight and his vision blurred with the tears that seemed never far from the surface with him lately. He came softly to stand behind her and put a hand on her shoulder. She finished the song, touching her hand to his where it rested on her shoulder. He turned his, clasping her fingers and squeezed them with gratitude.

Letting go reluctantly, he took his seat in the chair by the bed. He ought to relieve her, send her back to bed, but selfishly he wanted her to stay. In silence, they kept vigil together for another hour or so until Ewen woke, distressed and hot.

She fetched cold water and wrung out cloths for cold compresses, and he bathed his son's burning body trying to bring the wretched fever down.

Toward dawn, it began to ease again, and he sent her back to her room firmly.

"You must go, it is unseemly for you to be found with me like this. For your own sake go, but know you have my undying gratitude." He kissed her hand, and she left.

Full daylight found him nodding in his chair, bleary eyed and exhausted, but Ewen slept peacefully, and he hoped the fever was broken.

The promised nanny arrived midmorning. She was a pleasant woman in her forties, with a cheerful smile, restful manner, and generous bosom. She came with excellent references and, upon learning that her youngest charge was ill, took control immediately of the situation. The weary viscount, assured that the woman knew what she was doing and that Ewen seemed happy enough under her care, relinquished his post and sought his bed.

Chapter Ten

ANNIS SENT A note to the girls to say there would be no lessons for the morning and went back to bed upon hearing of the arrival of the new nanny, glad to surrender the responsibility for the children to her for a while. Annis was exhausted from the events of yesterday and overnight.

She slept until just before midday and woke hot and slightly depressed. It took her a while to figure out why. Kicking off the sheets, she lay sheened in perspiration and let her thoughts roam over the events of the last few days. The viscount figured prominently, and she realized with a jolt that she had derived no small degree of pleasure from his company.

Which explained her melancholy mood. The man was so sweet and so hurt, her heart was wrung for him. His devotion to his wife and children did him credit. Many men in his position would eschew the responsibility of the children, palming them off on servants, while losing themselves in drink or gaming, as so many dissolute peers did.

He was not a polished gentleman—his appearance was careless in the extreme. His jackets were clearly cut for comfort not style. His neckcloths, when he bothered with them, were knotted negligently, his boots and shoes were scuffed and dull, and his waistcoats frequently stained and unbuttoned. He seemed to shave only every three days or so, and his hair was too long and frequently looked uncombed.

For all this, he always smelled nice, so he washed daily at the very least. It was just his clothes he didn't care two pence for.

And under that careless attire, she had discovered yesterday, lay a firm, hard body with impressive muscles. She blushed, recalling the feel of him pressed briefly up against her as he pulled her and little Ewen into his embrace in the water. His body had been shockingly hot in the cold water, and the outline of his broad chest and pinkness of his flesh was clearly visible through the wet fabric of his shirt. He might as well have been naked from the waist up.

At the time, she had been too preoccupied with Ewen to really notice, but the memory came flooding back now in vivid, visceral detail, and her whole body flushed with heat.

A twitch and tingling dampness between her legs made her catch her breath.

No! No, no, no! I cannot not think of him in those terms. I will not. For he was far above her station. So far above that he was completely out of reach. Viscounts did not marry bastards—which was what she was, after all—even if he wanted a wife which, given his circumstances, she was absolutely certain he did not. *But he might entertain the bastard-born daughter of a lord as a mistress? Might he not?* whispered a wicked voice in her head.

No! She had fought so hard to hide the truth. If the duke and duchess knew, they would turn her off without a reference. One baseborn such as she could not be allowed anywhere near the duke's innocent sisters.

Exposure was what *he* had threatened her with. She shuddered with memory, as the dam wall she kept up between her and her past broke free.

She huddled against the wall in the darkened room, terrified out of her wits, as the figure dressed all in black, with a mask covering his face, loomed over her and rasped "You shall say nothing, you hear me?"

She whimpered and nodded, flinching as he leaned even closer, crowding her against the wall.

"Because if I get so much as sniff that you have confided in any-one—anyone!—you'll lose more than your post, my girl! You'll be branded a bastard and you'll be snuffed out faster than a candle! They'll find your body in a ditch so badly mutilated you'll be unrecognizable! You understand me?"

She made a garbled noise of terror and nodded again.

"Tell me you understand!"

"I-I und-derstand," she stammered.

"Good!" He straightened and moved away. She sagged against the wall, her legs so weak they threatened to give out.

He turned back, and she tried to shrink away. "Did she give you anything? Some token?"

"N-no!" Her teeth were chattering so much it was hard to get the word out. The ring was all she had; she wouldn't give it up.

"Are you sure? If you've lied to me . . ."

"I'm s-sure. I s-wear. I have nothing!" Would he believe her? Her heart thudded so hard she thought it would jump out of her chest.

"Hm."

She blinked, watching him as he appeared to be gathering himself for something. Then he turned back to her, and his gloved hand seized her throat and squeezed. She tried to say she was sorry that she lied, but then she couldn't speak. Couldn't breathe. She was going to die here, now, and no one would know what happened to her or why.

Blood pounded in her head as she struggled frantically, trying to prize his fingers away from her throat, but it was a futile endeavor. As the room went dark and she lost consciousness, she thought she heard a very faintly whispered "I'm sorry . . ."

She had woken in a backstreet in a pile of filth, her throat bruised and her head aching. Retching from the smell, she staggered to her feet and out into a street she recognized. Weeping and shivering from shock, she ran, limping. She had lost a shoe somewhere. She ran until she reached the seminary in Queen Square, Bath.

Circling to the rear entrance from the mews, she waited until she was sure there was no one about and dashed in the rear door and up the servants' stairs to her room on the second floor. Reaching the sanctuary of her room, she locked the door, stripped off her clothes and washed them and her body and hair, before slipping on a nightgown and sliding under the covers, where she lay shivering and shaking for a good hour before sleep finally overtook her.

Even now, after seven years, the memory made her shudder. Driven from her bed to get away from the clinging fingers of fear, she plunged her face in cold water to clear her head and sponged herself down thoroughly, enjoying the cold shock of the water on her skin driving out the past.

She put her hand to the chain round her neck where the ring hung suspended. No one knew she had it, for she always wore it hidden beneath the high necklines of her gowns. She touched the ring and tried to breathe through the tears that threatened.

She had been offered the opportunity by the owners to take over running the seminary on her mother's death, but the incident with the man in the mask had made her so terrified, she declined it and left Bath soon after the attack, driven by terror to put the whole episode behind her. She'd soon got another post in London with Lord Dowton's family, quite a step-up for a Bath seminarian. Her fears continued to plague her, though, and she sought some way to learn to protect herself. It was a conversation overheard between two of the footmen that had given her the idea.

"How much you gonna bet on Bloody Mary to beat Saucy Sue?" asked one.

"Nothin'" retorted the other. "Saucy Sue'll do fer 'er in five minutes flat!"

The other guffawed, "Not on yer life!"

The conversation had continued, but Annis wasn't listening anymore, the notion of a fight between two women for money was so fantastical she couldn't credit it. Yet further investigation proved it to be true. In the seedy backstreets of Cheapside, one could witness pugilistic events where the combatants weren't men, but women.

On her day off, Annis had gathered her courage and ventured into the area to find one of these fights. The noise, the smell, the coarseness of the audience, and the raw brutality of it all sickened her. But she screwed up her courage and watched an entire bout, trying not to flinch. At the end of it, she'd waited until the winner had received her accolades and payment and retired to the bar for a drink before approaching her. The winner's name was Brutal Betty. When she heard what Annis was proposing, she spat out her beer and laughed until the tears ran down her grubby cheeks.

But when she'd realized Annis could pay, she grew canny and demanded up-front payment. Annis offered half before and the rest at the end of the lessons. Much haggling later, they reached an agreement and Annis had begun visiting Betty weekly on her day off for a lesson in fisticuffs and knife fighting. She practiced each day and slowly improved.

If her mysterious attacker came for her again, she would not be helpless this time.

After a year in the Dowtons' employ, she saw the Duke of Troubridge's advertisement for a governess for his sisters. She applied for and miraculously was hired for the post with the Laynes and escaped to the country in a household that treated her with kindness and respect. She loved her charges and began to relax and feel safe.

As safe as anyone could with her history.

Lingering weariness and the cobwebs of the past made her slow, and she took her time dressing and rang for a tray in her room. When the maid came, she asked after Master Ewen and was told he was sleeping. She wanted to ask after the viscount, too, but that would not be proper. The governess had no business asking after his lordship. And if she did, it would be all over the house in five minutes.

Having eaten, she felt fortified enough to venture out for a stroll in the rose garden. It was another fine day, so she put on her broadest brimmed hat and took a basket and some pruning shears outside with the intention of picking some blooms for the duchess's drawing room. She wandered about the rose beds smelling blooms and selecting a range of different colors. Bees buzzed and the sun shone gloriously, its heat tempered by a nice breeze. Another perfect summer day. They were really most fortunate with the weather this year.

"You make a picture, Miss Pringle," said the viscount behind her, making her start and almost drop the basket. She flushed remembering her illicit thoughts about him earlier this morning.

"Are you fully recovered?" he asked, coming level with her.

"Yes, I am. Thank you," she said, attempting to cover her discomposure. "And you? And more importantly, Ewen?"

"Ewen is sleeping, I've just come from his bedside. The inestimable Mrs. Green has him in hand and the other children also. She appears to be highly competent."

"That must a big relief for you."

"It is. I must thank you again—"

"It is unnecessary—"

"No, it is not! Your quick action saved his life. I was moments behind you, that is true, but in a situation such as that, moments count!" He took the basket from her and set it on the ground. "You must allow me to thank you, to express my gratitude, although I am at a loss as to how to do so. Nothing I can say or do would ever be enough!" The rough emotion in his voice threatened to overset her, and when he captured her hands and brought them to his lips her heart flipped over in a cascade of beats that set her pulse racing.

She gazed up at him startled. His eyes were a stormy green, his expression quite anguished. "My lord—!"

"You don't understand, Miss Pringle. If I had lost him"—his throat worked—"I don't know that I would have been strong enough to withstand it!"

Her heart clenched in sympathy, and she leaned forward, seeking some way to comfort him. "I do understand! You have already suffered a terrible loss. To lose a child as well would be unthinkable." She freed a hand from his grip and touched his cheek.

AT THE TOUCH of her hand, so soft and light upon his cheek, and the glow of compassion in her eyes, he lost what little control he still had of his faculties and reached for the back of her head. He brought her mouth to his and kissed her.

Her lips were soft and sweet, and the tingling pleasure of their touch sent his senses reeling. He hadn't kissed any other woman than Caro in over ten years, and he was unprepared for the flood of heated desire that the touch of her lips provoked in his body.

He swept an arm round her waist instinctively, to draw her against him, and moved his mouth over hers, exploring and appreciating. Those luscious breasts he had been lusting after pressed against his chest as he moved his head to savor her lips. She didn't draw back, but remained frozen a moment in his embrace, and then he felt her soften and respond tentatively to the movement of his mouth over hers.

He groaned in his throat with the delight of her and parted his lips to lick tentatively at the seam of her mouth. A gasp from her gave him access, and he swept his tongue into her mouth to taste her. His arm tightened round her waist, as he deepened the kiss, exploring and teasing as she responded in a way that fired his blood and made him hard as iron.

He moved the angle of his head, tightening his hold, wanting her closer, his mouth wanting to claim and devour. Dimly, somewhere in the back of his head, he knew this was wrong, but he couldn't seem to stop kissing her. She was water in a desert to his parched soul, and he wanted to drown in her.

A bird call nearby disturbed the peace of the afternoon, and she jerked as if coming back to herself and pulled away, fought her way out of his embrace. Reluctantly he let her go. Dazed by the passion of their kiss, he stared down at her dumbly.

Her eyes were wide, their pupils full and black, her lips swollen from the punishment of his mouth, her breasts rose and fell rapidly in the confines of her modest gown.

"This is wrong, my lord. I could lose my post!" she said, breathless. She backed away and fled, leaving the basket at his feet and the scent and feel of her branded on his soul.

He closed his eyes a moment, adjusting to the loss of her from his arms.

She was right. She was Robert's employee, and he had just taken advantage of her like the lowest and most disgusting of reprobates. He had always despised men of his class who took advantage of the servants. Even as a goatish young lad, he had not done it. Perhaps it was because his sire had been so free with the chambermaids, and he saw what it did to his mother. They were both dead and gone now, but that didn't mean he had leave to start emulating the worst aspects of his sire's behavior.

Disgusted with himself, he turned aside, and then seeing the basket of roses she had left, he picked it up and took it back to the house, leaving it in the duchess's drawing room for someone to find. He then went to the library in search of a drink.

ANNIS GAINED HER bedchamber once more, shaken to her core. Hot tears stung her lids and rolled down her cheeks as shame excoriated her soul. She was so close to becoming what she had vowed she never would be: a fallen woman.

All her efforts would be in vain if she let him have his way and, God forgive her, she wanted him to. His kisses had scalded her, his hard lean form pressed against her had been delicious, his lips even more so, the tingling pleasure igniting the fire between her legs and making a strumpet of her.

She stumbled to the bed her hand to her mouth to stifle her sobs. A governess's life was lonely, caught between upstairs and downstairs, never belonging in either. She hungered for the felicity of connection and rapport, and even more perhaps for physical touch, for no one touched the governess. No, that was not entirely true. Her charges gave her hugs on occasion. But a young lady's hug was a different matter to an embrace from a virile man.

The truth was she did hunger for the viscount's touch. It had crept up on her over the past few days as she spent increasing amounts of time in his company, as he took her hand to help her down a set of steps or over a rough bit of ground, as he smiled at her and engaged her in conversation as if she were an equal. As he hauled her and his son against his hot, lean body in the lake.

She was a wanton. There was no way round it. She had let him kiss her, encouraged it, responded in the most brazen fashion to his passion. *How am I ever to face him after this?*

Annis kept to her room for the remainder of the afternoon, only descending to dinner after a lengthy debate with herself over whether she could face the viscount. But she reasoned that she would have to face him on the morrow anyway, and it was better to get it over with sooner rather than later. And besides, she didn't want him to think she was going to make a fuss about it.

She would behave completely appropriately; her demeanor would give no hint of what had transpired between them. The sooner it was forgotten the better. And she would be careful not to be alone with him again. It was essential that no one guess there was anything between them. Her reputation and the security of her position depended on it.

Chapter Eleven

EMRYS WAS UNSURE if Miss Pringle would appear for dinner and even less sure how he would handle it if she did. As it transpired, she was perfectly composed and treated him in a cool and professional way. She was never forward in company anyway, seldom participating in the dinner conversation, so to others she would appear no different than usual.

But to him, there was a silent constraint. She kept her eyes modestly on her plate, partook only lightly of the meal, and was careful not to look in his direction. He knew this because he couldn't help looking in hers, try as he might not to.

While keeping up a dinner conversation with the duke and duchess, he caught himself sneaking glances at her down the table. She was seated on the opposite side to him, flanked by the two princesses. He smiled to himself; he would forever think of them that way, he was sure.

"Master Ewen has taken no lasting hurt, I trust?" asked the dowager.

"He has not, Your Grace, for which I am profoundly thankful."

"Did Robert tell you about the time *he* fell into the lake?" she said.

"No," he threw Robert a glance, and the man rolled his eyes.

"He and Hereward had taken out the rowboat against their father's orders, and they got into an altercation in the middle of the lake. The craft, as I understand it, became unsteady and Robert fell in. Hereward was forced to rescue him."

"That is not precisely how it happened," said Robert.

Emrys let Robert's words wash over him, his attention snared by the fact that Miss Pringle was engaged in a softly spoken conversation with Heather and Mary. He couldn't hear what she was saying, nor their responses, but he was captivated by the softening of her expression as she spoke. She appeared to have relaxed somewhat for the first time this evening. He was glad of that. It distressed him to think that his behavior had caused her discomfort.

When the ladies rose at the end of the meal, he had hoped he would see her later, but when he and Robert rejoined them in the drawing room, he discovered that she and the young misses had retired early. He was still tired himself and made his excuses to retire, too.

On his way, he visited each of his children, tucked up in bed asleep. The girls were sharing a bed. Quite a large one for two tiny things. They looked so sweet in sleep, he just sat with them a bit in silence, watching them. He must pay them some more attention.

Finally dragging himself away, he popped in to sit with Ewen for a while. Mrs. Green was there, and he spoke with her quietly. She said that Ewen's temperature had spiked a little but then settled back down. She expected him to be better tomorrow.

Reaching his own room at last, he didn't bother ringing for his valet. Stripping off his clothing and slipping into bed, he lay on his back and finally let the thoughts he'd been holding at bay swamp him in sensation.

He couldn't pretend Miss Pringle's kisses hadn't roused him to an extraordinary degree. Reliving the moments that he held her in his arms and lost himself in her mouth, his body demanded release, and he gave it, closing his eyes in the aftermath and letting the peace soothe him.

He had no idea what he was supposed to do with this inconvenient lust for a woman he had no business thinking of in this way. He could only conclude it was a part of the grieving process and that it would pass. It didn't feel like that, but it must be the case.

He had never loved anyone but Caro. The fact that she had betrayed him at the end was sometimes hard to remember, because he just missed her so. Yet when he did think of it, his primary emotion was anger and a kind of dull despair. He wondered that he didn't feel more bitterness. He should, yet he couldn't muster the energy.

He sighed and rolled over, closing his eyes. He was deathly tired.

RETURNING TO HER room, Annis congratulated herself on having got through dinner with the viscount with no untoward incident. It was true that his eyes had strayed toward her rather more often than they should, but he had made no attempt to speak with her, for which she was grateful. And she rather thought no one else would have detected any change in her demeanor toward him or in his toward her. The whole thing could hopefully be put behind them and never spoken of again.

She must put his behavior down to an overexcitation of emotions triggered by his son's near drowning and her role in his rescue. It was nothing more than that on his part, she reassured herself, and the fact that she felt such a strong attraction toward him . . . well, she would just have to suppress such inappropriate reactions and thoughts. For if she didn't, she would be ruined. The price of pleasure for one such as she was far too high.

Having reached this satisfactory state of mind, she pushed her bedroom door open and gasped with shock.

Her room had been ransacked.

Stepping in and closing the door hurriedly, she leaned against the door a hand over her fast-galloping heart. Fear prickled over her skin.

Her drawers had been pulled out and their contents upended on the floor, her bedding pulled off and heaped in the middle of the room, her clothing ripped from the wardrobe and strewn about the room.

Tears started to her eyes, and she covered her mouth with her hand to stifle her sobs. Her other hand stole to the ring on a chain about her neck under the cloth of her gown.

A breeze disturbed the curtains by the window, and she stepped over the mess to the window and looked out. It was still daylight, being only half past eight. She had left the window open to allow the evening breeze in to cool the room. She looked down and noted the scrape marks on the windowsill. As if something sharp had gouged the wood. Whoever it was had entered, and presumably left, this way. And they had done it in broad daylight, which suggested a desperate act.

She swallowed the panic which threatened to bring up her dinner. *I have not been imagining things the last few weeks.* Someone *was* stalking her—like an animal—and here was the proof. She turned back to survey the mess in her room. *For whatever reason, he is back. My nemesis.*

She leaned against the windowsill, shaking with pure terror. What could she do? If she told anyone, he had promised he would kill her and not nicely . . . *They'll find your body in a ditch, so badly mutilated you'll be unrecognizable!*

She moved stiffly, picking things up and restoring them to their rightful places. Clothes back in the wardrobe. Sheets, coverlet, and pillows on the bed, stockings, reticules, belts, and personal effects in the dresser drawers. It was as she was restoring the drawers to the dresser that she noticed it. A folded piece of paper fallen into the empty coalscuttle by the fireplace.

She stared at it in horror for several moments, her heart

thudding loudly in her ears. Bending she picked it up and with shaking fingers and opened it.

> *Firstly, you will tell no one, for you know what will happen if you do. Secondly, you will meet me at the ruins at midnight tomorrow night. Thirdly, you will bring the ring.*
> *You will come alone on foot. Do not be late.*

She dropped the paper with a whimper from nerveless fingers. *He will kill me for certain this time. As soon as he has his hands on the ring, he will kill me.* He must have figured out that she had lied and been watching her for a while to plan this attack. But how? And why now? Clearly when he couldn't find the ring, he'd settled for leaving the note, but what had he intended if he'd found the ring in her room?

Lay in wait for me to return and murder me in my bed . . .

She gasped, tears squeezing out behind her scrunched-up eyes. *He wants me dead, but only after he gets his hands on the ring. I am the only clue to its whereabouts. He won't kill me as long as I don't give him the ring.*

She clenched her hands tightly into fists, a long-stoked rage building under her ribs. *This has to stop, or my life won't be worth living. I cannot, will not, continue to live my life in fear like this. This man, whoever he is, must be stopped.* She swallowed. *I should tell the duke, or the viscount. Surely, they will protect me.*

> *Firstly, you will tell no one, for you know what will happen if you do.*

She shuddered. The threats of her attacker rang in her head, husky and dark, making her body quake with renewed terror. No, she couldn't involve the duke or the viscount. What if this desperate madman decided to take his vengeance out on one of the children?

She must deal with this alone. She would not be responsible for bringing such a threat into the lives of innocents. Only then would this menace go away.

Can I do it?

I have to. It is his life or mine.

She shuddered again, wrapping her arms round her stomach, her skin goose-bumped with horror. She felt sick.

Sitting down on the newly made bed, she closed her eyes and just breathed. Finally, she rose and went to the window and drew the curtains. Then she turned to the small writing desk set beside the window and sat down. Drawing pen and paper toward her, she mended the pen, stuck the nib in the ink, and began to write.

My dearest Emrys,

If you are reading this then I am already dead, for I do not plan for you to ever see this letter, but I feel that in the circumstance of some ill befalling me, I will owe you some explanation for my disappearance.

I am also giving into your safekeeping a ring that belonged, I am told, to my father. I do not know his identity, only that I am his baseborn daughter and that he is a peer of the realm, of what degree I do not know. My mother was Miss Janet Pringle. For most of my life I thought she was my aunt and that I was the daughter of her brother, Mr. Jeremiah Pringle, and his wife Adela. They died when I was a baby, and I do not remember them. It was only on her deathbed that I learned from my Aunt Janet that she was in fact my mother as well as the identity, such as it is, of my father.

Since her passing, I have been subjected to the most horrible persecution by a man of unknown identity seeking to obtain the ring and kill me. I had thought for a number of years that he had given up his persecution of me, but lately he has resurfaced.

I know this must sound raving, but I assure you he has attacked me before and has now threatened me again. I don't know why my existence or that of the ring is worth such drastic action, but it is terrifying. I am tired of living in fear and must act now myself.

I am taking steps to eliminate the threat once and for all.

But it is essential that he not get his hands on the ring, for if he should do so, he will assuredly kill me. Thus, I am leaving it in your possession, unbeknownst to you. I do not anticipate you will find either it or this letter before I execute my plan.

In the event that I am successful, you will never know of it or of this letter, for I shall take them both back and destroy the letter. But in the event that I am not successful, I wish you to know that I treasured your kisses. You are the kindest, most attractive man I have ever known, and I hold you in the highest esteem.

I recommend that you destroy the ring and tell no one about any of this, for I truly do not wish for you or your delightful children to be placed at risk. I honestly think the risk will die with me, because it seems clear to me now that my existence is the true threat this man wishes to eliminate.

I remain ever yours,
Annis Benedicta Pringle

She read over the letter carefully, sanded it dry, folded it, and placed it and the ring from around her neck in an envelope upon which she had written his name. She folded it in half and, clutching it in her hand, buried it in the folds of her skirt. She then opened her door and checked the hallway. Seeing it empty, she closed and locked her door behind her.

She then walked rapidly to the servants' stairs and, slipping through the door, made her way to the floor below, where the viscount's suite was located. She emerged in his dressing room, checking carefully first for the presence of his valet, who was mercifully absent.

It took her a few minutes to select an appropriate hiding place for her little package, but finally she chose the pocket of a quite resplendent evening jacket, which she had never seen him wear and thought he was highly unlikely to wear in the next forty-eight hours. It was the sort of thing he might wear to a ball, being made of black satin, and there were a pair of matching breeches. Satisfied that this was a very unlikely item of clothing to be called into service between now and midnight tomorrow night, she slipped her package into the breast pocket, closed the wardrobe door carefully and slipped back into the servants' stairs and made her way back to her room.

She had merely to get through the next twenty-four hours as if nothing were wrong. A feat that would call upon all of her acting skills. But having made up her mind to her course of action, she was remarkably calm and focused. She was even, to her surprise, able to sleep soundly.

The next morning Annis spent with her pupils, and since the weather was for the first time in days inclement, the children were forced to remain indoors and play games in the nursery, supervised by Mrs. Green.

This freed Annis to spend the afternoon putting her affairs in order, not that she had a lot to do. She owned very little, but she did want her room to be tidy and her few possessions in good order in the event that the worst should happen.

Just before tea, she popped into the nursery to watch the children wistfully. *If this is the last I will see of them . . .* She swallowed a lump in her throat and was forced to clear it hastily when Miss Elizabeth bowled up to her and demanded her opinion of her latest artwork. Not to be outdone, Miss Charlotte wished to show her a sculpture she was making in clay, and she found herself on the floor with the two of them providing artistic advice when the viscount appeared above them.

"Papa!" squealed both girls, flinging themselves at him. He didn't seem to mind this assault, not even the fact that his clothes were threatened with red paint and wet clay. Hugging both little ladies in turn he got down on the floor, too, and offered his opinion of their artistic efforts.

"Don't you think he is a little lopsided?" he asked Charlotte of her sculpture.

"He is *supposed* to be, Papa! He's a monster. See he has a hunchback and uneven legs."

"Oh, I see, and what is this that he is chasing?" he said, pointing to the second figure.

"A little girl, of course!" she replied, rolling her eyes.

He glanced at Annis, the smile in his eyes inviting her to share the joke. She smiled in return, relieved that the children seemed to be providing a bridge to cover any awkwardness they might feel after their encounter in the rose garden. She was glad. She would prefer that their last interaction, should it turn out to be so, not be attended by unpleasant feelings.

"Do you like my sunflowers, Papa?" asked Elizabeth claiming his attention.

"I do," he said.

"This is you and Miss Pringle," she added, pointing to the two figures standing among the sunflowers, apparently holding hands.

Annis flushed when he raised his eyebrows at this, and she thought crossly, *so much for no awkwardness.*

"At first I was going to make it Mama, but then I thought it was better if I made it Miss Pringle, because she is here, and Mama isn't." Elizabeth's mouth turned down and Annis's heart contracted. *Gosh, if anything happens to me, the children will miss me. I didn't think of that . . .*

The viscount cleared his throat and seemed to be groping for another topic of conversation when the welcome interruption of afternoon tea being served saved the situation. Leaving the children to their afternoon feast, she left the nursery with his lordship.

She should leave him, as well, but found herself completely unable to do so, walking with him to the stairs down to the next floor and the next. If she had been thinking about it, she might have assumed he was heading to the drawing room where she anticipated afternoon tea for the adults was being served. But she wasn't thinking much except that she wanted to remain in his company as long as possible. And when they reached a door on the first floor, he pushed it open, holding it for her.

It was the library, she registered stupidly. Her heart accelerated when she realized he had shut the door and was moving toward her. *Oh, no! He is going to kiss me again!*

I should stop him, but . . . if this is my last opportunity . . .

He stopped before her and his eyes told her everything she needed to know about his intentions. They positively smoldered.

"Miss Pringle—Annis! I have been wholly unable to stop thinking of you since yesterday."

She gasped as he put his arm round her. "I know this is wretchedly unfair of me," he said thickly, "but I cannot resist you!" He pulled her tight against him and kissed her.

It was a rough, devouring kiss that completely decimated any defense she might have tried to raise. In any case, this was perhaps her last chance to experience the delight of his embrace. She surrendered, returning his kisses with fervid ones of her own, parting her lips for him and even using her tongue to taste and devour him as much as he was her.

She molded her body to his in wanton abandon, feeling the heat and hardness of him through the layers of their clothing, tingling wet heat gathering between her thighs. Her arms crept round his neck, her fingers pushing into his long hair, cupping his scalp, her breasts squashed flat against his chest. He was wearing more clothes than usual today, including a jacket and neckcloth, to her regret.

"Annis," he murmured, breaking the kiss, his breath hot and rapid in her face as he leaned his forehead against hers. "Annis, will you marry me?"

Her eyes widened in shock, her heart turning over in her breast. She pulled back and stared at him, bereft of speech.

"The children already love you, I can tell, and they need a mother. A nanny alone won't do. I think you're fond of them, could love them in time? Hm?" He nuzzled her cheek with his nose. "And God help me, but I want you. I don't understand it. There has been no one but Caro for me for over ten years, and suddenly you're all I can think about."

Oh, God! Her heart clenched with anguish. *How can this be happening?* She could never marry him. Even if he never found out she was baseborn, she was still only a governess and no fit bride for a viscount. *And with what I plan to do tonight . . .*

Tears, never very far from the surface, stung her lids and she swallowed with difficulty.

"I cannot, my lord! I'm so sorry!" She tore herself from his embrace and fled the room, racing up two flights of stairs as if the hounds of hell were after her. Reaching her room, she unlocked the door with shaking hands, barely able to see through her tears. Getting the door open she flung herself through it, then slammed it and locked it. Leaning against it, she slid slowly to the floor sobbing.

⤐⤜

EMRYS, LEFT STANDING in the library alone, suppressed the urge to go after her, they couldn't have an argument in the middle of the hallway or stairs. He had taken her by surprise. *Hell, I surprised myself!* He had not intended to propose marriage—the words had just burst from him. With her unbridled response to his kisses, he had lost all sense, and suddenly it had seemed the perfect solution to all his woes.

The children *did* need a mother, and a nanny alone would *not* do. And she was perfect for the role. It was obvious the children loved her, and she was fond of them at the very least. And in his fevered state, he thought he would do anything to have her.

He had not expected her to refuse him. Her physical response told him she wanted him as much as he wanted her. He acquitted her of fakery in that regard. Annis Pringle was no seductress. Her emotional responses were pure and without artifice, he would swear to it.

She was no young miss either, but a mature woman. A virtuous one all the same, he'd stake his balls on that. For all her honest passion, she was not experienced, he was certain. Something in the way she had hesitated yesterday told him she was not accustomed to kisses. She was no flirt, no coquette. She dressed plainly with no adornment, her dresses so modest they drove him mad wondering what was underneath.

I did surprise her, he reiterated to himself. He would give her time to consider all the benefits of his proposal. *Then I will ask again, for her refusal has done nothing to assuage my longing for her. In fact, it's made it worse.*

Chapter Twelve

ANNIS REMAINED IN her room for the rest of the evening, claiming a headache and having a tray brought to her room, which she was unable to touch. Her state of turmoil was such that food was the last thing she could think about.

The viscount's proposal was a bittersweet thing in the face of what she had to accomplish tonight, and should she survive the night, she would deal with it tomorrow. She wasn't entirely sure how or in what fashion, but first and foremost she needed to ensure her own survival. Once she had dealt with that, she could consider what to do about the viscount.

Time dragged interminably toward midnight. At half past eleven, she left her room, dressed in a cloak and stout boots, with a small sharp knife in her reticule and determination in her heart. She was never gladder of her lessons in knife fighting than now.

She crept down the servants' stairs to the rear entrance and made her way around the house toward the ruins. There was intermittent moonlight between the scudding clouds to light her way. The air was cool and damp, the wind tugging at her cloak.

Her heart thudded hard in her chest as she approached the black outline of the ruins. Terror stiffened her limbs and threatened to make her teeth chatter. Everything in her willed her to turn tail and flee. *I should go to the duke, throw myself on his mercy, and hope that he will not dismiss me for lying about my birth and my past. Or the viscount? Can I . . . no, I cannot! The man has enough troubles. Embroiling him in mine is unthinkable.*

But seven years of unrelenting fear made her push on past her doubts. It would end tonight. She would no longer live her life in fear.

If I am free of this, perhaps I can consider the viscount's offer, my birth notwithstanding.

The notion strengthened her resolve, and she came to a cautious halt beside the tower, looking around for her assailant.

A shape separated itself from the shadow of the tower, and she gripped the knife in her reticule. She wished she had been brave enough to steal one of the duke's pistols.

The figure stepped slowly toward her. He seemed of a different build than the figure in her memory, more slender. She seemed to recall the man who had terrorized her mind for seven years as being bulkier, bigger. But then he could have lost weight, or perhaps he had just loomed large in her recall because she was so afraid of him. Like her, he wore a cloak, and his face was hidden. A shudder of fear raced through her body.

He stepped close. "You brought it?" he asked.

His voice was not as deep as she recalled, but again, perhaps her memory was faulty.

He stepped closer, holding out a hand. "Give it to me!"

Slowly she extracted her hand from her reticule, the knife clutched in it, and she struck with all her might, bringing the knife upward under his ribs as she had been taught.

He cried out and staggered. "You bitch!" he gasped.

She pulled the knife free, but contrary to her expectation he did not go down. Instead, he tried to grapple with her. She brought the knife up again, and it scraped across his cheek, making him howl with surprise and shock. He staggered then, falling to his knees, and she turned and ran. She glanced back once but could discern no pursuit.

She reached the house, panting and faint with horror. She

went in via the servants' entrance and staggered up the stairs to her room, trying to be as quiet as possible. Her hands were shaking so much she had difficulty unlocking her door. She finally got the key in the lock. Shutting the door of her room, she inspected her clothes and person for blood. Sure enough, there were splatters on her gown. If there were any on her cloak, they were not visible against the dark cloth.

With unsteady hands, she washed the knife in the bowl of water and spent some minutes rubbing the stains from her gown. She then emptied the bowl of bloody water out the window and sank down with shaking legs upon her bed, her head in her hands. *Have I killed him? I can only hope so, or he will come after me again.*

She shuddered. Surprisingly she shed no tears. She was beyond tears at this point. She had crossed the Rubicon. She was a murderess. She would never be the same again.

My letter to the viscount! She started up. *It is more imperative than ever that I retrieve it!* She left her room silently, slipped into the servants' stairs and emerged again in the viscount's dressing room. The room was in darkness, and she crossed on silent feet to open the curtains slightly to let in a little light. She paused, getting her bearings, and headed toward the wardrobe. Groping in the darkness, she finally found the satin evening jacket and inserting her fingers into the breast pocket she extracted her little package. *Exactly where I left it!*

Relief coursed through her. As she closed the wardrobe door, however, she half expected the viscount to appear and catch her red-handed. *Perhaps I even hope that he might?* However, the door to his bedchamber remained shut. She crossed to the window and twitched the curtain back into place. She paused to listen, but there was no sound from the next room. She could only conclude he was asleep. With a wrench, she resisted the temptation to look at him while he slept and crept back to the servants' stairs and to her room.

The fire was banked. She stirred it up, removed the ring from the envelope, and threw the letter into the flames. She watched the paper catch fire, crinkle, and turn to ash in moments. Letting out a deep sigh, she sank down once more on the bed, rethreading the chain through her ring and fastening it round her neck.

She sat a few minutes with her eyes closed, clutching the ring and fought the tears. Finally, she gave in and sobbed. She must have been mad to think she could go to the viscount after this. *I am a murderess!* She couldn't remain here, under the duke's roof, teaching his innocent sisters and pretending she wasn't a black-hearted sinner. She deserved to hang, and if she were caught, that was what would happen. *Why did I think this would solve all my problems? They will find the body in the morning. I can't face it. I will give myself away.*

When the tears had run their course, she rose and began packing a bag. She would flee to London and lose herself there. She could change her name and earn her living as a seamstress. *But what to tell my employers to stop them pursuing me?*

She penned another letter, this one much shorter than her one to the viscount.

Your Grace, I do beg your forgiveness for leaving in this fashion. I have received bad news of my aunt, the woman who raised me. She is dying, and I must go to Bath to attend her.

Yours sincerely,
Annis Pringle

There, that was sufficiently vague to prevent them finding her, and by the time they realized that she wasn't in Bath and wasn't coming back, it would be too late to find her in London. And hopefully her disappearance would not be linked with a body in the grounds, either.

The fact that her aunt had died some years ago might come to light if they asked questions, though. The duke would know from her original references that she was raised by Janet Pringle of the Pringle Academy for Young Ladies in Bath. But he would likely have to search through his records to find that information. All of which would take time.

With any luck, they would not realize she was missing for several hours. No servant would come to her room if she didn't ring for one. If she left a note in the servants' hall for them to inform the young ladies that there would be no lessons in the morning as she was unwell, no one would trouble her for some time.

Pleased with this stratagem, she crept downstairs, left the note for the servants and let herself out of the house for the second time that night. She would have to walk to Leicester and hope that the stagecoach would arrive before anyone came looking for her.

Chapter Thirteen

I T WASN'T UNTIL after lunch that they discovered Annis was missing and her note to the duke was found.

Emrys and Robert were having a postprandial whisky in the library, the weather outside being still wet, when the duchess poked her head in the door.

"There you are!"

"What is it, love?" asked the duke, looking up from his newspaper. Emrys glanced up from the book he was reading—or attempting to read. Thoughts of Annis kept intruding. He had been in a worry about her the instant he heard she wasn't well and was keeping to her room. *Have I made her ill, or is it a female malady that ails her?*

The duchess came in and very improperly perched on the arm of her husband's chair. Emrys hid a smile. The buttoned-up duke would never have tolerated anything so casual prior to marrying Sarah. But the Watsons' friendly ways had rubbed off on him to good effect.

"I just discovered that Miss Pringle has left for Bath at some ungodly hour this morning—on foot, for goodness' sake! I cannot understand why she would do this. Surely, she knew we would lend her the carriage?"

Emrys dropped his book, leaning forward in shock. "Bath!

Why would she go to Bath?"

"Her aunt who raised her is dying apparently," said the duchess. "But why she wouldn't wait and asked for the carriage I cannot fathom. Surely, she wouldn't think we would refuse to let her go."

"Of course not!" said Robert. "This is a most distempered freak. Why would she do such a thing?"

"Oh, God!" said Emrys. "I think I may know. You have to let me go after her."

"Emrys what are you on about? If it's anyone's responsibility to go after her it is mine. I'm her employer, after all!" said the duke rising.

Emrys shot to his feet. "No, Robert. I need to go. She—I—" He stopped, flushing crimson.

The duke and duchess goggled at him, and he rubbed his head, tousling his hair. "I asked her to marry me yesterday," he said somewhat sheepishly. "I fear that may be why she has fled."

"Good God, man, have you taken leave of your senses? She's the bloody governess!" said the duke explosively.

The duchess was grinning hugely and said, "What has that to do with anything? She is perfectly delightful, and the children adore her." She bounced off the chair arm and gave Emrys a hug, with a defiant look over her shoulder at her indignant spouse. "Of course you must go after her, Emrys!"

"You mean this nonsense about an aunt in Bath may be a fudge?" said Robert, very heroically ignoring his wife's provocation. "No, wait a minute though, didn't she come from some seminary in Bath?" He turned toward his desk and began pulling out drawers. "I'm sure I've got her papers here somewhere."

"I believe she does have an aunt in Bath," said the viscount. "I'm sure she mentioned her at some point. Though I got the impression she was already dead. However, I suppose I must be mistaken if she really has gone to Bath to attend her on her deathbed." He frowned. *Perhaps I am jumping to conclusions, blaming her exodus on my proposal. Bit of a coxcomb aren't I, to think my attentions might have driven her from the house?*

"Whether she has gone to attend her aunt or not is irrelevant!" said the duchess impatiently. "The thing is she should not be allowed to continue all the way to Bath on the stage. It will take days and be vastly uncomfortable."

"Ah! Here it is!" exclaimed the duke, pulling out a sheet of paper. "Queen Square, Bath, the Pringle Academy for Young Ladies!" he said triumphantly. He raised his eyes from the paper and smiled at his audience. "Yes, my love, you are perfectly correct. We cannot allow Miss Pringle to journey all the way to Bath on the humble stagecoach."

"In that case," said Emrys, "I had best make haste. If I take a horse I will make much better time, and with this weather, the stage will be moving cursed slowly anyway. With any luck, I'll catch her before nightfall."

"Aye, well, don't catch your death in this wet!" said Robert. Emrys waved in acknowledgment, passing out the door to the sound of the duke saying, "Well, I'd never have thought it of Emrys. What was he thinking? The governess!"

"Don't be so stuffy, Robert! I think it's romantic!" said the duchess.

Emrys found the butler and requested him to find his valet and get the man to pack him an overnight bag and to send to the stables and get his horse, Inigo, saddled. He then ran up two flights of stairs to find his children. Mrs. Green had all the small fry on the rug reading them a story.

"Sorry to interrupt, Mrs. Green. Might I borrow my three for a moment?"

She nodded, and he beckoned them over. Crouching down, he said, "Miss Pringle has had to leave on an urgent personal matter, but she has gone without an escort, and that is not proper. I am going to fetch her, make sure she is safe, you understand? I may be gone a couple of days. Will you be all right?"

Lizzie stiffened, and he watched her struggle. Ewen, who had recovered now from his dunking in the lake, eyed him somberly. Charlie screwed her face up and said tearfully, "You can't leave us, Papa!" She wrapped her arms round him.

He hugged her close. "It won't be for long, poppet. I promise."

"It's all right, Papa. I understand," said Lizzie, manfully trying not to sniffle. "Charlie, he's going to get Miss Pringle. You want Miss Pringle to come back, don't you?"

Charlie sniffed and nodded.

"Well then," said Lizzie.

"Miss Pingle?" said Ewen.

"Yes, Miss Pingle," said Emrys with a smile, despite the ache in his throat.

Hugs all round, and he left with a brief word to Mrs. Green to take care of them.

"Of course, my lord, they will be fine until you get back. Do not worry." Emrys nodded and left to collect his bag, check he had sufficient funds for a journey, and make his way to the stables where his superb, dark chocolate-colored gelding, waited for him.

The skies were a leaden gray, and the fine rain that he started out with grew progressively heavier as he rode. It was just gone three o'clock in the afternoon when he reached Leicester and proved what he had already suspected. It was impossible to reach Bath from Leicester by any publicly available form of transport. Reaching Bath required either one's own horse or carriage, or alternatively to travel to London and thence to Bath from there, a journey that would take well over a week all told.

Finding the stagecoach inn at Leicester, he established the Royal Mail had passed through Leicester at around 10:30 that morning. As to whether a young woman meeting Miss Pringle's description had boarded it, the proprietor of the inn couldn't say. With the worsening weather, that worthy noted pessimistically that the mail would be running several hours late and likely not to reach its destination of Watford that evening at anything like its scheduled time.

It was just past Swinford, well after five o'clock and almost dark due to the heavy cloud cover and persistent rain, when he ran across the mail coach mired in the mud. Its passengers sat damply by the side of the road on their luggage, while its officers and such male passengers who deemed themselves capable attempted to unstick the carriage's wheels from the mud.

Scanning the passengers in the gloom, he found her sitting on her bag under the branch of a tree and huddled in her cloak, with her head down. She didn't even see him as he approached and dismounted his horse. He squatted in front of her. "Miss Pringle?"

Her head came up abruptly, and she stared at him wide-eyed. Her face was so pale as to be almost white in the gloomy light, and she seemed to sway slightly as she stared at him uncomprehendingly. Fearing she was about to swoon, he put his arms round her and murmured, "It's all right, I've got you."

"Emrys?" she said faintly. "Is it really you?"

"Yes," he said, smiling at her use of his name. "Come, I'm taking you home."

"But—"

"No buts. If you truly wish to go to Bath, you shall go in the duke's carriage suitably escorted. But for right now I need to get you somewhere warm and dry before you catch your death of cold. Your cloak is soaked through. And you're shivering!" he scolded.

She seemed to subside at this and nodded dumbly. He scooped her up, plopped her on his horse, where she sat sideways, clinging to the pommel, while he tied her bags to the saddle and then got up behind her. Wrapping his arm round her waist he turned Inigo and set off back toward Swinford. He would find an inn for the night. She was done in, and no wonder—she had walked goodness knows how far, carrying a heavy bag, and then sat in an uncomfortable coach for hours, followed by at least an hour sitting by the side of the road in the cold and wet.

She subsided back against him and mumbled, "How did you

find me?"

"It wasn't difficult. Hush now and rest," he said, pulling her back against him.

She wrapped her arms round his middle and nuzzled her face into his chest, which made him smile despite the inclement conditions. *She is wet through and exhausted, I need to get her warm and dry as soon as possible.*

"I think we should stop in Swinford for the night. And given that we are arriving on one horse I think I should say you are my wife, or it is going to look dashed peculiar, and I'd rather not wrangle with the landlord over proprieties," he said, tightening his arm round her as he urged Inigo into a canter.

She looked up at him dazed.

"Don't worry. I won't do anything you don't want me to. You're safe with me, Annis."

She bit her lip and nodded, subsiding against his chest again, and he said nothing more until he brought Inigo to a halt in the courtyard of the Blue Rose Inn.

He nudged her gently. "We've arrived."

"Hm?" she straightened up. "Where?"

"Swinford." He dismounted and drew her down into his arms and set her gently on her feet. She clutched at his arm to steady herself. *I am right—she is completely done in, and cold to the bone.* "Here, hold onto something while I get our bags," he said, putting her hand onto the pommel. He unlashed both bags and turned just as a servitor appeared.

"May I help you, sir?"

"Yes, take these. I require a room for myself and my wife, a hot bath for the lady, and a meal for us both served in the room. And see that my horse is attended to."

The man, recognizing him for quality from his speech, bowed. "At once, sir." He indicated to the ostler to take the horse. "Come this way."

Emrys turned his attention back to Annis. "Can you walk, or would you like me to carry you?" he asked quietly.

"I can walk," she said faintly, grabbing his arm. Deciding that she couldn't after all, he swept her up and carried her into the inn and up the stairs after the man with their bags.

The room he showed them to wasn't elegant, but it was clean. It boasted a fireplace where a fire was already lit, and there were several candles and two lamps to give them light in the gathering gloom. There was also a large bed covered in a cozy red coverlet and piled high with pillows, a small round table with two chairs, a small two-seater couch drawn up to the fire, and a dresser with drawers, on the top of which rested a ewer and bowl.

"You shall have the bath and hot water directly, sir, and a meal soon after." The man left, and Emrys set Miss Pringle—Annis—down on the settee and began unlacing her cloak. "Let me get this off you," he said.

She let him, and he divested himself of his own coat as well, which was also wet, but being made of thicker material, had withstood the soaking rain better. He turned to his pack and found the flask he carried and took that to her and offered it. She needed something immediately to buck her up a bit.

"Here," he said gently.

"What is it?"

"Brandy. I think you could use a little, yes?"

She took a swig and coughed. But it brought a little color to her cheeks.

A knock at the door heralded the arrival of the bath and a procession of buckets of hot water. The chambermaid left towels and a cake of hard soap.

"I'll leave you to your bath," he said. "Do you require help with your laces before I go?"

She shook her head.

"Lock the door behind me," he said and left to go and check on his horse. He stayed away for half an hour, and judging that was long enough, he returned to the room, knocking for readmittance. "It's me."

After a few moments, she unlocked the door and let him in. She had changed into a robe over a nightgown and her hair was down in a plait—the same as when she sat vigil with him over Ewen that night. "They just brought the meal," she said, indicating the dishes and plates on the table.

He joined her at the table, conscious of the constraint between them, but unsure how to bridge it. She seemed disinclined to talk. He wasn't sure if that was from fatigue or some other cause. In either case, he was ravenous and fell to with enthusiasm. The meal was plain but good fare. A thick meaty stew, fresh bread and butter, with cheese and fruit.

She ate quickly, too, as if half starved, and he wondered when she had last eaten.

A red wine of reasonable quality accompanied the meal, and she drank the glass he poured for her as quickly as she had eaten the meal. He topped up both their glasses and sat back in his chair, regarding her over his glass. She toyed with hers but stared at the fire as if it were the most fascinating thing in the room.

"Were you going to Bath?" he asked gently.

She shook her head.

"Your aunt isn't dying?"

"She's already dead," she said flatly.

"Did you leave because of me?"

"In a manner of speaking," she said, sipping her wine and transferring her gaze to the glass, twisting it about as if watching the play of light on the blood-red liquid.

He closed his eyes a moment, a lance of pain in his chest. Then, leaning forward, he took her hand. "I never meant to drive you from your home. If my proposal was that abhorrent to you—"

"No!" She looked at him then, her eyes full of some kind of deep sorrow he could not comprehend. "You just tempted me beyond reason!"

"I don't think I understand, Annis. Will you please explain?" he said gently.

She looked down. "Yes, I suppose I owe you that, having put

you to so much trouble as to come after me." She drew in an unsteady breath and let it out slowly. "I'm not sure I know where to start." She paused as if considering. "Do you recall when we visited Kegworth? And we took a stroll up the street? You noted that I was pale and asked me if I was well?"

He nodded. "Yes, you were as white as a sheet. I was quite concerned about you."

She swallowed. "Yes, well, I fancied that someone was watching me. Have you ever had that feeling? A kind of prickling between the shoulder blades as if someone were staring at you very hard?"

"Yes. Not often, but I have felt it." He leaned forward, watching her face intently. So many emotions were flitting across it, he was having trouble keeping up. Whatever was going on here had been provoked by more than his proposal.

"It turns out they were. Watching me that is. I—" She stopped, her throat working. She took another sip of wine. "When I explain, my lord, you will understand why I refused your proposal and why being here with me at this inn will be— must be—the last time you see me. Tomorrow, you must let me go."

He opened his mouth to protest and shut it again, his mind baffled by her cryptic words. "Go on," he said a mite grimly.

She looked down at her hands clasped tightly in her lap and took another one of those breaths. *Whatever this was, it was difficult for her.* He gave her his full attention.

"Seven years ago, my aunt died. On her deathbed, she gave me something—a ring." She drew a chain from beneath her robe and showed him a plain gold ring with a flat oval top, as if it ought to have something carved into it but didn't. "It belonged to my father, apparently. I don't know who he was, she didn't tell me. I gathered, though, that he was a member of the aristocracy." She swallowed, looking down at her hands. "Up until that point I had believed myself to be the daughter of Aunt Janet's brother and his wife Adela. Aunt Janet raised me, you see."

"The Pringle Academy for Young Ladies in Bath."

"Yes, that is where I grew up."

"Go on," he said taking another sip of the wine.

"It—it was shortly after that, that a man—I don't know who he was—kidnapped me off the street and took me to a—a room somewhere. I don't know where it was, for he put a hood over my head and only removed it once we were in the room. It was ill-lit. He was dressed all in black, and he had a mask on his face. He—he threatened me."

Emrys started at this and opened his mouth to say something, but she went on, oblivious to his reaction, and he kept silent.

"He seemed to think I knew who my father was. When I protested that I didn't, he refused to believe me. He—he said that if I breathed a word to a soul, he would kill me." She swallowed visibly. "He said they would find my body in a ditch, and I would be so badly mutilated that no one would recognize me."

"Oh, God!" Emrys got up and came round the table and pulled her up into his arms and held her tight. "No wonder you were frightened. And you think this man is still after you?" He buried his face in her hair, his heart thudding hard.

She nodded, her face pressed into his chest. She turned it slightly and said, "My room was ransacked two nights ago. He was looking for the ring. When he couldn't find it, because I had it on me, he left a note and told me to meet him by the ruins last night at midnight."

"My God, you didn't go?"

"I did." She swallowed.

"Why didn't you tell me? Tell someone? The duke if you didn't trust me?" He almost shook her with frustration at the danger she had put herself in.

"Did—did they find a—a body?" she asked shakily.

"What, at the ruins?"

"Yes. This morning, did—"

"No, why?"

"I—think I might have killed him, you see. I stabbed him

under the ribs. After the first attack I learned how to defend myself so if he ever came after me again, I'd be prepared." She babbled, her eyes wide, the pupils blown.

"There was no body reported."

"They may not have found it yet. Who would go there to find out?" she said chewing her lip.

He cupped her face in his hands and stared into her eyes. "I cannot believe that you have killed anyone."

She smiled, but it was awry, and her eyes for the first time showed a glimmer of tears. "Does it matter whether I did or not? I intended to, and that is just as bad. I decided I'd had enough of constantly living in fear. I wanted it to end. Especially after—" She stopped, closing her eyes, but the tears seeped out and rolled down her cheeks.

"Annis," he whispered. "Don't, sweetheart. I can't bear it." And he kissed her.

She pulled back. "Stop—Emrys, you can't still want me after this."

"Let me show you how much I want you," he said soft and low.

"Emrys, no! I'm a murderess confessed!"

"You are no such thing. If you did kill him, which I highly doubt, it was in self-defense. In any case, as my wife you would not be prosecuted."

"I'm not your wife."

"You will be." He lifted her chin up to look at him. "We are alone in a bedchamber for the night. You are entirely ruined even if I don't lay a hand on you. I have to marry you."

"No one here knows who we are. And I'm only the governess, Emrys. You most emphatically do not have to marry me. I'm not a lady."

"You are to me."

"I don't even know who my father is!" she said helplessly.

"I don't care." He cleared his clogged throat. "My children love you; they need you. You make them happy. Damn it, you make *me* happy!"

"Emrys I—" But he cut her off with a kiss. If his words weren't enough to convince her, he was willing to use other methods of persuasion. He lifted her up, carried her to the bed and laid her down on it.

He looked down at her expectantly, his gaze fairly burning into hers. With every look and action he had tried to make it clear what he wanted, but he wondered if she would object. He knew she wanted him as he wanted her, knew her objections were founded on some notion that she was damaged goods. But he also knew he could show her how wrong she was if she'd let him. She stared up at him a moment, then shed her robe and slid under the covers, and he set about divesting himself of his wretched clothing.

Chapter Fourteen

ANNIS WATCHED HIM remove his neckcloth, jacket, and boots, then his waistcoat and shirt. He left his breeches on, which was a courtesy typical of him. Her heart skipped and thudded hard. *Oh, how you tempt me, Emrys!* He even tempted her to believe he meant the words he spoke so emphatically. But they were driven by passion, surely? By desire. Could she trust such words, such promises?

On the other hand, does it really matter? she wondered. *I'm ruined anyway.* Her life—her old life—was over. She couldn't go back to being the duke's governess after this. She was a murderess confessed in intent of not in deed. And the viscount couldn't mean to make her his wife after that. *I won't let him, anyway. He and his precious, darling children deserve better.*

She would leave in the morning before he woke, saving him the embarrassment and awkwardness of retracting his offer. But for now? *Now I will seize this one moment of happiness and pleasure that he offers me, for when will I ever get the chance again?*

This dear, gorgeous man. Her eyes ran over his bare chest appreciatively. He cut a good figure out of his ill-fitting clothes, which did nothing to enhance his appearance. And she didn't fail to note the bulge in his breeches. She had no doubt at all of his intent as he approached the bed, after a quick wash of his face and upper body and a snuffing out of all the candles, bar the ones beside the bed.

He pulled back the covers and slid into the bed beside her. He drew her into his arms, pulling her against his chest and kissing her hair. "Annis," he murmured, "you must be so tired."

"I am," she admitted.

He pushed her chin up. "Can you stay awake long enough for a little pleasure?"

She felt herself blushing and nodded.

He smiled, and the softened expression in his eyes made her heart turn over. He lowered his head and kissed her, bearing her back into the pillows, his thigh coming down between hers, half his weight pressing her into the soft mattress.

His mouth on hers elicited all that hot tingling pleasure between her thighs again as he kissed her with determined, deliberate, slow passion. Breaking the kiss and diving back in for more, his tongue moved in delicious exploration, his lips a soft caress and nibbling pleasure. His touch so gentle, yet passionate, filled her with warm yearning. *Oh, to have this forever . . .*

He moved to her neck, pressing soft kisses on her flesh to the line of her nightgown's high collar. He touched the ribbon tying it closed and said, "May I?"

She nodded, her heart beating a tattoo in her breast as he ·pulled the ribbon, parting the neck of her gown to expose the base of her throat and upper part of her bosom.

He uttered a soft groan and nuzzled into her neck, tracing damp kisses over her skin. She felt powerful and desired for the first time in her life. It was a heady mix.

"You know," he said, raspy voiced, "it was your breasts that had me fascinated first. I couldn't take my eyes off them, and I couldn't sleep for wondering what they looked like under your so-proper gowns, what they felt like." He buried his face in her cleavage and cupped each breast in his hands, uttering a soft growl.

"Really?" she said breathlessly, trying to work out when he

had noticed.

"Hm," he kissed across the tops of her breasts and then squeezing the soft flesh in his hands, fondled and scraped his thumbs over her nipples, making her jump and gasp at the jolt of pleasure his touch caused.

He lowered his head and suckled on one through the fabric of her gown. She hitched a breath and moved her legs restlessly; the heat and suction of his mouth was arrowing straight to the place between her legs. Despite her best efforts to suppress it, a whimper escaped her, and he said, all growly again, "You like that?"

"Hm, yes!" She gasped as he did it again to the other breast. His hands ran over her belly, massaging her through her gown, squeezing her waist and hips. "Do—do you want to take it off?" she asked as he blew on the damp fabric making her nipples tighten even further.

"No, I want to save that for our wedding night," he said, sucking again on a nipple and making her back arch. "If you'll have me?" he added with an arched eyebrow and wistful expression that quite broke her heart.

"Oh!" an exclamation of pleasure and shock at his words. "You can't still want to marry me, Emrys!" she said, panting.

He lifted his head and stared down at her with a frown. "I can, and I do!" He insisted, in low tone that she found entrancingly erotic. He was devasting her with desire.

"Oh," It was very hard to think clearly when he was touching her like that. She wanted so much to believe him, but it seemed like a fairytale, and she had been taught by her mother not to believe in fairytales. Even when you found your true love, a happily ever after didn't always ensue.

But she lost the thread of that thought and whimpered as his hand moved lower, pushing up her gown. He splayed his hand over her lower belly. The muscles pulled taut under his touch, and she fought the impulse in her hips to buck. She could never recall feeling like this before. Such pulsing longing between her legs, such damp heat.

"May I touch you between your legs?" he asked between kisses through the fabric on her belly.

"Yes!" she gasped. *Oh, the relief! Something to assuage the tingling longing.*

He pushed the bed covers down a bit and moved her gown up her legs with both hands, sliding up her thighs to her hips and revealing the patch of hair at the apex of her thighs. She should feel embarrassed to be so naked to him like this, but she didn't. She felt brazen and wanton. She wanted him to touch her so much she ached with it. "Please . . ." she breathed.

"Oh Annis!" Her name was a prayer and a groan, and she realized with a jolt how much he must be longing for her, too, to sound like that. *To inspire such need in a man. In him . . .* He touched her gently with a fingertip, sliding it between her nether lips. "You're so wet," he whispered and found her mouth with his in a deep exploratory kiss.

Raising his head, he nuzzled her face with his nose and traced kisses along her jaw, while his fingers wreaked havoc between her legs. The tingling heat was so sharp it almost hurt. She gasped as his fingertips found a spot so intensely pleasurable it made her feel faint. "Oh! Oh!" she moaned, her hips bucking and her body shivering.

"Have you ever climaxed, Annis?" he asked gravelly and low.

"O-only in my sleep!" she gasped, her face flushing.

"Oh, sweetheart," he groaned. "You've never done this to yourself?"

"No! I was taught it was a sin . . ." She gasped again as his fingers continued to trace a scalding path between her lips.

"You've never had anything inside you?" he asked raspy, growly, deep. "No fingers, candlesticks, tongues, or *cocks!*" He made the last sound so absolutely filthy she blushed fiery red.

"Candlesticks?" she gasped, bewildered.

He chuckled. "Some girls use them as dildos sweetheart. A substitute for a man's cock"

"I never have—not anything!"

"Can I put my fingers inside you, Annis?" he whispered, nibbling on her ear lobe.

"Yes, yes, anything . . ." she almost sobbed. His sliding, slippery touch was driving her to madness.

"Just fingers for tonight, darling," he murmured. "The rest will keep."

"Oh!" She subsided back against the pillows, then jerked up again with a whimpering moan as he slid a finger inside her.

"An aroused woman likes the feeling of something long and hard inside her," he said low and rumbly. "Conversely, if she's not aroused, it isn't pleasant."

"Ah huh!" she nodded, panting, as his finger slid in and out in a mesmerizing rhythm. His thumb stroked that sensitive spot again, and she almost leaped off the bed. She clutched the sheets, her hips bucking, and she wailed, "Emrys!"

"Yes, sweet Annis, that's it, let go and fly. It will feel so good, sweetheart. Just let it happen," he murmured, finding a nipple and sucking hard.

A bolt of pleasure jolted through her as his thumb traced round and round, and he added a second finger to the first inside her, increasing the pace and sending the pleasure spiraling upward to an impossible peak.

"Ah!" A sound between a groan and a gasp escaped her as the pleasure exploded and sent a thousand rainbow tingles through her body in a pulsing wave of bliss, flowing outward from the place where his hand was weaving magic.

"Oh, oh, oh." She cascaded down the slope and collapsed in a limp heap on the mattress.

He withdrew his fingers and cupped her gently, pressing a kiss against her neck. "You're so beautiful when you come apart," he murmured.

She blinked, gazing at him dazedly.

"Sleep," he said softly.

"But don't you want to . . ."

"You need sleep," he said gently and tucked her in against his chest. And truth to tell she was too relaxed and weary to argue. She nuzzled into him, and she was soon asleep.

EMRYS LAY BESIDE her listening to her breathing as she slipped over the border into slumber. His groin was hot and achy, but he ignored it until he was sure she was fast asleep. Then he unbuttoned his falls and released his rigid, throbbing cock. *Fuck!* He swore under his breath with relief, the last hour had been an exquisite form of torture. He spat on his palm and took himself in hand, stroking firmly, stifling the groans that rose in his throat, trying to keep his body as still as possible so as not to wake her.

His mind ran back over everything he had done to her and the exquisite touch, taste, and smell of her. Her innocent reactions, the feel of her soft round breasts in his hands, her jutting nipples, the wetness between her legs. It took all of a few minutes to reach his peak and he gasped softly, his mouth gaping in a silent groan, his head flung back into the pillow as pleasure flooded his body and his seed spurted all over his belly.

He used the sheet to clean himself up and then rearranged the bedclothes round them, snuggling into her warm body.

She felt very different to Caro, who had been tiny. He'd always felt clumsy and big beside her, afraid of hurting her or breaking her; afraid of overwhelming her with his passion, if he was really honest. He'd worshipped her, but he'd been afraid of letting loose the really earthy side of himself in front of her. He kept that to his imagination and solo sessions with his hand. He had the feeling that he wouldn't need to do that with Annis, provided she'd consent to be his wife. Once he got her accustomed to the full deed, Annis, he thought with satisfaction, might like his wolfish side. He was certainly looking forward to educating her in all the ways a man and woman could pleasure each other.

He closed his eyes, snugging her close, breathing in her lovely scent. All the worrying things she had told him tonight seemed to matter very little in the face of the physical comfort of her body. For the first time in months, possibly in years—he realized with a shock—he didn't feel lonely.

Chapter Fifteen

ANNIS WOKE TO the unaccustomed sensation of being cuddled by a large sleeping male. Emrys had his arms round her, snugging her into his chest, and a thigh between her legs. It was remarkably comfortable and comforting. It was also quite late in the morning, judging from the amount of light coming through the window.

Which wasn't what she had planned at all. She had meant to wake early and abscond before he woke and stopped her. But then last night hadn't gone as she had expected, either. Far from him taking her for his pleasure, he had pleasured her and forfeited his own. This was not how she had imagined congress between a man and a woman would progress. Everything she had been led to expect was that the primary purpose (apart from procreation) was to bring the man relief from his physical urges.

She had heard precious little about the pleasure to be obtained by the woman from the act. Not that they had performed the act, as she understood it. He'd made reference to it with his salacious comment about fingers, candlesticks, tongues, and *cocks.* The word curled inside her, deliciously wicked. *And women desiring long hard objects . . .* She bit her lip to silence the involuntary sound that wanted to escape. She had made a lot of involuntary noises last night. She flushed remembering how she had behaved.

He stirred, making a snuffling noise, and murmured something unintelligible. His arm tightened round her and pulled her closer against him, his thigh pressed deeper between her legs. He lifted his head blinking.

"Annis." His voice was thick and deep this morning. "You feel delicious," he murmured, nuzzling her neck and pressing kisses into her skin.

Was he even awake?

"Emrys?"

"Yes, love?"

Love? What did he mean by that?

"Shouldn't we be getting up? I think it is quite late."

He rolled onto his back and stretched. "I suppose so. I'd much rather stay in bed with you."

She flushed. "Would you?"

He grinned wolfishly. *When did my gentle paladin become a wolfish rogue? And when did I start thinking of him as mine?*

He rolled toward her, pushing her back into the pillows. "I can't wait to start teaching you things. I feel you are going to be a very apt pupil, my governess."

"What—what things?"

He slid his hands over her body rubbing the fabric of her nightgown over her nipples and cupping her breasts, his head dipping to nuzzle at her neck. "You're so delicious I don't know how I'm going to keep my hands off you until I get a ring on your finger."

"About that—" she began, and yelped when he grazed her neck with his teeth. "Did you not pay attention to anything I said to you last night?"

"I paid very close attention to everything you said last night," he said, transferring his mouth to one breast and suckling a nipple.

She panted. "Then—then how can you contemplate letting me anywhere near your children?"

He let go of the nipple slowly and lifted his head. "Annis, my children have grown to care for you. You must know that."

She nodded, trying to suppress the lump in her throat. "And I for them."

"Nothing else matters," he said simply. He sat up, swinging his legs over the side of the bed. "I will apply to the Bishop of Leicester for a license to wed and we will be married in Robert's chapel."

"You're being very feudal, my lord."

"Yes, I am, aren't? It's very unlike me, you know. Generally, I'm the most easygoing of chaps."

"You cannot force me to marry you." she said quietly.

"I know, and I would not want to." He turned to face her. "Do you not wish to marry me, Annis?" She bit her lip, and he went on rather doggedly. "I'm no oil painting, I know. But am I such a bad bargain? One slightly worn widower with terrible dress sense and three small children . . . Well, perhaps there are better options."

She threw a pillow at him. "Don't pretend to be pathetic. It doesn't suit you!"

He grinned and pounced on her, pinning her to the bed. "Annis Pringle, once you're Lady Ashford I am going to do terrible things to you," he said, nuzzling and blurting his lips against her neck.

"What sort of terrible things?" she asked, trying not to laugh and failing.

"I'm going to destroy your feminine sensibilities with pleasure and obscenity," he said, kissing her exposed bosom. "You are going to discover that your husband is a filthy beast with lascivious appetites who will devour and ruin you." He transferred his mouth to her breast again, sucking through the fabric. "You, my lady, are not going to be able to walk when I have finished with you." His hand crept up under her gown and cupped her between her legs.

He raised his head and stared straight into her eyes. "I want you, Annis, all of you. Tell me don't want me even a little bit, and I'll let you go."

She swallowed. "I want you, Emrys," she whispered.

A small smile of relief broke across his face, and he lowered his head to bury it in her bosom, murmuring softly, "Thank God."

They reached The Castle just after five that afternoon, after a three-hour wait to see the Bishop of Leicester. Emrys lifted Annis down off Inigo and passed her into the duchess's hands. He saw his horse taken care of and their baggage dispatched. Having divested himself of his damp overcoat, he followed the duke to the library and collapsed in a chair near the fire. If he was tired, he hated to think what Annis must feel like.

"Where did you find her?" asked the duke, passing him a generous tot of whisky.

"Just south of Swinford on the side of the road. The mail coach had become mired in mud. It was raining. She was soaked and out on her feet. We stayed the night at Swinford." He paused to drink the whisky. "I've obtained a license from the bishop. I plan to marry her tomorrow in your chapel, if you've no objection?"

"You're set on this course?"

"I am."

"Well, who am I to stand in the path of—well, I'm not sure what this is. Do you love her?"

"I want her," Emrys admitted, flushing. "And the children need her. I'm not sure I'm capable of exactly loving another woman after Caro. I don't entirely trust my feelings at the moment. But I think we could suit each other. And she needs my protection." He finished off the whisky and stood up. "Also, there is something we need to check before it gets dark," he said, heading for the door.

The duke swallowed his own whisky hastily and followed him. "Where are we going and why?"

"I'll explain on the way," said Emrys, leading him to the front entrance and donning his coat again, as it was still drizzling out. He had debated all the way back on what to tell Robert and had decided that he needed to know part of the truth at least. The attack had taken place on his land, after all, and involved his employee. If there was any danger to anyone in his household, he needed to know.

They struck out toward the ruins. "Annis has been persecuted for some time by a man. I don't know his identity, but I mean to find out. He wishes to take something from her that was left to her by her aunt, Miss Janet Pringle. The lady is deceased—she died some years ago, I gather. The reason Annis fled two days ago was because she met with this man here in the grounds, by the ruins. She took steps to defend herself and she fears that she injured him, possibly fatally. She is quite convinced we will find his body."

Robert huffed. "That is quite a tale. Why the devil didn't she come to me with this?"

"She feared she would lose her post, Rob. She is alone in the world, has no one to rely upon, no one to support her if she were turned off without a reference, for example."

"I would never do that! Good God, she is part of the family. She has been with us close on six years. The girls adore her."

"I know, but I don't think she is accustomed to trusting people. This man—" Emrys stopped to swallow the incandescent rage building under his ribs. "This man threatened her horribly. She was afraid. She has been living with this fear for several years. It has made her wary."

"But what did she hope to gain by fleeing?"

"To be honest I don't think she was thinking clearly. She panicked, fearing the worst."

The ruins loomed up out of the gathering gloom, the gray cloud cover had obscured the sun and was making things abnormally dark for this time of year. The drizzle was persisting, and everything was damp and unpleasant. The ground, soaked now with two days of constant rain, was muddy, with standing pools of water among the grassy tussocks.

To Emrys's relief, there was no immediate sign of a body. Though if there had been any blood or signs of a struggle initially, the wet would likely have obliterated that by now. It was still possible that the man may have staggered away to fall and die somewhere else.

"Let's widen the search, make sure he is not hidden in the bushes farther afield."

Robert nodded agreement, and they scoured the surrounding area for a good half an hour and found nothing.

Thoroughly soaked now and feeling the chill, they headed back to the house.

"He may have left the property and subsequently died of his injuries or even now be languishing somewhere. We have no way of knowing, but at least you are not implicated if the body hasn't been found here."

"That is true and, I admit, a big relief. I'd as soon not have the place crawling with Bow Street Runners."

"Indeed."

"And knowing all this, you still wish to marry her?"

"I wish to marry her all the more—she needs me. If the man comes after her again, he will have me to deal with. He'll not find me so easy to intimidate. He may hesitate also to offer violence to a viscountess as opposed to a mere Miss Pringle, Governess."

"Are you not concerned for the children's safety?"

"I don't believe there is any threat to them. This man's threats are specific to Annis and Annis alone. It seems he wishes to obtain the item that her aunt left her. I can take steps to secure the item and keep her safe. As her husband I will have the law on my side should he attempt to attack her again. An attack against a peeress will be seen very dimly by a magistrate. I think such a deterrent would be enough to keep him at bay."

"And if he is dead?"

"Then he is no longer a threat. He appears to have been acting alone. In all honesty, I do not believe she killed him. She may very well have injured him, however. Sufficiently that he may rethink his course of action and stop his persecution going forward."

"Hm. Well, keep me apprised of what you find. I will post some guards to patrol the grounds in future. I don't like the idea of strangers wandering around with violent intent. The girls, Mother, or Sarah could be in danger, to say nothing of the children or any other guests we might invite."

They had reached the house at this point, and Emrys divested himself of his coat once more and went upstairs to see his children and change for dinner.

Lizzie pounced on him as soon as he entered the nursery and demanded to know if he had rescued Miss Pringle.

"I did," he said. "She is safe home once more."

Charlie barreled at him for a hug, followed by Ewen. When hugs had been duly had all round, he sat down on the floor with them and said gravely. "I have some news that I hope you will like."

"Yes?" asked Lizzie with bated breath.

"I am going to marry Miss Pringle tomorrow here in the chapel. What do you think of that?"

"I told you so!" said Lizzie with a broad grin.

"So, you approve?" he asked smiling with relief.

"Of course," said Lizzie. "She makes you happy."

Charlie hung back, however, a troubled look on her face. "Don't you love Mama anymore?" she asked, chewing the knuckle of her thumb. It was a habit he noticed she had adopted since Caro's death. Her question cut him to the heart, and he swallowed, blinking his eyes.

"I will always love Mama," he said slowly. And it was true. In spite of her betrayal, a part of him would always belong to Caro—his youth, his past. But his future, for good or ill, belonged to Annis. "Do you like Miss Pringle?" he asked, worried that he'd overlooked Charlie in his plans. She was always in Lizzie's shadow. Lizzie was the outspoken one, but Charlie was sensitive and felt things she didn't always express.

Charlie nodded. "Yes. She saved Ewen."

"She did," he agreed.

"Miss Pingle," interjected Ewen at this juncture, crawling onto Emrys's lap. "Miss Pingle is nice. I love her." he said pushing his head into Emrys's chest. He put his arm round his son and squeezed, a warmth blooming in his chest. He put out his other arm to the girls, and they crowded in for a group hug.

Chapter Sixteen

THE DUCHESS SUPERVISED getting Annis undressed, bathed, fed, and into bed herself, and Annis subsided into her familiar bed and slept like a proverbial log. She was woken the next morning by the duchess at the very late hour of ten o'clock with the news that her wedding was set for two o'clock in the afternoon.

After that, things were a whirlwind, as the duchess swept her off to her own suite to select a suitable gown to be quickly altered to fit her, as none of Annis's gowns were fit for a bride, being too plain and worn. The gown selected was a lovely pure-white muslin, so fine and sheer it needed a chemise and petticoat for modesty's sake as well as to widen and stiffen the skirt in the new fuller fashion. The bodice was so small and cut so low as to be almost indecent in Annis's view. She blushed looking at herself in it.

The gown was adorned with gold ribbon and gold embroidery, with elaborate puffed sleeves with layers of embroidered muslin falling over them like the petals of a flower. Fortunately, the duchess had similar-sized feet to Annis, and Annis was able to pair the gown with white satin slippers, a reticule, a fan, and a matching satin shawl with gold embroidery. The whole ensemble was so exquisite and rich, Annis felt quite overwhelmed.

When the duchess produced a string of milky white pearls to go with it, it was too much, and Annis burst into tears.

"My dear, don't cry! This is supposed to be a happy day!" The Layne girls were also present, like a flock of pretty birds, but the duchess chased them away in the face of Annis's distress and sat her down on the bed.

"Now tell me, do you not wish to marry the viscount?"

"Of course I do! It's like a fairytale," blubbered Annis, wiping her eyes.

"Well, that is a relief! I am very fond of Emrys—he has such a kind heart!"

"Yes, he does," admitted Annis with a lachrymose smile.

"Oh, you love him!" said the duchess accusingly.

Annis nodded, kneading the handkerchief. "Is it so obvious?"

"Only to me. I was madly in love with the duke, too, before we were married. I was deathly afraid he was going to break my heart. Fortunately, he realized eventually that he also loved me, and everything was wonderful. My dear, Robert tells me Emrys is mad for you. What is distressing you so?"

"He loves his wife—it's been too soon, I—"

"It is quick I grant you; I was surprised. But there is perhaps something you don't know. Caroline betrayed him before she was killed. The children don't know, of course, and we tried to hush up it after that unfortunate misunderstanding than led to Robert punching him in the eye. Particularly after she was killed so tragically. She broke his heart, poor lamb."

Annis's heart contracted. *Why hadn't he told her?* "I didn't know."

"Well, there. So, you see it is perhaps not so surprising that he has fallen in love with you—"

"Oh, but he hasn't! It's all physical!" She flushed scarlet. "And being a gentleman and wanting to protect me and give the children a suitable mother. They're fond of me, you see, and I of them. He has never pretended that he loves me, though."

The duchess regarded her for a moment in silence. Then she

patted her hands and squeezed them. "Give it time. One look at you in this gown and I expect he will lose his head entirely. With gentlemen the physical attraction often comes first." She glanced at Annis sideways. "He's not the handsomest of men. Are you attracted to him?"

Annis closed her eyes and whispered. "Oh, yes." She swallowed. "His clothes don't do him justice."

Sarah blinked, flushing faintly. "I think, my dear, that might be a shade too much information. But I am glad you find him attractive, for that really is essential in building a lasting bond."

The duchess then organized for her to have another bath and for her hair to be dressed by her own maid. She was dressed in the hastily refitted gown with all the accoutrements and led to the chapel by the waiting duke, where she found her soon-to-be stepdaughters had been pressed into service as flower girls. The whole household, including most of the servants, had turned out to witness her nuptials, and Annis had to fight tears all the way down the chapel's short aisle to the point where the duke left her beside Emrys and took up his other role as Emrys's groomsman.

Emrys was wearing that black silk evening jacket and breeches, for once his neckcloth was tied with precision, and his too long hair was confined with a black ribbon. He had shaved too. He looked quite resplendent, and to Annis's partial eyes, as handsome as any man could be.

Emrys's gaze widened at sight of her, and he flushed faintly as his eyes took in her gown and it's low-cut, narrow bodice that threatened to spill her breasts free for all to see. She wore the pearls and the chain with her father's ring which nestled it in the space between her breasts. When he took her hands, he murmured, "You look beautiful," in a tone that made her blush.

She said breathlessly back, "Black suits you, my lord."

The ceremony was short, and the whole thing passed in a blur for Annis. After signing the parish register, the party decamped to the ballroom, where tables had been set out for the whole household to eat, including the children and servants.

THE DUCHESS HAD given them the rose suite for their wedding night and had all their belongings moved there. From the moment Emrys clapped eyes on Annis in that dress he'd been in a fever to get her alone. It seemed like hours before he was able to sweep her off upstairs and into their rooms.

Closing the door on the world, he set her on her feet and turned her in his embrace, staring down at her exposed bosom with hungry eyes. "At last! Do you *know* how delectable you look in that gown?" he asked hoarsely.

"About as delectable as you look in that suit," she said softly with a delicate blush.

He groaned, "Annis! There is no comparison!"

"Well, it's all the duchess's fault! I would never have chosen anything so—so brazen. I feel half dressed!" she said with an exasperated smile.

"It is very different from your normally staid dresses. I think that is why I'm losing my mind." He cupped her face. "It is going to be very difficult for me to restrain myself." He kissed her softly and groaned again. "God, I've missed you, I feel like I've hardly seen you since we got back yesterday."

Her delicious bosom heaved with a breath and made his already hard cock twitch. "It is true, we have hardly seen each other since then."

"I missed you last night in my bed," he confessed. "I like cuddling up to you."

She smiled and blinked at him. "Really? Well, it might be something I can get used to, too."

"I hope so. I don't mean to sleep alone again. I don't like it." His eyes roved over her, devouring. He felt like a starving man at a feast, not knowing where to start. "You got my note about there being no body near the ruins, didn't you?"

"I did. Thank you for that. It was—a big relief." Her face

showed a flicker of distress, and he drew her closer, stroking her back comfortingly.

"For what it's worth, I don't believe you killed him," he said, kissing her hair. She smelled of roses.

"Perhaps not," she said with a sigh. "But if that is the case, he is still out there."

"Yes, but you have me now. And the protection of my name. As a viscountess he won't be game to touch you."

She nodded, but he got the feeling she wasn't convinced.

"I really don't want to talk about that right now, do you?"

"No." She put her hands on the lapels of his jacket, and he leaned forward to kiss her. Her hands slid up round his neck and he pulled her closer against him, his heart thudding in his chest. He needed to take this slowly for her sake. He wanted desperately for it to be good for her. His memories of the first time with Caro haunted him. It had taken months to recover from that. Given the way things had ended, he wondered if they ever truly had.

"Just let me get rid of this damned neckcloth and jacket," he said pulling back from kissing her. God, he was as nervous as a boy, which was ridiculous—he hadn't been nervous two nights ago. No, he hadn't, he thought as he ripped off his neckcloth and struggled out of his jacket, because he'd had no intention of taking her that night. It had been all about her pleasure. What had him tied in knots now was the prospect of causing her pain, or at least discomfort, all in the name of his pleasure. That made him uncomfortable. The thought subdued his lust a bit, which was all to the good.

He needed to recapture that playfulness of the morning before they left the inn. He needed to relax and just let things flow. He had promised her pleasure, he would give her pleasure, and be damned to the rest—it would happen when she wanted it to. *I have learned a few things since I was twenty-two, after all.* He kicked off his shoes and removed his waistcoat and turned back to her.

She eyed him, speculatively he thought, and she surprised

him with her next question. "Aren't you going to remove your shirt?"

"Do you want me to?"

She nodded, blushing faintly. "I like your chest," she confessed.

Pleased, he grinned and complied, ripping the fine cotton off over his head and discarding it carelessly with the rest of his clothing. He only wore his breeches now, and he had no intention of taking those off, yet.

He took her in his arms again and surveyed her with satisfaction. "Now with you, I think we will start with your hair and your shoes and stockings. I want to savor this bosom for as long as possible," he said, dropping kisses on her forehead, cheeks, and nose before finding her mouth.

She wrapped her arms round his neck, and he pulled her closer, deepening the kiss and losing himself in the delight of her.

He broke the kiss when he felt his control starting to slip and said with quickened breath, "Annis, you are a delicious, delectable delight. And I want the husband's privilege of seeing your hair down and loose." He examined her coiffure, which was an intricate confection of braids and curls garnished with combs and flowers and, he guessed, a hundred pins.

He reached for a pin and then another, removing and discarding them as her curls and braids came down one by one to fall about her shoulders like a chestnut waterfall, burnished deep brown with a hint of red. He tossed aside the roses and the combs and undid the fine braids, combing them free with his fingers until all of her glorious hair was flowing round her shoulders and down her back. He plunged his fingers into it and lifted handfuls to sniff the rose smelling fragrance and feel the soft silky strands running through his fingers.

"Your hair is magnificent," he said.

"I like yours," she responded, removing the ribbon from his and running her fingers through his wild mop of unremarkable brown hair. Her fingertips scraped his scalp, and he closed his eyes and purred.

"That feels good," he murmured.

After a moment or two, he opened his eyes and, lowering his head, he kissed her again. *Will I ever grow tired of kissing her?* He didn't think so. Leaving her mouth reluctantly, he worked his way slowly along her jaw to her soft, chewable earlobe, and her neck, her delicious, elegant neck. Annis carried herself with a quiet dignity and part of that impression was down to her swanlike neck. He nuzzled and nibbled at it, and she arched it to give him better access, making little whimpering noises that just encouraged him.

He finally reached the base of her neck and began, very slowly, to work his way over the delicious expanse of her bosom. The gown had confined and pushed up her round, plump breasts so that they were served up to him perfectly. The hollow between them beckoned his tongue and those soft pillows begged to be kissed.

Unable to resist any longer, he brought his hands up to cup those gorgeous globes and squeeze them gently. "Annis," he whispered, his tongue delving into the hollow between her breasts and lifting out the ring that nestled there with his teeth. He tossed the ring aside, and it slid over her shoulder, the chain slithering against her throat, then he returned to his worship of her half-exposed breasts. He was saving the nipples, but it wouldn't be long before he could wait no longer to see them. His thumbs grazed over them through the fabric of her bodice, teasing them to full hard peaks. She gasped and clung to him. *God, yes!*

He gave them one last fondle and squeeze before walking her backward toward the bed, where he eased her down to sit on the edge and knelt at her feet.

"What are you doing?" she asked.

He reached for a foot and eased off her slipper. "Removing your stockings," he said, taking off her other slipper.

He glanced up at her watching him. Her expression seemed

slightly bemused. "I can't believe you're on your knees for the governess," she said.

"I'm on my knees for my viscountess," he said, easing his hands up under her skirts to slide up the length of her legs. He found the tops of her stockings by feel and began to loosen one garter. Her thighs were warm and smooth under his fingers, and her delicious bosom was level with his eyes. He wanted desperately to rip the dress off her and expose the full glory of her breasts to his gaze, but he made himself wait.

Transferring his attention back to what his fingers were doing, he got the garter loose and began to slide the stocking down her leg. The stocking appeared from below her petticoats, and he discarded it, reaching up under her skirts to remove the second one. When he had got rid of both, he slid his hands back up her legs, enjoying the smoothness of her skin.

"Part your legs for me and lie back," he said, husky voiced. She did, and he pushed her skirts up slowly to reveal her legs and, most importantly, the treasure at their apex. He ran his hands up her inner thighs, sliding and caressing, his thumbs swirling over her skin. *So smooth!* He leaned forward and set his mouth very gently against her nether curls. They were dark and slightly crinkly with flashes of flame. He drew in a breath through his nose to inhale her scent and groaned softly.

She jerked at his touch and uttered a soft gasp. "Emrys!"

"I hope you will enjoy this," he murmured, his voice dropping to a low rumble.

Parting her with his thumbs, he set his tongue delicately to her dewy, satin flesh and tasted her. *Exquisite, slightly salty, slightly sweet. Musk and rose and entirely delicious.* He shifted his position to relieve the compression on his cock, trapped inside his breeches. He was likely to make a mess of himself before he was finished here. *It didn't matter.*

"Emrys!" her body jerked more strongly, and he leaned in, using his arms across her thighs to hold her in place as he licked again gently. Testing what she liked, he used his tongue to lick and pet her flesh, swirling it around but not directly on her bud. In his somewhat limited experience, women preferred a less direct approach to the seat of their greatest pleasure. Judging from her reactions, Annis was no different in that regard.

Her hands clutched at the coverlet as he increased the assault with his tongue on her defenseless flesh, as her body arched and jerked and she uttered the most delicious noises. Holding her down with an arm across her pelvis he moved a hand to caress very gently at her entrance, his tongue busy with her bud. Swirling around the entrance, he slid his finger inwards, palpating her bud very gently with his tongue.

Annis moaned, her body arching against the downward pressure of his arm. "Emrys!" Her voice was husky and had taken on a pleading edge that made his cock jerk in his breeches and threaten to spill.

He added a second finger and applied a rapid swirling of his tongue, moving his fingers in and out, curling the tips forward searching for that spongy spot that seemed to drive a woman crazy. *Would it have the same effect on Annis?*

He found it and rubbed vigorously, and the result was spectacular. Annis gasped and groaned, her body going taut, and her flesh fluttered and clenched on his fingers. A deep moan escaped her, and her legs trembled as her frame shook for several moments and then she subsided into the bed, gasping for breath. He stilled his tongue and withdrew his fingers. Pressing a kiss softly to her flesh, he raised his head and wiped his chin with his hand as he observed her lying limp, her eyes closed, her magnificent bosom rising and falling rapidly as she got her breath back.

She opened her eyes and blinked at him. He smiled. "Good?"

She nodded, as if slightly dazed. She held her arms out to him dumbly, and he was very tempted to crawl up over her and just take her like that, his cock certainly thought that was a good idea, but he restrained the impulse. He'd ruin her gown for one thing, and for another there was something he'd been anticipating for a while—he wasn't going to deny himself the pleasure now. The other could wait a little longer, and if he came in his breeches while he did it, so be it.

He reached out and drew her upright, wrapping his arms round her. He said, hoarse with desire, "The time has come to release your ladies, I think."

She leaned into him as he reached for the laces on the back of her gown, moving her hair out of way, and began to loosen them. When they were loose enough, he leaned back a little to kiss her gently. A savoring sort of kiss, his hand still resting against her loosened laces and the layers of corset and chemise revealed beneath. Rising to his feet, he drew her up and slowly slid her gown off her shoulders, until the bodice fell away from her breasts and pooled round her waist, caught on the petticoats beneath. His quest still had layers to go before the prize would be fully revealed. Her corset sat under her breasts, half cups pushing them upward over the low-cut chemise beneath and blocking his view of the nipples.

He turned her round and began loosening the ties of the corset. When it finally came free, he let it drop to the ground and pulled her back against him, his hands going to cup her breasts over the fine cotton chemise. He squeezed them with a soft growl, rubbing his face alongside of hers, pressing kisses against her cheek. They felt so good in his hands, soft and full. He found her nipples with his fingers and thumbs and squeezed gently, she jerked and gasped, and he groaned in response. *So delicious! I can't wait to taste them!*

"Annis. Annis," he whispered.

His hands went to the tie of her petticoats at her waist and loosened it, letting the whole ensemble of petticoats and gown drop and pool round her feet. She was now dressed only in her thin chemise which stopped at her knees. He stepped back a moment to admire the outline of her body through the translucent fabric.

"Beautiful," he murmured. Stepping closer, he clasped her waist and ran his hands up and down her sides and cupped her bottom briefly and squeezed. *Ugh, yes!* A growl in his throat. Running his hand back up and round to her belly, he pulled her back against him and hugged her close, pressing his sorely tried cock against her rump. He wanted desperately to press it hard against something to ease the ache. To his delight, she pressed back against him, molding herself to his body. "Oh, Annis!" he moaned softly. He found her neck and nibbled on it, pressing intense kisses to the warm flesh. Her scent made him dizzy with desire.

Then he turned her to face him, his eyes running over her body, and coming to land on the swell of her breasts, the nipples a pink haze, poking hard peaks beneath the fabric, almost, but not quite, visible. He couldn't stifle a groan of anticipation. The moment of full revelation had arrived. She smiled tentatively and he grinned with delight.

"At last!" he murmured.

With his cock jumping in his breeches, he bent and lifted the chemise slowly upward, and she raised her arms as he dragged it up and off her body and discarded it behind him. His eyes glued to her lovely, lovely breasts.

They were perfect, round, white globes, the skin so translucent he could see the blue veins beneath. The nipples and areolae were a delicious raspberry pink, perfect crinkled circles topped with jutting pink buds just begging to be suckled.

"Annis!" he breathed, just staring at them a moment to take in their perfection.

Then he bent, picked her up, then laid her down in the center of the bed and crawled on top. His pulse thudded in his veins and throbbed in his cock. Anticipation was in every breath.

She spread her legs for him without him saying a word. His whole concentration was on her breasts as he settled himself in the cradle of her hips, his hard cock inside his breeches pressed against her sex.

With his weight on his elbows, he cupped each breast and lowered his head to trace kisses over them, licking and sucking and losing himself in them. Finally he took one nipple in his mouth and sucked. He growled with delight and suckled and licked, taking as much of her breast in his mouth as he could. His left hand squeezed and fondled the other breast, and she moved under him, making noises and pressing her hips and sex up into him.

He rutted and rubbed his cock against her, heedless almost of what he was doing, his mouth full of wonderful nipple and breast. He swapped his attention to the second breast, hands swapping likewise.

The feel of her nipple and breast in his mouth as he sucked and licked and pulled on it was heaven. The hot need in his groin spiked as his hips rutted harder. *Fuck, he was going to come!*

"Annis!" he groaned helplessly. His frenzied need erupted as he buried his face in her breasts and came spectacularly inside his breeches, thrusting and rubbing on her, groaning and grunting like a beast.

Panting, he collapsed on her, his face still buried in her breasts, and he felt her hands on him stroking his head and shoulders.

Chapter Seventeen

"T HAT ISN'T QUITE what was supposed to happen," he murmured into her breasts.

"Does it matter?" she asked, stroking his hair. *God, I love him!* The reality of it hit her hard.

He raised his head. "Not if you don't mind, I suppose."

"Why should I mind? I enjoyed it, too."

"Did you come?"

"Not quite, but I was close when you stopped."

He stroked a tangle of hair off her face. "Next time I'll make sure you do. I might be a little less worked up and can last longer."

"When we do it properly you mean?"

He flushed. "Yes, when we do it properly."

He hesitated, and she said, "Go on."

"It will likely hurt you a bit the first time." *He looks uncomfortable, bless him.*

"That's all right. I'm prepared for that." She smiled to reassure him.

He swallowed. "I hurt Caro the first time. It took her a while to forgive me."

"Well, you were both young, weren't you?" She hid the fact that him talking about his wife at a moment such as this made her wince internally.

"Yes, damnably." He rolled off her and sat up. "I'll just get rid of these breeches and clean up a bit," he said, picking his way across the debris-strewn floor. She watched him strip and wash. Then he brought her a cloth to wipe herself, too.

"Would you like a drink?" he asked, returning the cloth to the bowl and waving at the bottle of wine and glasses on the table.

"Yes, please," she said, sitting up and banking the pillows behind her.

He uncorked the bottle and returned with two glasses. She ran her eyes over all of him, now that he was naked, and liked what she saw. His member was no longer engorged. It would be interesting to see what it looked like in that state. It had certainly felt enormous and hard, pressed against her earlier. It looked much less alarming at the moment. His legs, like his forearms and chest, had hair on them.

He put the glasses down on the bedside table and climbed into bed beside her. Handing her a glass, he raised his in a toast. "To married life, my lady!"

She touched her glass to his and they both took a sip. He laid back against the pillows with a sigh, and she wondered in panic if he was regretting it.

"Why did you do it?" she asked, smoothing the soft cotton sheet with her left hand.

"What?"

"Marry me?"

"I thought I explained that. Lots of reasons."

"Yes, but I would have thought, considering what happened, you wouldn't want to marry again. Especially so soon . . ."

"Sarah told you about Caro, did she?" he said, looking a bit dour.

She nodded.

He shifted on the pillow to face her. "I actually like being married. I've been married most of my adult life. I missed having someone to hug at night and get miffed at me across the teacups!"

he said with a whimsical smile. He looked down, the smile fading. "I loved Caro. I had no idea—" He stopped, swallowing visibly.

She put out a hand to cover his, her heart torn by his obvious distress. "I'm so sorry," she whispered.

"Thank you," he said quietly. After a moment he drank his wine and motioned to hers, which was still half full. "Do you want it?"

"Not right now," she said surrendering it. He took it and set both glasses on the bedside table. Turning back to her, he took her in his arms and pulled her close against his chest.

With his face resting on the top of her head as she buried hers into his slightly scratchy chest, he said softly, "I'll try to be a good husband to you Annis. I want you to know you can rely on me. I'm the dependable sort by nature. Not especially exciting or romantic, but dependable. I hope that counts for something."

"It's everything," she said softly, blinking back tears and squeezing her arms round him.

"Good," he said, clearing his throat. "And as for reasons," he said, lifting her chin up, "the fact that I can't keep my hands off your delectable body is certainly one. I've become a ravenous wolf where you're concerned, wife!" He gave one of his delicious growls, pushing her back into the pillows and kissing her, the weight of his body coming down on her and his legs tangling with hers.

Annis wrapped her arms round his neck and reveled in his kisses as he showered them over her face and neck and bosom. He made her feel so adored with the way he worshipped her breasts with such lascivious delight and wrapped her up in affection with hugs and kisses. He was both wolf and lamb, going from affectionate playfulness to libidinous desire and back in the blink of an eye.

She kissed him back, shyly at first. She wasn't used to showing physical affection, let alone desire, but he broke down all her barriers and made her feel safe to express all her stored-up affection.

He was at her breasts again and sending jolts of desire to the juncture of her legs with the delicious things he was doing with his mouth. She moaned, arching her body and clutching at him, desperate for more. He growled again—*I love it when he does that!*—as he renewed his assault on her breasts. After a bit he raised his head, his face pink with effort, his breathing rapid. "Forgive my crudity, but I so want to fuck you. Will you allow me to prepare you to take me?"

She smiled, panting a little, shocked and thrilled by his blunt speech. "Of course." She added awkwardly, "I want you, too."

He groaned. "I'm so afraid of hurting you, but I want you fiercely. Please forgive me if I lose control."

She swallowed, her body convulsing with a deep throb of desire and flood of wetness between her legs. "I doubt you will hurt me, and even if you do, it will be momentary, I'm sure. I—I am quite desperate for you Emrys. Please touch me, I want to feel you."

"Annis!" He reached for her mouth and kissed her. A devouring savage kiss that made her lose the last of her reserve and fling herself against him, undulating with pent-up desire, pressing her sex against his thigh with wanton abandon, anything to assuage the throbbing ache between her legs.

He shifted over her, moving to situate himself between her legs, and reaching down to stroke her swollen, wet flesh with his fingers, he pushed one and then rapidly two fingers inside her, and she groaned with the relief. She had not known it was possible to ache with the desire to have something thrust inside her. She remembered his talk of candlesticks and would have laughed if she weren't so overwrought with longing.

His hard, hot cock poked into her belly. It was plenty huge now; she could feel it. *Would it fit? His fingers were one thing, but that great stave?*

He added another finger, sliding them in and out rapidly, his thumb tracing circles round the place she felt the most intense pleasure, she was nearly out of her skin with wanting.

He widened his fingers, stretching her, and she gasped at the pinch of discomfort. He murmured something soothing against her neck and did it again, adding a fourth finger and pushing them deep. She gasped, stiffening at the burn. He twisted his hand, turning it inside her, back and forth, then in and out. His thumb returned to its teasing, and she pushed up into his touch with a moan. Discomfort or not, she wanted more.

"There, that should do it, I think" he said thickly, withdrawing his hand and fumbling between her legs. Then she felt the press of something hard and round against her entrance. He lifted his head and found her gaze with his. "Ready?"

She nodded, and he pressed forward with a slight grimace. She felt a momentary resistance, a stinging tear, and he was suddenly inside. He slid deep and stopped with a groan. Their bodies flush against one another. He watched her face anxiously for her reaction and she smiled to reassure him. She felt full and peculiar, a sort of achy pleasure-pain.

"All right?" he asked, hoarse and breathless.

She nodded and then found her voice. "Yes, it feels strangely pleasant."

He huffed a laugh. "It feels more than pleasant to me. I shall have to do more if it is only pleasant."

She shifted, bringing her legs up which eased her and made it feel better. He uttered one of his growly curses. "Fuck, Annis!"

"What? Is that wrong?" she asked anxiously freezing her position.

"No, on the contrary!"

"Oh good, it feels better for me."

"Good! That's good!" he panted. "Lift your knees up a little more."

She did, and he slid a hand under her knee, holding her open in a way that ought to feel obscene but felt absolutely wonderful. He moved then, pulling almost out and back in again in a hard rush that made her moan.

"Does it hurt?"

"No!" she panted. "No, please, don't stop."

"I won't. God, Annis, you feel so fucking good!" He groaned and moved again, beginning to thrust in a way that jarred her frame and sent tendrils of pleasure chasing themselves through her body. He moved his hand, pushing his arm under her knee and grasping her hip and thrust into her repeatedly with escalating, rapid strokes.

He closed his eyes and groaned again, then shifted his position once more and reached between them to touch her, rubbing his fingers rapidly over that sensitive spot. He was panting loudly by now and growling in his throat with each thrust.

His fingers were causing a maelstrom in her body. Between that and the deep thrusts stirring her from the inside, the rush of pleasure overtook her in a breathless wave, and she cried out, her body convulsing round his.

"Fuck, yes!" he bellowed, and she felt the heated burst within her as his member jerked and spilled his seed. She gasped for breath in the aftermath as he collapsed in a grunting, cursing heap on top of her.

"Annis. Annis," he whispered against her neck. She stroked his back, her body lax and sated beneath him. "My dear, are you all right?" he asked, lifting his head.

She nodded, smiling. "Oh yes, Emrys, I am fine," she said and kissed his nose.

He laughed and kissed hers back. "Thank God," he groaned, extracting himself and rolling off her. "We will get better at it with practice, I promise you," he said, flopping onto this back.

"It seemed pretty good to me," she said mildly.

"Pretty good! Pretty good!" he expostulated in mock indignation. "I'll have it known it can be a lot better than that!"

She laughed. "I'm only teasing. It was wonderful." She rolled toward him and traced patterns on his chest.

He looked down and seized her hand and kissed it. "*You* are wonderful," he said softly. "Are you sore?"

She rubbed her thighs together feeling the moisture seeping

out of her. *His seed. I could be with child soon* . . . The thought made her heart skip a beat. She had never thought she would have the chance to have children of her own. She swallowed and said, "Not really. I just feel a bit swollen and very wet!"

"I'll fetch you a cloth," he said leaping out of bed and fetching the cloth for her before she could protest. His propensity to wait on her was as startling as his consideration between the sheets. The governess was not used to such things. Annis Fitzgerald, Lady Ashford, would have to get used to it, she supposed with a little sigh of contentment.

Chapter Eighteen

Annis woke the next morning to her husband plastered to her like a limpet. He was wrapped round her tighter than a cloak, his arm across her belly, his knees tucked into the back of hers and his face buried in the back of her neck. He snuffled when she moved and tightened his arm round her, pulling her back into his chest.

She sighed, smiling and stroking the hairs on his arm.

"That tickles," he said.

She turned her head and twisted round to face him. "Do you realize you sleep-hug?" she said.

He smiled lazily. "Is that a variation of sleepwalking?"

"Yes. Every time I wake up, you're wrapped round me tighter than a boa constrictor. I'm not complaining, though. I like it," she hastened to add with a softening smile.

"Good, because I don't plan to stop," he said. Then he added, "I don't even know that I could. I'm not aware that I'm doing it. I've been waking up hugging pillows for the past four months," he admitted a little sheepishly.

Her heart melted, and she slid closer, wrapping her arms round him and kissing his nose.

"Well, I'm here now. You don't have to hug the pillows."

"You're far better than a pillow," he said kissing her. "Let me show you," he said diving under the covers.

She squeaked when his mouth landed on her belly and blurted, and she giggled and shrieked helplessly when he tickled her.

"Emrys, stop!" she begged breathlessly between giggles. *I have never giggled in my life! What would Mama say to me behaving with such abandon?*

He did stop, but then he did something else that extracted a different kind of noise from her. His mouth moved lower, and his lips and tongue made her groan.

"Emrys . . ." she said faintly.

A little while later she was limp and breathless as he sat up looking pleased with himself and wiped his face on the sheets.

His cock jutted out from his groin, large and pink as he knelt looking at her.

She sat up on her elbow to get a better look at it in its fully engorged glory. She put out a hand. "May I?" she asked, shocked at her own boldness, but she wanted to touch and feel it. Stroke it.

He nodded. "Go ahead. It won't bite, but I don't guarantee it won't leak." He smirked.

She stroked it with a tentative finger, and he gasped. It was hot to the touch and when her fist closed around the shaft, she found it silky smooth, the skin so soft it almost felt like velvet. A velvet-encased, hot, iron shaft, with a bulbous head peeking through a hood of skin.

"Annis, that feels very good," he said, his voice gravelly and strained.

She looked up at his face which had taken on that twisted grimace he got when most aroused.

"Can I make you come?" she asked and squashed the outraged voice squawking in the back of her head.

"Yes, very easily," he said, his growly voice making something inside her hum. "You know I made myself come with my hand thinking of you lots of times," he said lying down beside her, so she could continue to stroke him.

"Really?" she said, arrested a moment in shock. "When was the first time you did that?" She resumed stroking him.

"The day we went to Kegworth. I first noticed your breasts the night before when we played cards with the dowager and Lady Ava. Do you remember that evening?"

"Yes." She stroked him steadily, and he began moving his hips into her hand.

"You were wearing a little seed pearl brooch in the middle of your bosom. Your gown was so modest, not a skerrick of flesh anywhere, but the cloth of the bodice clung to your shape. I couldn't take my damned eyes off your breasts. They haunted me. I was obsessed with them. And I couldn't stop wondering what they looked like, would feel and taste like. Now I know." He moved a little closer and dropped his head, pushing her back against the pillows, so he could get to her breasts.

"I don't think I'm ever going to get enough of them," he said, opening his mouth over her nipple and engulfing as much of her breast as he could. Beneath him, she arched up into his touch and reminded herself to continue stroking his cock with her hand while he moved his hips.

He let the nipple slip from his mouth with a soft moan. "You're going to drive me to madness if you fall pregnant. They'll get much bigger and more sensitive." he said hoarsely.

She jerked at the mention of pregnancy. "You want more children?" she asked, slightly breathless.

"Of course. Why wouldn't I? You'd make a wonderful mother—you already do. Watching you with Ewen and the girls . . ." He sighed, closing his eyes, and thrust into her hand with more determination. After a few moments he said hoarsely, "Do you mind if I finish inside you?"

"N-no," she stammered, her body pulsing at the notion.

"Good, I'm feeling quite wolfish today." He nudged her legs apart and settled between her legs. His fingers traced along her channel and then thrust inside firmly. She gasped.

"Good or sore?" he asked quickly.

"G-good," she said.

"You're wet enough," he muttered. "Are you sure?" He moved his cock to her entrance but stayed his thrust.

"Yes," she said, quite breathless. Her body was pulsing, the ache deep inside gnawing at her. If he was feeling wolfish, she was feeling wanton and deeply needy.

He pushed forward hard and groaned as he sank all the way into her, driving a reciprocal groan from her.

He rolled onto his side dragging her with him and hitched her leg over his hip and arm, his hand resting on her rump, where it squeezed in involuntary rhythm with his thrusts. This position was different, the angle catching her in more of the places that felt good. He kissed her, using his tongue deeply.

The hand on her rump slid lower, and she felt his fingers stroking between her legs from behind, touching her where his cock slid in and out of her. The sensations were so unexpected and naughty, her flesh throbbed, and a pleasurable rush began to build. She pressed closer, her hips moving with involuntary passion in time with his. She whimpered and moaned into his mouth as he thrust harder and deeper. His other arm crushing her against him.

The pleasure burst in a shower of sparks and throbs, and he groaned loudly, his thrusting becoming jagged as she felt the hot rush once again of his seed inside her. He held her tight against him as the spasm shuddered through his body and he grunted and moaned with it. "Annis! Annis!" He let out a breath and sighed, going gradually limp.

They lay in mutual silence in each other's arms for several minutes after that. Eventually he stirred enough to say, "I hope that will stay my appetite sufficiently so that I can behave with decorum today, but I wouldn't guarantee it. Prepare to be ravished behind a curtain at unexpected moments," he said with a smile.

She laughed which made his softening flesh retreat. They separated slowly with little kisses.

"Shall I call for a bath?" he asked.

"Oh, that sounds heavenly," she said, realizing with a shock that she could have as many baths as she chose now. The change in her status was going to take a bit of getting used to.

EMRYS WASHED AND shaved in the hot water brought by the servants and left his wife to her bath while he disappeared into the dressing room attached to their new bedchamber to let his long-suffering valet dress him. He would need to organize a maid for her and give her an allowance to buy clothes. He wasn't the kind of man to take much notice of what women wore, but even he knew her old wardrobe wasn't going to be suitable for her new title.

As he wrestled with his cravat—*drat, I hate the bloody things*—he reflected with satisfaction on his second wedding night. A great deal better than his first, which had ended disastrously with his new bride in tears and himself feeling like the biggest monster in creation. Not that he had meant to hurt her, of course, but his inexperience and her lack of knowledge—no one had told her what to expect!—had presaged an encounter that left her a little sore and disappointed and him dismayed and embarrassed. He had made it up to her and thought all was well, but with hindsight he wondered. In any case, he was decidedly more confident that Annis had derived almost as much pleasure from the night and morning's activities as he had.

Finally satisfied with his neckcloth, he combed his unruly hair and realized that there was something more than pleasure he had taken from the experience: comfort. Comfort, a warm feeling in his chest and belly. Annis gave him comfort. It was a shock after months of depression to realize he actually felt happy.

Happier than he had felt in a very long time. With the perspective of hindsight, he realized that well before Caro's betrayal and death he had not actually been happy. He thought he was, he thought he was content. He knew life wasn't a constant state of bliss, but he thought he was happy. The truth was the youthful love he had shared with Caro had withered slowly and silently on the vine of marital decay. He had still loved her, but she had not loved him. And the woman he thought she was had become largely a figment of his imagination. He hadn't really known her.

How all this had happened he still wasn't sure; except he knew he hadn't paid enough attention. He hadn't tried hard enough to be the husband she needed. He'd let her down and hurt her. All unknowingly, all unintentionally. But he could not afford to make the same mistakes again, not with Annis.

Chapter Nineteen

A PPEARING DOWNSTAIRS AS the newly minted viscountess made Annis feel odd.

"Good morning, my lady, my lord." The footman held the door for her as she entered the breakfast parlor. The duchess greeted her with a kiss and the duke a smile.

As she was seated at the breakfast table beside Emrys, she was reminded of her birthday breakfast when they all made a fuss over her. But this time was different. Her status was elevated permanently now. She was no longer in that debatable zone between family and servant. She was in the family camp. It made her eyes sting. She blinked them hard and accepted the cup of coffee poured for her by Emrys. He glanced at her and snuck his hand under the table to give hers a reassuring squeeze.

He knows! He knows I am feeling odd and overwhelmed! Her heart felt like it would burst with how much she loved him. *If he can only learn to love me back a little . . .*

The duchess had very kindly lent her two day dresses and a dress suitable for dinner to tide her over until they returned to London, which was planned for the end of August. Which meant she no longer had to wear her governess dresses. She was still adjusting to the lower décolletage for even the day dresses, with the narrow bodices and shorter hems. It all felt indecent to her, but she could see by his expression that Emrys approved.

"So, what do you two have planned for the day?" asked Sarah, helping herself to toast. Before either of them could reply, Ava swept into the room, resplendent in jonquil muslin trimmed with forget-me-nots and blue ribbons. She immediately swooped on Annis and hugged her.

"Good morning my dearest Annis! Or should I address you as your ladyship now?" she asked with a cheeky smile and a curtsy.

Annis blushed and hugged the girl back. "No, no, Annis please, Ava."

"I plan to teach Annis how to ride," said Emrys, surprising her. "If you would like to learn?" he asked, cocking an eyebrow at her.

"Um, yes, I suppose," she said uncertainly. Horses made her a little nervous.

"Splendid idea," said the duke. "Ava, will you lend Annis old Sandy to practice on?"

"Yes, of course. You will recall my old mare, Annis. She is by far too lazy to throw you off, but you will be flat out getting her to move unless you offer her an enticement. She is very sweet, however, so you needn't worry she will nip you or kick."

Annis nodded. "Yes, I remember her."

"You can borrow one of my riding habits, too," said the duchess.

"You're so kind—"

"I know exactly how you feel," said Sarah with a gentle smile. "I felt that way, too, to begin with. A change in status is always a challenge, but you will get used to it remarkably quickly, and you're among friends here, so you have no need to be nervous or uncomfortable."

"See?" murmured Emrys in her ear.

And it turned out that old Sandy was indeed very placid and sweet tempered. She was dun colored, hence the name, and she stood quietly while Emrys boosted Annis into the saddle and she arranged herself with her leg over the pommel.

"I'll teach you to ride astride next. If you can master this, riding astride will be easy," he said. "But you'll need to ride sidesaddle in London, or you'll shock everyone."

She leaned forward to pat her mount who flicked her ears in acknowledgment. "Yes, I know. When you brought me home from Swinford, that was the first time I'd ever been on a horse. But I think I was too tired to be nervous, and with your arms around me I felt safe. Inigo is a fine horse," she said, eyeing the chocolate-colored gelding.

"He's a lovely boy." Emrys stroked the horse's nose affectionately. "Right. Are you comfortable?"

She nodded, "As comfortable as I can be perched up here on something that moves!"

He chuckled. "You'll get used to it. I'm going to lead you for a bit, all right?" He tugged Sandy's rein gently, but the horse refused to budge, and with a sigh he dug into his pocket and drew out a bit of carrot, which he offered on his palm. The mare lipped it up and then let him lead her. The movement of her gentle steps still made Annis sway in the saddle, but she corrected for the movement after a bit as they took a walk around the yard. Inigo followed placidly beside, led by his master's hand on his rein. When they had done three full circuits, Emrys asked, "Ready to try going for a walk across the fields?"

"Yes?"

Emrys grinned. "Don't overdo the enthusiasm."

He mounted Inigo, and setting a gentle walking pace, he led Sandy beside him out of the yard and into the fields behind the stables. "All right, we're going to walk to that stand of trees over there."

Annis shifted slightly to relieve the pressure on her leg, and they set out. The ground being a little less even than in the yard, there was more movement to accommodate for, but she found herself moving with it after a bit and relaxing. They reached the trees and Emrys held out the reins to her. "Now we will go back. If you need Sandy to move faster, kick her gently in the ribs with your heels." He demonstrated with Inigo, and the horse leaped forward. He brought him back around. "If you need her to stop, tug on the reins. If you need her to go to one side or the other, tug on the side you want her to go." He demonstrated all of that for her.

"And don't worry. I'm right here. If she spooks, I'll catch her and pull her in for you, all right?"

Annis swallowed and nodded. Her heart was pounding faster than it should really. *Everybody rides. It can't be that difficult.*

They set off across the field, Sandy happy enough to plod along next to Inigo. Annis's hands held the reins tightly and her whole body tensed up at first.

"Relax," he said with an encouraging smile. "Sandy isn't going to bolt on you. She's more likely to stop and have a snack."

Annis laughed and forced herself to relax. By the time they had gone back and forth to the trees three times she was feeling more confident, and Emrys praised her.

"Good, I think that's enough for one day. I don't want you getting too sore. At least not from riding a horse!" he said with a growly leer.

Annis laughed, blushing faintly, and let him lift her down from her placid mount. Set gently on her feet, she looked up at her husband, and the kind light in his eyes made her heart melt. Ignoring the stable hands who were collecting the horses, she slid her arms round his neck and kissed him. "Thank you. You're very patient. And so is Inigo. Don't you need to take him for a proper run?"

His hands tightened on her waist. "I do, but I'll do it later. Come on." He tugged her away, and they set off across the field once more to that stand of trees.

"Where are we going?" she puffed to catch up with his lengthened strides.

He shortened his stride a bit and said gruffly, "I want to kiss you properly and not with an audience."

"Oh. Well, you did warn me. But there are no curtains out

here," she said, trying to make light of it. Her body was twitching at the notion of more of his attention. *Really this was ridiculous. Surely, I had enough this morning?*

"No, we'll have to make do with trees instead." *Trees? Good heavens, anyone could see us.* But the idea was wickedly arousing.

"Emrys, wasn't this morning enough?" she teased.

"Apparently not."

She smiled at the ground, pleased she wasn't alone in her wanton desire.

They reached the trees, and he pulled her into the shelter of one, pressing her up against the trunk and kissing her.

"You don't need to thank me, you know, for a riding lesson or for anything else," he said, husky voiced. "This ledger is by no means unbalanced. In fact, if anything, I feel it is tipped the other way. You're giving me so much, Annis."

"I am?" She stroked his cheek, pushing a stray hank of hair out of the way. Love billowed up in her heart. She just adored him.

"You are. Apart from being an irresistible delight between the sheets, there is the way you are with the small fry, and you're putting up with me. I'm a wreck you know."

"Emrys, there is nothing to put up with," she protested. She felt so tempted to blurt out how she really felt, but his still-evident attachment to Caroline stayed her tongue. He needed time to sort out his own feelings, and having hers dumped on him at this point would likely be a burden. She feared she would drive him away, if he knew how deeply and hopelessly she had fallen in love with him.

"Let me make you feel good," he murmured, nuzzling her neck and reaching for her skirts.

Chapter Twenty

LAWRENCE CLUNG TO the saddle by instinct, barely conscious. Fortunately, his horse knew where to go. The pain under his ribs was a constant, nagging scream along his nerves. Blood seeped out and soaked his clothing. He was cold . . . so cold . . .

Hot . . . so hot . . .

Disembodied voices . . . "It will be a miracle if he survives . . ." Sobbing . . .

Who would cry for me? My family are all dead . . .

Chapter Twenty-One

EMRYS ROLLED OVER in bed and groped around. *She is gone!* He sat up and bellowed, "Annis!"

"Yes, Emrys?"

He blinked, bringing her into focus. She was sitting at the writing table under the window in her robe.

"What are you doing over there?"

"Writing to the girls," she said composedly.

"Well stop it and come back to bed," he said grumpily.

She cocked her head at him, and he added, "I want my morning cuddle." *I sound like Ewen. What is wrong with me?*

They had spent the rest of August at The Castle and returned to Cavendish Square in London three days ago. *The truth is I am struggling.*

She rose and came toward the bed, shedding her robe. She climbed in beside him, and he pulled her close.

After a bit she said softly, "What's wrong?"

He sighed and kissed her hair. "I'm sorry. This is the bed I used to share with Caro. I feel like she's haunting me."

He felt her stiffen slightly and cursed himself for being too blunt. She placed a hand on his bare chest and said calmly, "We can change rooms or change the bed. Would that help?"

"Perhaps." He stroked her back. "Thank you."

She nuzzled her head into his chest. "I thought you were restless."

"Hm," he grunted. "Thank you for being so understanding."

"It's only been five months, Emrys." She spoke quietly.

"It feels like an eternity."

"I'll get us moved into a different room and have this bed replaced, shall I?"

He hesitated a moment and then nodded. "Yes, that would be best. I had all of her things removed, but . . ." He trailed off. "The place still feels like her. She chose all the colors and the furnishings. The whole damned house feels like her," he admitted.

"Then perhaps I need to do some redecorating?" she said quietly.

He nodded.

"Are you sure?" she pressed, searching his face. "If I sweep everything away, will you resent it?"

He paused to consider this carefully. *Will I?* If Caro had just been killed without the drama and betrayal, it would all be different. He wouldn't want his past eradicated. It was highly unlikely in that circumstance that he would have chosen to marry again at all. He would still be mourning her, still wallowing in sorrow . . .

But that wasn't what had happened. He couldn't recapture the fantasy he had been living with Caro, because it didn't exist. It had all been an illusion, and he knew that now. He couldn't put the genie back in the bottle. And the truth was he didn't want to. He had Annis and the children and a new life. He didn't want to cling to the old one.

"No," he said slowly. "No, I want to start over, fresh. But you might check with the children. I don't want them to feel they have lost touch with their mother. They still need to feel connected to her."

She nodded. "Of course. I'll be careful."

His throat suddenly seized up, and he felt the prickle of tears under his lids. He closed his eyes and tried to swallow, but the lump was stuck and wouldn't be pushed down. He had cried tears of rage and hurt in the immediate aftermath, but he hadn't cried much since. He was surprised to find it happening now. But Annis's sensitivity and understanding undid him.

He slid down the bed a bit and buried his face in her bosom and cried.

"Oh, Emrys," she said softly. And she held him and stroked his hair and murmured things that made no sense but were comforting all the same.

When the storm passed, he sat up sniffing and wiped his tears on the sheets.

"Emrys, you're such a grub!" she said affectionately and reached for a handkerchief from the bedside table and handed it to him. He blew his nose and noticed her wiping her own cheeks.

"I made you cry!" he said, conscience stricken.

"Sympathetic tears," she said bracingly, sniffing. He handed her the handkerchief, and she found a dry bit to use.

"Do you feel better?" she asked, putting the handkerchief aside.

"Yes, I do." He kissed her hand. "You're a treasure, and I don't deserve you."

"Nonsense!" She shook her head, flushing faintly. "You have done so much for me—"

He cupped her face and kissed her. "We have already had this conversation. I consider the ledger well and truly balanced." He pulled her against his chest and heard his stomach rumble. "I think it is time we got up. What do you have planned for the day?"

"Apart from redecorating the house?" she said playfully.

He nodded, smiling. Annis's ability to make everything fun was one of the things he liked about her.

"Getting better acquainted with the servants and the way this house is run. Sarah is going to take me shopping for dresses on Friday, which will save you that chore. I know it's not something you would relish."

"Thank you, Sarah," he said, shoving back the covers and rolling his legs out of bed.

"Yes, as reluctant as I am to deck myself in finery, even I recognize I can't go out in public in my governess dresses. And I can't keep borrowing Sarah's clothes!"

"I like your governess dresses," he protested. "Don't get rid of all of them. You can wear one in private for my libidinous fantasies."

She laughed, rolling out the other side of the bed. "Really?"

He came round the bed and wrapped his arms about her. "Yes, really. I told you the prim and proper cut of the bodice drove me mad."

"You did," she admitted.

"Well, now I know what's underneath, I like the idea of you wearing them to continue to drive me mad. Because I can have the pleasure of revealing your lovely bosom to my gaze slowly and torturously." He cupped her breasts and massaged them through her semitransparent nightgown. "They are by far my favorite of your assets," he said, bending and kissing first one and then the other.

"I don't have assets!" she protested.

"Oh, yes, you do!"

"I was never a beauty, even when I was young."

"You are beautiful to me, Annis," he said softly and kissed her lips. "And you aren't *not* young!" he scolded, letting her go and striding over to the water jug to wash and shave. He used not to bother shaving daily, but he didn't want to scratch his wife's soft skin with his stubble, so he had begun to adopt the habit. *Perhaps I will get my hair cut, too. It is getting very long.*

AFTER BREAKFASTING WITH her husband and their joint morning visit with the children and Mrs. Green, Annis repaired to the servants' quarters to consult on the logistics of rearranging their sleeping arrangements. After that, she sent a note round to Sarah, asking if she could recommend someone to consult on redecorating the house. The duchess had mentioned that she was slowly making changes to The Castle and the London house.

The duke and duchess had followed them to town and arrived yesterday. Sarah had her sister Deborah with her, whom she was planning on presenting in the little season that was about to begin. As she would be taking Deborah for dress fittings, she had generously offered to include Annis. Annis suspected the duchess knew that she hadn't a clue how to go about selecting a fashionable wardrobe, and that, unlike many more dandified husbands, Emrys would be no use whatsoever in that endeavor.

Annis had been adjusting to her new status since the wedding. Spending the better part of a month at The Castle had helped to ease her into it, but she was woefully aware of her shortcomings and quite dreading going out into society. She was more than grateful for the duchess's guiding hand.

Having sent off her note, she returned upstairs to relieve Mrs. Green of the children and institute the first of her daily lessons with them. She had discussed this with Emrys and pointed out that while they could engage a governess and a tutor for Ewen, and probably should when the children were older, she wanted to initiate their lessons herself to begin with.

"For the girls have been without a governess for too long—you said so yourself, Emrys—and that will not stand them in good stead later. I can teach all the foundational skills the girls and Ewen will need, for I was taught mathematics and science as well as the arts, history, languages, and literature. And I would love to do it. Please say I may."

"Of course, if you want to, but won't it be a lot of work?"

"A labor of love," she smiled. And it was true, but she didn't reveal that she had an ulterior motive. She needed to keep up her skills, for if something went wrong . . . She didn't want to think of it. She was so deliriously happy at present. But the fear that her nemesis would suddenly reappear and rob her of her happiness persisted, no matter how hard she tried to suppress it.

And when things like this morning happened, she was re-minded of how much Emrys loved Caroline and how far away was her secret dream of earning his love for herself. His tears had wrung her heart. But a little flame of hope burned persistently still. For he was fond of her—his open affection made that blatantly obvious, and he wanted her physically in the most powerful way. She could only hope that with time, Caroline's hold over him would fade and leave room for him to love her a little. *Perhaps if I bear his child . . .*

She swallowed and wiped her eyes. It would not do to dwell on that. She stopped outside the nursery door to compose herself before opening it and stepping inside to be rapidly enveloped in the squeals and hugs of Emrys's children, who were her own now. That felicity alone was enough to cement her heart and commitment to Emrys, for she loved the darlings so much. Each day was a revelation as she came to know them better and understand their individual personalities and quirks, their likes and dislikes.

To all intents and purposes, she had her dream come true, if only she could be sure of her place in Emrys's heart.

EMRYS SPENT THE morning with his secretary, catching up on correspondence and the list for the House of Lords that was now in session. He supposed he would have to put in an appearance. But not today. This afternoon he was going to take his wife riding. He had continued her riding lessons while at The Castle, and it was time to show her off in Hyde Park.

He had visited Tattersall's yesterday and purchased a gentle mare for her. The beast had just been delivered to the mews behind the house. It was a surprise, and he looked forward to her reaction.

Going in search of her, he found her in the morning room, writing letters. He supposed they must be the ones she began this morning that he had interrupted.

"There you are," he said coming in and going to her side. She looked up and smiled. They had dined together at lunchtime but spent the morning and the two hours since occupied about their own business, she with the children, he with his secretary. *Why did it seem so long a time? Really my dependence on her is extraordinary. It hadn't been like this with Caro, had it? Even in the beginning? I can't remember. I don't think so.*

"Do you need something?" she said, putting down her pen.

He suppressed a lewd response and smiled, picking up her hand and kissing it. "I have a surprise for you. Come."

Standing, she raised her eyebrows in inquiry, a faint flush staining her cheeks. "What surprise?"

He grinned. "You'll see. Come with me." He tucked her hand in his arm and led her from the room, through the back of the house, out into the gardens at the rear, and through the gate to the stables.

Waiting for them was his head groomsman, holding the bay mare.

Annis's eyes widened at sight of the lovely horse. "Emrys?"

"She is yours, my love," he said with a grin. "I bought her for you yesterday. Isn't she a beauty?"

Annis stepped up to the mare and stroked her withers tentatively. "She is. Emrys, really you shouldn't—"

"I should," he said firmly. "You need a horse to ride in London. She has a gentle, sweet temperament, but she is a little more lively than old Sandy. She has been trained to be a lady's mount, however. I think she will suit you well."

"Oh, Emrys, you are so thoughtful!" she hugged him, and he hugged her back, well pleased.

"I thought we could go for a ride in Hyde Park, put her through her paces?"

"I—suppose." Annis eyed the lovely mare with some trepidation.

"I'll be with you. I won't let anything happen," he said reassuringly.

Annis nodded, biting her lip.

"Good. Shall we go now? You could go and put your riding habit on."

"It's not mine—it's Sarah's. I suppose I will need to remember to order one made when we go to the modiste's. Thank you, Emrys," she said shyly and kissed his cheek. He wanted to kiss her properly, but with the groom standing there, he restrained himself.

Fifteen minutes later she returned arrayed in her borrowed riding habit. It was blue and fitted her lovely figure to perfection. She would have her own gowns soon, after the promised shopping expedition with Sarah on Friday. He was grateful to Sarah for saving him from that torture.

Having gotten her settled comfortably in the saddle, he mounted Inigo and led the way out of the mews at an ambling walk.

"What will you name her?" he asked.

"I'm not sure," Annis leaned forward to pat the mare gently with one gloved hand. The ears twitched, and the horse shook her head.

"Oh dear, doesn't she like that?"

"I don't think it's you. There is a fly bothering her."

"Oh." Annis waved away the insect and settled into her seat. She looked every inch the elegant lady perched on the mare.

They entered the main thoroughfare, and the mare held steady. She had been trained in traffic and was not easily spooked, he was glad to see. Annis was a little tense but trying to hide it.

"Relax," he murmured. "Everything will be fine."

"Sorry, I'm such a ninny. I've never done this before."

"I know, hence why we are practicing before London is swamped with people again. If we do this every day, you'll get the hang of it in no time."

"Thank you," she said with a grateful smile.

He nodded encouragingly.

They arrived at Hyde Park and entered the grounds. It was a bit early for the most fashionable time to be seen, which was five o'clock, so there were fewer people to contend with. And as he had noted, the little season wasn't in full swing yet.

They ambled slowly down Rotten Row among the other riders and the occasional carriage, the pedestrians walking to their left on the footpath.

"Have you been here before?" he asked.

"Oh yes, when I worked for the Dowtons in London, I used to bring my charges here for walks in the afternoons. But I have never visited London while in the duke's employ."

"You will see some changes then in six years."

"Yes, no doubt."

"Ah, there's the dowager with Lady Ava and Ravenshaw," he said, waving. They brought their mounts to a halt and Ava exclaimed, "Oh what a pretty mare, Annis. I am green with envy!"

Annis smiled at her erstwhile pupil, a little flush of pleasure at the compliment. Jerome DeVere, the Marquess of Ravenshaw, bowed at the waist and gave Annis one of his devilish smiles which had her visibly flustered. The dowager asked her how she did, and under cover of her response, Ravenshaw murmured, "An unexpected start, Emrys. The governess?"

Emrys stiffened, bridling at the implied criticism of Annis. "And why not? You're hardly in a position to preach propriety, Ravenshaw!"

Ravenshaw raised his eyebrows and smirked slightly. "Like that, is it? Congratulations, I hope you're happy."

"I am," said Emrys, somewhat mollified.

Ravenshaw lost his smirk and nodded. "I'm glad," he said simply.

The sincerity in his tone smoothed the last of Emrys's ruffled feathers. Just then Ava claimed Ravenshaw's attention with a touch on his arm and Emrys was struck by the picture they made. Two of the best-looking people in London, a petite, pretty blonde and a handsome, dark-haired Corinthian. Ravenshaw was too old for her, of course, even if he were the marrying sort, which he wasn't. And in any case, Rob would have his guts for garters if he so much as looked at Ava that way. But they did make a picture.

He and Annis took their leave of the other party and ambled on, turning at the end of the Row and ambling back.

"I think I shall call her Charis," announced Annis. "It means *grace* in Greek you know. Thank you so much, Emrys. She is lovely," she said, smiling at him with such warmth his chest filled up to bursting.

"Don't keep thanking me. I'm your husband—it's my duty to see you properly mounted." His wicked sense of humor asserted itself, and he added, "Although that's something I'll be doing more in private!"

"What?" Eyes widening in comprehension, she flushed. "Emrys! Not here!"

"Exactly!" he said, smirking. "In private."

Later that night, in the privacy of their bedchamber, he looked up at her straddling him as he drove upward into her, and her delicious breasts swung before his face. "I trust you feel well mounted my lady?" He grinned at his joke even as he panted, gripping her hips and thrusting hard enough to jolt her whole body.

She moaned softly, "Emrys!"

"Yes, love," he panted. "Come for me, sweetheart." He groaned. "God, Annis, I'm not going to be able to hold off much longer." He moved his hand to rub her furiously and she arched her body, flinging back her long neck and thrusting forward her magnificent breasts. He reached up and captured a nipple in his mouth and dropped back against the pillows as he lost the battle and came hard. Pleasure spiking and flooding his senses, her body milking his to completion as she flopped forward on his chest with a replete moan, panting in his ear.

Who would be without a wife? he thought muzzily, stroking her damp back and pulling up the sheets to keep her warm.

Chapter Twenty-Two

S ARAH CALLED FOR Annis on Friday morning and whisked her off to Bond St. for a marathon shopping expedition. Annis, unaccustomed to being able to afford lace and ribbons, let alone a whole wardrobe of sumptuous gowns, was a bit overwhelmed. But Emrys had impressed upon her over breakfast that she could spend what she liked.

"You won't bankrupt me for a few gowns, my dear. I can assure you, my estates are in good heart. Caro used to buy something new every week, if I recall. Just tell them to send the bills to me. I will organize you an allowance in future, and you can manage for yourself, as I'm sure you'd prefer, but for this once just get what you need, and be guided by Sarah."

Seeing Annis's discomfort in the first shop, Sarah said quietly, "I know how you feel. I was reluctant at first when I inherited my great-aunt's fortune. But Daphne—you remember Lady Holbrook?—she convinced me it was an investment in my future, and it did pay off. In your case it's different, of course. But you must dress as befits your station, as I do now. We need to ensure we don't become sources of gossip or put our families to the blush, my dear, not over trifles like clothes. That doesn't mean I countenance squandering money unnecessarily; I would much prefer it went to charity. But with the title comes certain responsibilities, you understand?"

Annis nodded. It made perfect sense, and she did want to make Emrys pleased with her appearance. To see the warmth in his eyes when he looked at her was worth more than gold.

She was glad to make the acquaintance of Sarah's sister, Miss Deborah Watson, again. She was an exceedingly pretty young woman with dark hair and blue eyes, a stunning combination. Despite her looks, Miss Watson wasn't in the slightest bit affected in her manner. She seemed oblivious to her appearance and entered into the process of acquiring a wardrobe with similar trepidation to Annis. Despite the seven years between them, Annis felt a certain kinship of spirit with the younger woman.

The modiste, Madame Therese, had both of them up on pedestals while fabrics were draped and pinned on them, and patterns and styles were discussed with Sarah. Once this part of the proceedings was completed, they tried on several made-up dresses, which were adjusted to fit with pins and promised for delivery later that day or tomorrow. The gowns to be made bespoke would take a couple of weeks to arrive.

Since both of them required everything from corsets, chemise, and petticoats, to shoes, bonnets, gloves, and shawls, it was a very long day traipsing from shop to shop. They stopped for luncheon, and Sarah allowed them a respite at Hatchard's bookshop for a blissful hour where they all three poured over the new catalogue of novels and chose some volumes for their respective libraries.

By the time Sarah dropped her at home, Annis was exhausted. She went up to her dressing room with the intention of putting away all her new purchases, the footmen trailing her, carrying up all her packages, and was confronted by the sight of a young woman in an apron and mob cap waiting for her.

"My lady," she said with a smile and dipped a curtsy. "My name is Bess Harper. His lordship sent me to help you with your wardrobe, if it pleases you?"

Annis recalled Emrys muttering something about getting her

a maid and she had meant to ask Sarah how to go about it but forgot in all the kerfuffle. It seemed he had done it for her. Generally, she enjoyed the things he did for her, but choosing a personal lady's maid was rather more delicate than choosing a horse. Not entirely sure she liked this high-handedness, she still smiled at the young woman and said, "Thank you, Bess. There are a few things to put away."

The footmen deposited the first lot of boxes and packages and went back down for the rest. It took them four trips.

By the time they had gone, Bess was already helping her unwrap and unbox everything and making *oh* and *ah* noises over her purchases.

"Oh, my lady, these are lovely!" she said, eyeing a pair of dancing slippers in pink silk with rosettes.

Annis stared at everything laid out before her and nodded. "There is a ball gown coming to match them."

With Bess's help, she got everything packed away and realized it was time to dress for dinner. She had brought one gown home with her. In sea-green silk with a gauze overskirt, it had fitted her perfectly without the need for alteration. It was secretly her favorite of all the gowns she had tried on, and she was quietly excited to wear it for Emrys.

Bess proved highly competent with dressing her hair, a luxury Annis had hitherto not had. And it was in need of a cut. Sarah had promised to send round a hairstylist tomorrow to give her a fashionable crop.

When she mentioned her plans for her hair to Emrys over dinner, he dropped his fork and said, "Oh, no! But I like your hair the way it is!"

"Oh! Well of course if you—"

He sighed. "No, you're right, you need to look fashionable, and of course you should have it as it pleases you. I shall just have to get used it." He chewed thoughtfully. "I should get mine cut, too, and try not to embarrass you with my woolly mop." He shook his head, and his hair fell over his face.

"Oh, but I like yours!" she protested.

"We both need to be shorn like sheep," he said. "We shall accustom ourselves and be fashionable, at least for the season. We can go wild in the off months."

She smiled and forked up some peas. "As you like, my lord," she said demurely.

He grinned at her. "I know I said it before, but it bears repeating—that dress really suits you. Something about that color."

She flushed. She soaked up compliments from him like a sponge. "Thank you. Yes, I like it very much myself. It's my favorite shade of green."

⊁⟫⟩⟨⟨⟨

THE FOLLOWING MORNING, Emrys shocked his valet by asking for a haircut.

"Certainly, my lord. The usual slight trim?" asked Felton, getting out his scissors and comb.

"No, do what you want with it," said Emrys, seating himself before the mirror.

Felton stood behind him and said, "I beg your pardon, my lord. What do you mean?"

"Cut it, Felton. No doubt you know how to achieve something . . . fashionable?" He winced internally but faced the mirror manfully, reminding himself that if it looked awful, the hair would grow back.

Felton opened his mouth and shut it. "As your lordship pleases." He draped a towel round Emrys's shoulders and set to work.

Twenty minutes later he held up a mirror to show Emrys the cut from the back. All the length had been cut, and his thick, slightly wavy brown hair clung to the shape of his skull. At the front, a bit more length had been retained.

"Your lordship's natural curls give body to the hair and support the romantic look. I have refrained from adopting the extremity of the Brutus, but I think this style frames your face well. If you choose to adopt the fashion of sideburns, my lord . . .?" He stopped delicately, clearly not wishing to overstep.

Emrys regarded his reflection with slight surprise. He would never be handsome, but the cut was an improvement, even he had to admit. "I'll consider it, Felton. Good job," he added.

Felton bowed, a slight smile curling his lips.

"I think I'll get some new boots, too," said Emrys.

"And some pantaloons, my lord?" asked Felton hopefully. "A pale biscuit is tasteful, while being in the first stare of elegance."

Emrys's lips twitch, "Don't get too far ahead of yourself, Felton. You'll never turn me into a Brummel, you know."

"I know, my lord," he said in a hollow voice.

"Do I pay you enough, Felton?"

Startled, Felton said, "Your lordship is most generous. I have no complaints about my remuneration."

"I'm glad I pay you enough to put up with me, then," said Emrys, rising and stretching. He shook his head, dislodging some of Felton's carefully arranged curls.

"If you won't consider pantaloons, my lord, would you at least consider purchasing some jackets and waistcoats that fit your trimmer figure? I have done what I can with your breeches, my lord, but I'm no tailor, and the jackets and waistcoats are beyond me."

Emrys looked down at his flatter stomach, running a hand over it. "I suppose so. I hadn't really noticed. This slimmer me seems to be the new normal version. But I won't purchase coats so tight you have to use a shoehorn to get me into them, mind."

"Of course not, my lord."

Emrys smiled and accepted the neckcloth Felton handed to him and attempted to tie the damned thing with a bit more precision than usual. He would never master the art of the cravat, he was sure. Dressed in one of his ill-fitting waistcoats and jackets and his rather scuffed boots, despite Felton's best efforts with the bootblack, he reflected that the least he could do for Annis was pay a bit more attention to his wardrobe, and he resolved to pay a visit to Scott and Hoby.

Some time later, having spent an hour with his delighted tailor, he headed toward Hoby in St James's to purchase some new boots and ran into the duke.

"Turning fashionable, Emrys, or did Felton threaten to resign unless you chopped it off?" said the duke, referring to his hair cut.

"Neither."

"Ah, then I detect the influence of Annis."

Emrys shook his head. "Annis likes my hair long. But you're right—I did it for her. She is making strides to be fashionable and look the part of the viscountess; I don't want to embarrass her by being shabby next to her. I'm heading to Hoby now to get some new boots."

"I'll come with you," the duke said, falling into step with him. "Sarah mentioned she had both Annis and Deb at the dressmakers. Must have been quite a day. I know Sarah was tired after it."

"Yes, Annis was, too. There are a dashed lot of bits that go into a lady's toilette. Makes it damned tricky to get her out of all those layers."

Rob grinned but didn't comment.

After finishing with Hoby, the two men headed to Gentleman Jackson's, where the duke was in the habit of practicing the pugilistic art regularly.

Emrys consented to go a couple of rounds with him and enjoyed it so much he resolved to continue the practice. After that, they repaired to their club for a meal.

Cutting into his steak, Rob said casually, "You look happy."

Emrys sipped his wine and nodded. "I am. Annis is the perfect wife I never knew I needed."

Rob nodded and said quietly, "I'm glad. No one deserves happiness more than you."

"Well, I fancy I'm not the only one." Emrys forked up some mashed potato and gravy with a quizzical look across the table.

Rob flushed faintly. "I am exceedingly happy. In fact"—he

stopped and picked up his glass of wine—"you can be the first to congratulate me. We're not making it public yet, but—"

"Sarah is expecting?"

Robert grinned and raised his glass to the one Emrys offered. "She is, and I couldn't be happier. I'm so looking forward to it."

Emrys nodded. "It is the best feeling in the world to hold them for the first time. Be warned, you will fall in love instantly and worry yourself into a frenzy about them for the rest of your life. Nothing will be the same again."

"I know. I cannot wait," confessed the starchy duke, already looking the very picture of a doting father.

They finished their meal and repaired to the billiard room for a game. This led to a card game or two, and it was in the card room that they were joined by the Marquess of Ravenshaw.

He started at the sight of Emrys's shorn head. "Good God, Ashford, I thought you were someone else. What brought this on?"

"His new wife," said the duke with a smirk.

Emrys opened his mouth to protest and gave up, shrugging. What did it matter?

"Careful, you'll turn fashionable," said Ravenshaw with a grin.

"I'll never be a peacock like you," retorted Emrys. Ravenshaw was not only stunningly handsome with dark hair and blue eyes, but also immaculate in his dress and appearance. His sporting proclivities prevented him from earning the sobriquet of dandy. Instead he was a noted Corinthian. He was also well known for his competitive streak.

"Care to play?" asked the duke, about to deal another round.

Ravenshaw sat down and ordered a bottle of Chambertin. "Ought to send round for Pendrell. We could play Whist with four," he said.

"You just want to beat us to flinders again!" said Emrys with a grin.

"That's a good idea. I'll send a note." Robert said. "The fellow is bound to be home; he never goes out unless one of us invites him. He's in serious danger of turning into a hermit."

Robert scribbled out a note and had it sent round to Deodonatus Kinninmouth's residence. Half an hour later he joined them. The Earl of Pendrell was a giant of man with a shock of red hair and freckles, and features that were more hawkish than handsome. He made a striking contrast with the Marquess of Ravenshaw who was built on slenderer and more aesthetically pleasing lines. Ravenshaw put one in mind of a black panther or a bird of prey. Beautiful, graceful, and deadly.

"Congratulations!" Pendrell said, giving Emrys a bear hug. It was the first time he had seen Emrys since the wedding.

Several games later it was getting on time for dinner. Seeing that his friends were determined to make a night of it, Emrys debated whether to leave them and head home to Annis. He missed her already, he realized. It was the first day they had spent apart since they were married.

But when he suggested he would be heading home, the outcry gave him pause. He couldn't spend every minute in Annis's lap, as much as part of him wanted to. And his friends were good company, and he'd been neglecting them. He opted to send Annis a note and stay.

WHEN ANNIS RECEIVED his note, she tried not to be disappointed. She had plenty to do, after all, between devising lessons for the children, her embroidery, and a book to read, but she couldn't help feeling a little heartsore. She missed him. But it was unreasonable for her to expect him to dance attendance on her every night, nor could she expect him to eschew his friends for her sake.

She tucked the children in and kissed them good night.

"Where is Papa?" asked Charlie fretfully.

"He is out for the evening, but he will be home later," Annis said with a reassuring smile.

Charlie pursed her lips and caught Annis's hand. "Will you sing a song for us?"

"Of course." She settled on the bed and chose a lullaby with a soothing cadence.

She glanced across the room where Ewen was tucked into his bed, his eyes already closed and his thumb in his mouth. Mrs. Green sat in her armchair, some sewing in her lap.

Lizzie settled herself and closed her eyes, but Charlie gripped her hand tightly and watched her as she sang. She clutched her doll in one arm and blinked as Annis switched to another song. Her eyelids slowly dropped and popped open again, and then again, and her grip on Annis's hand loosened. By the end of the second song her eyes remained closed, but Annis continued singing softly for a few more minutes to make sure. The little girl's hand lay loosely in hers.

Charlie's reddish-blonde curls escaped her plait and curled round her face, her skin so soft and translucent with the round-cheeked plumpness of childhood. She was a pretty child and would likely be a beautiful young woman one day.

Annis's heart felt full for these precious children she got to call her own. Her good fortune was hard to comprehend. She loved their father unequivocally. But she loved each of them, too, not simply because they were his, but because of who they were. Lizzie with her forthright personality and sunny disposition, Ewen with his sweet affection, and Charlie with her sensitivity.

Her compassionate heart bled a little for Charlie. She understood so well the insecurity that plagued the little girl. She of all of them seemed to have taken Caroline's death the hardest. It had rocked her world and turned it upside down. Her trust was broken. Charlie might resemble her mother most in appearance, but on the inside, she was like her father, sensitive and a bit insecure. She hoped she could fill the void for Charlie, as she hoped she was doing for Emrys. Gosh, she missed him. She was as addicted to his cuddling as he was to doing it. She sat a while, just watching them sleep and wiped a tear of happiness off her cheek.

Finally, she rose and left the room on quiet feet, smiling and nodding to Mrs. Green.

When Emrys still wasn't home at ten, she retired to bed and fell asleep over her book, jerking awake sometime later when the bed dipped and he murmured, "Just me."

He slid under the covers and reached for her. The book fell off the bed with a thump, but she ignored it as he pulled her close and nuzzled her neck. "Missed you," he said, husky voiced.

"Did you enjoy your evening?" she asked.

"Hm, yes, I did. Haven't seen the fellows for a while. It was nice to catch up." He kissed her neck, his hands running over her body through her night gown. "Bit bosky," he confessed. "We had a few." He found her mouth and kissed her. "What did you do this evening?"

"Planned tomorrow's lessons and reading," she said.

"And the children?"

"Charlie needed a song or two to go to sleep."

He nodded. "I stopped in to check on them on my way here. They were all sleeping. Including Mrs. Green. Did you know she snores?"

Annis chuckled. "Yes, I did."

"Should I be worried about Charlie?" he asked.

"I should think she'll grow out of it," Annis reassured him.

"Silly question, really. I'll worry anyway. Which reminds me—got some news!"

His grin, visible in the candlelight, told her it was good news. "Yes?"

"Sarah's pregnant."

"Oh, how marvelous. I did wonder the other day; she seemed a bit pale and tired."

"Rob's over the moon. He is completely soft under all that starch, you know."

"Yes, I do know. He was a very kind and considerate employer."

His hands were still stroking her. They now squeezed, one on her rump the other on her breast. "Feels like forever since this morning," he murmured, pushing her back into the pillows and moving a hand between her legs.

She sighed. He may have left her for the evening, but he was home now and wanting to make up for his absence. She wasn't inclined to stop him.

Only a few evenings later, Annis joined Emrys out in society among their friends. Her first appearance in society as Viscountess Ashford was a night at the theatre. The duke had a box in Drury Lane, and she and Emrys were to join the duke, Sarah, Sarah's sister Deborah, the dowager, Lady Ava, and the elder of the duke's two brothers, Lord Hereward, for a performance of the opera *The Fairy Queen*.

Her dress was a cream silk with blue piping and embroidery, finished with lace on the bosom, sleeves, and hem. The bodice was not cut so low as the gown she wore for the wedding, but it was still low enough for Annis to feel uncomfortable and for Emrys to eye it in a way that told her precisely what he would be doing when they got home. If he didn't whip her off into a secluded corner and do obscene things to her before then . . .

Since she was afraid he would wish to do precisely that, for Emrys seemed remarkably impervious to what other people might think of his behavior, she was only thankful that he didn't get the opportunity to try. They were never left alone long enough, which was a good thing, for Annis's nerves were stretched to breaking point as it was. Being presented as Viscountess Ashford couldn't help but make her feel like a fraud. She was terrified someone would step out of the shadows, point at her, and denounce her as a bastard. A lesser fear was that someone would recognize her as the duke's former governess, which would be bad enough. Quite humiliating in fact. But not as bad as the other.

She tried her very best to cover her fear and smile and nod and appear relaxed, and she thought she was doing quite well until Emrys murmured in her ear, "Relax. No one is going to bite you. You're among friends."

She flushed. "Is it so obvious?"

"Only to me," he said with an encouraging smile.

"I am so afraid someone will recognize me. You know, from before, when I was a governess."

"Even if they do, they won't say so. If you think anyone has more social credit than the duke, you would be highly mistaken. You're my wife and a friend of the Duchess of Troubridge. Robert is known to be a high stickler. If he approves of you, no one is going to gainsay him."

"Even the patronesses of Almack's?"

"Well, the dowager is bosom bows with Maria Sefton, so I wouldn't think so."

"Oh."

He kissed her hand and placed it on his arm. He was wearing a new suit, and this one seemed a better fit than the usual. Combined with his new hairstyle, he almost cut a fashionable figure. His hair was still a trifle long, but more fashionably so, with a rather romantic fall across his brow. And for once his neckcloth was tied properly. "Come and sit down and enjoy the performance. I guarantee you'll like it."

"Oh, yes. I loved *A Midsummer Night's Dream* and this is based on it, isn't it? We took the girls to a performance in Bath once. I was entranced."

Chapter Twenty-Three

ANNIS'S NEXT TEST was a ball held by the duchess to present her sister, Miss Deborah Watson, to the *ton*. Emrys knew this was going to be difficult for her, and he went to some lengths to make sure his own appearance did her credit. For the first time in his life, he was paying attention to how he looked. Not because he cared for himself, but because he wanted her to feel as confident as possible in her new role, and having him look a shabrag wouldn't help.

He'd taken to sparring with the duke at Gentleman Jackson's, too. He'd decided he preferred to keep off the extra pounds he had shed in the wake of Caro's perfidy and death. He knew he had a disastrous tendency to gain weight—he liked his food—so it behooved him to do some more exercise to keep it off.

Technically, he should still be in mourning and not attending balls at all, let alone with a new wife on his arm. He was a walking scandal after Caro's disaster, but the weight of public opinion was on his side, and he hoped that would be extended to Annis. He wouldn't dance, which was a shame, because he liked dancing, and he'd very much like to dance with Annis. He'd been giving her lessons round the drawing room at home, for she'd never danced in her life in public, although she knew the rudiments of the steps.

There was inevitably some gossip and some ill-meaning comments that he hoped fervently did not come to Annis's ears, for they would wound her terribly. The weight of the duke and duchess's approval counted for a lot and quashed much of the incipient scandal. But there were still a few who muttered that Annis was no better than she ought to be and had snared the viscount when he was most vulnerable.

"A governess, you know, no family to speak of—a nobody. Appalling, but she is received everywhere, for the Duke of Troubridge approves her, so there is nothing more to be said, really. He and Ashford have been thick as thieves since Cambridge."

Annis was to wear another delicious gown for the ball, green satin with something gauzy over it. A more sophisticated version of the one she wore to dinner with him the first night after her shopping expedition. He'd even had the foresight to ask Sarah what color her gown was, so he could get her something to wear with it. She had no jewels of her own except her father's ring, which he had stashed in the safe, and her sinful little seed pearl brooch, which still brought him undone when she wore it. So, he had ordered a teardrop-shaped emerald pendant set in gold with a gold chain just the right length to have the emerald nestle into the top of her cleavage.

She began to cry, of course, when he gave it to her and stared at it, nestled in its white velvet box, with her hand over her mouth. "Oh, Emrys, it's beautiful."

"I'm glad you like it. Sarah assures me it will go with your gown for her ball."

"Yes. Yes, it will." She sniffed and wiped her eyes. "Thank you. You are by far too good to me."

"I am not," he said roughly and put an arm round her. She put hers round his neck, holding the box in one hand, and kissed him.

"Let's see what it looks like on, shall we?"

She nodded, and he took the pendant out of the box. When

she turned, he set it round her neck and fastened it. Looking down from above he saw that it sat perfectly just where he liked it most. He slid his arms round her and kissed her neck, rumbling, "Perfect!"

His hands slid up to squeeze her breasts in her day gown, pushing them up and dropping the emerald deeper into her cleavage. "When you wear it with your ball gown, it's going to drive me to madness all night, you know."

She relaxed back against him with a sigh as he continued to massage her breasts. She lifted her chin as he nuzzled kisses into her neck and pressed his rapidly hardening cock against her rump. She rubbed against him suggestively, and he growled in her ear.

"Keep that up, and I'll want to fuck you, right here, right now." She glanced up at him, and he groaned, "Annis!" He kissed her hard and deep, pressing her back against him with a firm arm across her middle.

His hand moved down her front to cup her through her gown and press his fingers just where he knew she wanted them.

"Emrys!" she said, breathless.

"Just a moment, I'll lock the door," he said and crossed the room to shut the door and turn the key. He came back to her and pulled her back against him, renewing his assault with his fingers on the place between her legs.

"You'll ruin my gown," she protested, whimpering.

"Bend over the damned table!" he said, his voice gone gravelly with need. He couldn't fathom how much he wanted this woman. Repeatedly.

She bent forward over the small round table, her hands clutching the far edge as he lifted her skirts and nudged her legs apart a bit. He took in the view for a moment before he dropped to his knees and leaned forward to set his mouth on her exposed peach, his tongue circling and plundering her entrance. She whimpered and moaned, pushing back on him, and he reached down to undo his falls where his cock was being strangled by the fabric of his breeches. He brought his hand up between her legs to fondle and stroke her clitoris, making her jump and moan louder. Her flesh clenched under his mouth, and he groaned into her. His other hand distractedly stroked and squeezed his cock to assuage its throbbing ache.

"Please, Emrys!" she begged.

Rising he brought his cock level with her entrance and thrust firmly forward and sank to the hilt with a groan.

"This will be quick and hard!" he warned.

"Please!" She pushed back on him, and he grabbed her hips and jolted her and the table with the fierceness of his thrusts.

Hot, hard, quick! He leaned forward over her back and kissed the nape of her neck with an open-mouthed kiss that scraped her flesh with his teeth and bathed it with his tongue, reaching around to stroke her rapidly where she needed it. His other hand went to her shoulder, holding her steady as he pummeled her.

Fuck, yes!

She cried out, her legs trembling and her body convulsing round him. The sensation ignited his own orgasm, and he came hard, her name a loud groan disintegrating into grunts as he expelled his seed and slumped forward on her back in a knee-trembling heap.

"Fuck!" he muttered breathlessly against her neck. She slumped under him against the table and sighed.

"Oh, yes . . ."

"I'll have to give you jewelry more often if that is my reward," he rumbled in her ear.

She laughed and tried to clench on him as he slipped out of her.

She stood up slowly, her gown falling back into place. She put up her hands to her hair. "Have you ruined me?" she asked, turning to face him.

"No," he said, cupping her face and kissing her nose. "You look flushed and sated, very appealing." He did up his buttons and went to unlock the door. It was to be hoped that the servants hadn't heard them, but he rather suspected they might have.

They hadn't exactly been quiet. *But damn it, if I want to fuck my own wife in my own drawing room, in the middle of the afternoon, I bloody well will.*

THE BALL WAS a success for the duchess by all standards set for such things, and Deborah and Lady Ava did not lack partners. For Annis, though, it was a trial of sorts. Emrys was attentive. He had gone to the effort of purchasing a new set of evening wear, all black of course, and his attempts to look kempt for her sake touched her. All the same, she rather liked him rumpled and slightly scruffy. This new, more polished Emrys was a trifle too handsome.

What if he starts attracting the attention of other ladies? Can I compete? Her old insecurities gnawed at her. She tried to push them away. Emrys was the faithful sort. She didn't need to worry about him straying. *At least not yet.* He was as hot for her as ever, as this afternoon's little encounter in the drawing room amply demonstrated.

His cronies teased him about his new look, in particular Lord Ravenshaw, who was, as usual, impeccably dressed and extraordinarily handsome. To think of her, little Annis Pringle, mixing with dukes and marquesses! She quailed when she thought about what they would all say if they knew the truth about her.

She had never truly discussed the actual status of her birth with Emrys. She wondered if he had guessed. It was implied, after all, in the fact that she had her father's ring and that someone wanted her dead because of it. But he had never taxed her with it, and she was too afraid to raise it with him now that they were married. If her baseborn status came to light, it would cause yet another scandal for the poor man to bear, and she would hate to be the cause of that. For not even a duke's imprimatur could overcome such a stain.

When he left her with the ladies and disappeared into the

card room with his friends, Lords Ravenshaw and Pendrell, she tried very hard not to mind. After all, he couldn't dance, as he had explained to her, so what was the poor man to do, prop the wall all night? But she couldn't help feeling exposed not to have him at her side. They had been virtually inseparable since their wedding, usually spending a significant portion of each day in each other's company and all night wrapped up in each other's arms. The viscount was still sleeping wrapped round her like a limpet. She had grown used to it. If he stopped, she would miss it.

She sat with the dowager, as the duchess was flitting round the room as a good hostess should, and watched the young ladies being whisked off to dance. Which Annis was quite comfortable doing. As a governess, her lot had always been to sit on the sidelines and watch out for her charges. Although Emrys had assured her that she could dance if she chose, she didn't think it would be proper, and in any case, she would much prefer to dance with him. She had been so surprised to discover what an accomplished dancer he was. She knew he could sing, but she hadn't realized his talent for rhythm extended to dancing until he'd whisked her into a waltz.

She was therefore unprepared when Lord Hereward, the duke's great hulking younger brother, asked her to dance. He was slightly over six feet tall and very broad through the shoulders and chest, and quite handsome, with curly dark-brown hair and soft dark-brown eyes. She glanced at the dowager for help when he asked, and she waved her away.

"Go on, child. It will do him good."

He led her onto the dance floor for the Boulanger and said, "Mama insists we all dance."

"And you don't particularly enjoy it?"

He flushed. "I'm not much in the petticoat line, if you take my meaning. I tend to get tongue tied and develop two left feet if I like someone."

"Hence choosing me, because I'm safe?" suggested Annis understandingly. This young man was like a big, awkward, tree trunk with soft cow eyes.

"Yes," he admitted in a rush, and then reflecting on how that sounded, he said, "Not that I don't like you its just—you're a married lady."

She smiled and patted his arm. "I understand."

He relaxed then and said confidingly, "Kenrick's much better at his sort of thing than I am. He's my younger brother, but people often think he's older. He's a bean pole and charming and quite dissolute. That's him over there dancing with the chit in yellow."

"Gosh, she's quite beautiful, isn't she?"

"Yes, and she's an heiress to boot—Miss Cecelia Woodrow. Whoever her chaperone is shouldn't be letting her dance with Kenrick. Can't be trusted to keep the line. I believe she's engaged to Tavistock, but he's not here tonight. I heard he was ill or something. He'll be more ill if he hears of this."

⇶⤛

EMRYS WAS ENJOYING the company of his friends, even if they were still teasing him unmercifully.

"Setting up to be an Adonis now, Ashford?" said Pendrell with a nod to his attire.

Emrys pushed the fall of hair off his brow a trifle self-consciously and shrugged. "Just trying not to embarrass Annis."

"Must admit, took us by surprise a bit, old chap," said Ravenshaw. "Getting married again so soon. Especially in the circumstances."

Emrys flushed. "Aye, well, we needed each other, and the children need her, too."

Ravenshaw glanced at Pendrell and back before leaving that alone. "I will say you're the best advocate for marriage I've come across."

"Hardly, after what happened with Caro," he said shortly.

"That wasn't your fault, though."

"It was more my fault than you know," he said quietly.

"How so? You weren't unfaithful to her, I'd swear to it," said Pendrell.

"No, I wasn't." Emrys looked into the middle distance, his gaze going out of focus. "I just never knew her. I thought I did, but—" He shook his head.

"It will be different with—?"

"Annis? Yes, I think so. We've some things to sort out yet, but I believe we're on the right track. Marriage is a constant balancing act of compromise and small decisions that you make, mostly unconsciously, day to day. It pays to pay attention. That's what I've learned. Don't take things for granted, and don't make assumptions. Get clarity. Talk."

"Don't look at me, old chap, I'm not planning to get married anytime soon," said Ravenshaw, holding up his hands.

"What about you, Pendrell?" he asked.

"Chance'd be a fine thing," rumbled the earl. "I'm looking for a needle in a bloody haystack. The woman I want doesn't exist; I'm convinced of it. Or if she does, I'll never meet her," he said gloomily. "And even if I did, she probably wouldn't have me."

"You sound like Troubridge before he met his duchess," said Ravenshaw. "To quote you back to yourself, you're a bloody earl. Of course she'll have you."

The earl shook his head. "Not the one I want. You see she'll care a damn sight more about antiquities than she will about my title."

"Ah, good luck with that my friend," said Ravenshaw nodding in understanding.

"Advertise," said Emrys.

"What?" Pendrell squinted at him. *Does the man need his spectacles all the time now?*

"In one of those damned magazines you read so avidly. If you want a woman who shares your interests, reach out to her through a medium she will be reading."

Pendrell raised his eyebrows. "You may have got something there. Thank you, I'll think about it."

After an hour of playing cards with his friends, Emrys made his way back to the ballroom. He missed his wife. Being away from her made him anxious. *Is she coping? Does she need me?* He hadn't felt that way about Caro, but then Caro wasn't new to the *ton* and afraid people would judge her for her background.

He looked for her where he had left her with the dowager, but she wasn't there. He scanned the crowded ballroom for a green gauzy dress and found her dancing with Robert. An unaccustomed pang of jealousy shot through his chest.

Not that he was jealous of Robert—the man was devoted to his wife—but he was jealous that other people got to dance with her tonight while he couldn't because of some stupid rule about mourning for a wife who had so wronged him. He clenched his teeth, a rumble of annoyance rolling through him. He really had been more grumpy than normal lately. His emotions were all over the place. Crying one minute, laughing the next. He was usually the most calm and easy-going fellow he knew. Not this irrational idiot who couldn't control his impulses.

He wandered over to the dowager's side and greeted her.

"All's well I hope, ma'am?"

She waved her fan vigorously. "Yes, except for this infernal heat. I'm going to asphyxiate!"

"Would you like a turn in the gardens, ma'am?" he asked politely, really wanting to stay until Annis came off the dance floor.

"I would love to, but I cannot leave my post. I need to keep an eye on the girls. Not that Deborah is a worry—sweet girl and most obedient—but Ava!" The dowager duchess cast up her eyes. "That girl is trouble waiting to happen, I just know it!"

At this point, the music stopped, and the dancers began filing off the floor. "Perhaps Robert can take you for a stroll and you can deputize Annis and me in your stead?" he suggested.

"What a splendid notion, thank you. We won't be too long,

but I simply must get some fresh air. Robert!" She turned imperiously to her son as he bore down on them with his precious burden. Annis looked flushed but happy. His heart lifted at the sight. "Robert, you must take me for a turn in the gardens. I am like to expire in here! The Ashfords are going to keep an eye on the girls for me."

"Good luck with that!" said Robert sotto voce and bore his mother off.

Emrys took Annis's hand and smiled. "You're enjoying yourself."

She plied her fan, still catching her breath. "Yes, I am. I didn't expect to, but the duke's family are so kind. They have been most accepting of my change in status. I quite expected the dowager to arch up, but she never did."

Emrys knew that Robert had had words with his mother about that very thing. What exactly he had told her to calm her down, he didn't know, but she had been very nice to Annis ever since. He suspected it might have something to do with himself. The dowager had always had a soft spot for him. Unlike Ravenshaw, whom she barely tolerated. Pendrell, she treated like an overgrown schoolboy, which made the big man blush and stammer. Pendrell may be blunt in speech with his friends, but remarkably tongue-tied and awkward in company. He lacked the social graces.

Deborah appeared at their side, escorted by Hereward. "Would you ladies like a drink?" he asked. Since his own face was quite red, Emrys suspected this was not quite so selfless as it appeared. He must be cooking in that jacket.

"That would be delightful, thank you," said Annis.

Deborah murmured something similar, and the big man plunged off to find refreshments.

"Are you enjoying your first ball, Miss Watson?" he asked politely.

"It is not quite my first. I was at Sarah's wedding ball at The Castle, but it is my first London ball," she said with a smile. "And yes, I am enjoying it immensely. I just wish my sisters were here to enjoy it with me. Sarah has promised to bring Ruthie out next year, so I should have company then."

Hereward reappeared with the promised glasses of punch for the ladies, which they drank thirstily while Emrys scanned the room for the missing Lady Ava. He spotted her just leaving the ballroom for the gardens on the arm of . . . he thought Lannister. *Damn it! If Robert catches her with him, there will be hell to pay!*

"Excuse me a moment, I just have to retrieve Ava," he murmured and plunged off across the ballroom toward the French windows that led onto the garden terrace.

He reached the steps leading down into the gardens, looking around for his quarry and seeing no sign of her. *Damn and blast! Where is the little wretch?* He did not relish getting into fisticuffs with Lannister, either. It occurred to him that it would have been more proper for Hereward to be doing this—he was her brother, after all.

"Where is she?" asked a low rumbly voice in his ear. He turned and glanced up at the young giant. *Speak of the devil!*

"I'm not sure. I saw her come out this way with Lannister, but now I can't see them. Your mother and Robert are out here, too. If he should see her with Lannister, Robert will have an apoplexy!"

"You're not wrong," Hereward frowned. "The sooner that girl is married off the better! We can then let her husband worry about her! She is giving Mama more grey hairs daily!"

"Well, yes, but you don't want her married off to Lannister, do you? He hasn't a feather to fly with, to say nothing of his dissolute behavior. He makes Kenrick look like a saint!"

"True. We'd best find them. Divide and conquer—you go that way, I'll go this, and we'll meet in the middle. Try not to get into a fight with Lannister, and if you see Robert . . ." He flinched, trailing off.

"Yes, I know—lie through my teeth!" Emrys grinned and plunged off to his right. By the time he'd done a full circuit and got back to the starting point, he found Hereward coming up the steps with a disgruntled Ava on his arm. She was a little flushed and a shade disheveled, and he marveled that he was able to detect the difference. Six months ago, he would never have noticed. More recent events had sharpened his powers of observation.

Robert and the dowager appeared after that, and the group returned to Annis and Deborah. Disaster averted, Emrys bore his wife off to find the supper table. He was hungry, and there was no law against him eating at a ball at least.

Chapter Twenty-Four

RETURNING HOME TO Cavendish Square and going up to check on the children, they found Mrs. Green in her chair with Charlie in her lap.

"What is wrong?" asked Emrys sharply but keeping his voice low. His heart was hammering fast.

Mrs. Green patted the sleeping child and spoke softly over her head. "She had a nightmare, poor lamb, and wouldn't settle."

"What was it about? Did she say?" He had the occasional nightmare himself, and they were horrible. It would be terrifying for a little girl.

"Hard to tell—something about a monster and her mother, but it was garbled. She asked for you, my lord. It took me quite a while to quiet her."

Emrys heart clenched, and he held out his arms for Charlie. "I'll take her," he said, his voice thick. Annis, beside him, touched his arm in sympathy. He could feel her silent support without even looking at her.

He gathered Charlie in his arms, getting a nose full of her natural scent and the honeysuckle soap her hair had been washed with.

She moved in his arms. "Papa?"

"Yes, sweetheart, I'm here."

"Oh, Papa!" she flung her small arms round his neck and clung to him. "I had a bad dream and was frightened!"

"I know, darling, but it's all right. Nothing can hurt you, I promise."

"You weren't here," she said, blinking at him.

"I know, my precious. I'm sorry."

"How can you know I'm safe if you're not here?" Her big blue eyes looked glassy in the candlelight; her soft lower lip pushed out in distress.

"Because I wouldn't leave you if it weren't safe," he said quickly, his heart thudding.

"The monster got Mama! How can you know it won't get me, too?" Charlie frowned, one hand clutching a curl and twisting it nervously.

"Oh, my love!" he said his voice cracking. He squeezed her tight and pressed kisses against her curls. "There's no monster, darling. Mama was in an accident. Sometimes things like that happen if—if people aren't very careful, but I won't let that happen to you."

"Weren't you careful with Mama?"

Oh, God! His heart was going to crack. "I wasn't there, sweetheart. I couldn't prevent the accident happening."

"So how can you prevent an accident happening to me?" she asked, her face pressed against his jacket.

"Because I will take very good care of you. And Lizzie and Ewen." He rubbed her back comfortingly.

"How can you do that if you're not here?" she asked again, pulling back to look up at him, her eyes wide in consternation.

"I'm never very far away, sweetheart. And if leave you it will be with people who can look after you and keep you safe. Like Mrs. Green or your new mama." He nodded at Annis, who smiled reassuringly at Charlie.

Charlie swallowed, her little mouth setting in a hard line. "Then why couldn't you protect Mama?"

The knife in his heart twisted further. "She was too far away, sweetheart. In another country." He blinked the tears from his eyes and sniffed.

"Why was she there?"

"She—she was visiting a—a friend."

"Why did you let her go?" Charlie grabbed his lapel and tugged at it as if to emphasize her words.

"She wanted to go. I couldn't have stopped her." He swallowed and sniffed again. "Mama was a grown-up, darling. Grown-ups get to decide what they want to do."

"So, it was Mama's fault?" She went back to twisting her curl again.

"I—" He stopped helplessly.

"The driver of the carriage made a mistake, Charlie. Mistakes happen sometimes, but that wasn't your mama's fault," said Annis gently.

"Do *you* make mistakes, Papa?"

"Yes, sweetheart, all grown-ups do. None of us are perfect," honesty compelled him to say. Then he hastened to add, "But I won't make a mistake with you." He squeezed her tight. "You and Lizzie and Ewen are the most precious people in the world to me. I love you with all my heart, and even if I'm not right here in the house with you all the time, I will always love and keep you safe."

Lizzie was sitting up in bed by now, watching this. Ewen seemed to still be asleep.

"Papa won't leave us, Charlie. Even if he's gone for a little bit, he will come back. He always does. Papa is re-lia-ble!" she said, annunciating the long word slowly. He caught a smile from Annis at this. *Had she taught Lizzie that word?*

"What's that mean?" asked Charlie.

"It means he will always be here when we need him." Lizzie grinned at him, and her confidence in him almost made his knees buckle.

"Thank you, Lizzie," he husked. "Yes, I will always be here when you need me. Maybe not always in the exact instant, but not long or far away."

Charlie sighed and hugged him. "I love you, Papa."

"I love you too, Charlie-mine," he said, his voice choked. He walked over to the bed, depositing her beside her sister, and she crawled back under the covers.

Lizzie gave her a hug. "I'm here, Charlie," she said. "If you have a bad dream, I'll fix the monster for you. No monster is going to hurt my little sister."

"Thank you, Lizzie!" Charlie hugged her.

He hugged them both. "My precious girls!" he murmured. "Lizzie, I'm so proud of you!"

He tucked them both in and sat with them until they settled, Annis by his side.

When they finally left the nursery and repaired to their bed-chamber, a wave of fatigue hit him like a wall.

He sank down on the bed and put his head in his hands. Annis came to him and put her hands on his shoulders. He pressed his face into her belly and wrapped his arms round her.

"God," he said finally, "she just tears me apart. They both do!"

"They are extraordinary girls, both of them," said Annis, stroking his hair.

"It's moments like these that I am so angry with Caro!" he said hoarsely. "That is what I can't fathom. How could she do this to *them*? Me, yes. I understand her wanting to leave *me*. But not *them*. They're *innocent*. They didn't ask for this, and they don't deserve it!" He swallowed. *How much of it is my fault? If I had done something differently, would Caro have stayed? Not fallen in love with Greathouse? How could I have stopped it?* He shook his head, choking back a sob. He didn't know, and the pain tore a hole in his chest. An unaccustomed anger took possession of him. She had hurt his precious little girls, and he didn't think he could ever forgive her for that or understand it.

"How can a mother leave her children?" he asked, bewildered. "How can I have been so *wrong* about her?" His rage and confusion burst out of him. Tears trickled down his cheeks, and he wiped them away impatiently.

"I don't know, my dear," murmured Annis. "I don't know how she could leave any of you."

He clutched her close, burying his face in her belly fighting for composure.

"Thank God for you," he murmured, after a bit. "You always seem to know the right thing to say."

He was stifling in these clothes.

"Come to bed—I need to hold you." He sat back and ripped off his neckcloth and tore off his jacket. Rising, he flung them away and tore off the rest of his clothing. Turning to Annis, he helped her off with hers, flinging things left and right, careless of where they landed. Annis let him, helping him to get rid of her clothes as fast as possible.

They fell into bed in a tangle of limbs, and he pulled the covers over them, hauling her close.

"You," he muttered. "You are my sanity."

"Oh, Emrys!" She buried her face in his chest as his hands roved all over her.

"Lift your head, I want to kiss you," he growled in her ear.

When she did, he pushed her back into the pillows and kissed her, a devouring, deep, desperate kiss. *This woman is my everything. After so much betrayal, her support, her patience, her kindness . . . what would I do without her? Will she leave me, too? Grow tired of me?* Panic skittered along his nerves.

She responded to his kiss by wrapping her arms round him, her hands clutching at him, a whimper in her throat as his fingers slid along her slippery channel and plunged inside her. Reassured that she wanted him—*she couldn't fake a response like that!*—he pulled her leg over his hip and finding her entrance with his cock pressed inside her with an easy, deep thrust. His hand between them rubbed her furiously. *I need to feel her come.*

His thrusts were steady, firm, and deep as he pushed her toward a rapid climax. This was not one of those moments to savor. He needed to come and quickly. Panting in her ear, he said hoarsely, "Come, Annis! Fuck, I need you to come now!"

She jerked and cried out. *Thank fuck!* He felt the flutter of her climax in her body, and a groan was ripped from him as her response ignited his own. A spike of pleasure, a rush of sizzling heat, and he was coming hard. Gripping her hips, he rode it out with repeated grunting thrusts. The wavelets of pleasure slowly receded, and his body lost its tension, going lax and floaty warm. His breathing and heartbeat slowly sinking back to a normal pace.

"Thank you," he murmured, wrapping his arms round her. He was still inside her, and he stayed that way for some minutes until his softening flesh slipped out of her. He rolled onto his back, and she arranged herself on his chest.

"I'm exhausted," he murmured.

"Hm, sleep," she said softly.

"Hm . . ." He let his breath out on a soft exhalation. *They would talk about Charlie in the morning.*

ANNIS WOKE TO Emrys wrapped round her as usual and lay enjoying it for several minutes, her thoughts roaming back over Charlie's nightmare and Emrys's response. It was clear to her that he felt some kind of responsibility, as if Caro's defection was his fault. She clenched her teeth. Annis was generally a forgiving kind of person, but the thought of that woman brought tears of rage to her eyes. *How could she hurt him and those precious babies so?* It was beyond her comprehension how *anyone* could reject Emrys. He was perfect, the most wonderful husband any woman could ask for. Her love for him, never far from the surface, surged up and engulfed her. *I love him fiercely! And his darling children who are mine now to protect and love.*

Emrys snuffled and stirred, his arms tightening round her.

"Thank God you're still here," he muttered.

"Where else would I be?" she asked, looking up at him.

"Hm?" He opened his eyes and blinked. "What?"

She smiled and patted his chest. "Nothing."

He snugged her close and sighed. "What are we going to do about Charlie?"

"Be consistent and reliable," Annis traced patterns in his chest hair with a fingertip. "She needs to rebuild her trust that adults won't abandon her."

"How do you know these things?"

"I grew up an orphan. I had no father figure in my life, just Aunt Janet." He squeezed her in silent sympathy. "She was kind but strict, and very protective. She did everything she could to make me feel secure. It was only after she died that I fully realized how much she did to protect me. And how much she didn't tell me about what was really going on, how much of my truth had been an illusion." She looked up at him. "It destroyed my sense of trust in the world and people. I was an adult when that happened, but even so, it was difficult."

He dropped a kiss on her hair and gave her another squeeze.

"Charlie is a child," Annis continued. "It's much harder for her. We need to be patient with her and as I said, consistent and reliable, but not overly indulgent. We shouldn't pander to her fear—that will increase it. But we should show understanding of it. You did everything right last night. You were honest with her and reassuring, without making promises you can't keep, like that you will never leave her side."

He sighed. "How do you manage to always have the answers?"

"I don't think I do in most situations. But in this particular case, I feel I'm on safe ground to recommend a path forward. Lizzie was a great help last night, too. Her faith in you was probably more effective than anything you could say or do."

"Yes, she is splendid, isn't she?" He grinned, pride wafting off him in waves.

"As I said last night, extraordinary. They all are." Annis swallowed a sudden lump in her throat. "I feel very privileged to be their step-mama."

"A wonderful one you are, too," he said, kissing her hair again.

A warm flood of happiness washed through her at his praise, and she nuzzled her face into his chest. "Thank you."

"No, thank you for your words of wisdom. Patience, consistency, and reliability—I can do that."

She patted his chest. "Yes, you can, because you embody those traits absolutely."

He grinned. "I do, don't I? Who'd have thought that just being myself would be the right thing for once? Perhaps there is something to be said for being an ordinary fellow, after all."

"You are *not* ordinary," said Annis indignantly. "Like your children, you are quite *extra*ordinary. Kind and patient and reliable are rare traits to be prized."

"You think so?"

"I do." Annis said firmly, her heart thudding and spilling over with love for him. How she wished she could say what she was feeling. But his confusion and anger over Caroline just underlined how much further he had to go in that regard. She needed to keep her feelings to herself and not muddy the waters further. For now.

He rubbed her upper arm. "You're the extraordinary one." He tipped her chin up and kissed her. "Not sure what I've done to deserve you," he said, husky voiced.

"Oh, Emrys!" she choked. "I don't know what I've done to deserve you!"

"Now I've made you cry!" he said, dismayed.

"No, just happy tears, really!" she said wiping them away with her fingers and sniffing. "See? All gone."

"Hm," he kissed her again. "I'm convinced you're the best wife a man ever had."

"And you're the best husband," she said mistily. "And the best father." she added.

He sighed. "If only that were true."

"Back to Charlie," she said firmly, dragging the conversation out of dangerous territory. She was in grave danger of spilling all her feelings out if they kept this up. "I shall speak to Mrs. Green about the approach we have agreed on. I'm sure she will concur; she is a sensible woman. We are lucky to have her."

"Yes, I don't know where Sarah found her, but she is a treasure," agreed Emrys. He moved a hand lower to rest on her hip and squeezed. "I am tempted to drag you under the covers, but we should probably get up," he said.

"Yes, we should. I have a lot to do today. The decorator is coming, to go over new designs for the house. Do you want to be consulted?"

"Good God, no! I trust your taste—it's impeccable. Do what you think is fitting. Just send me the bills," he said, throwing off the covers and rolling out of bed.

Chapter Twenty-Five

EMRYS HAD BEEN giving some thought to trying to uncover the identity of Annis's assailant. While everything had been quiet on that front, he was not so sanguine as to think the issue had gone away. He wanted to know who the damned devil was and do something concrete to protect her from any future attacks. Assuming she hadn't killed the man, and he refused to accept that she had. She had certainly injured him, but he refused to think of his Annis as a murderess. In any case, even if she had killed the man, there might be others connected to him who would still come after her. The mystery needed to be solved.

Over breakfast that morning he said, "I've been thinking—your father's ring is the only clue we have to his identity and that of your assailant. I'd like to take it to a jeweler, see if they can shed any light on it. What do you think?"

Annis stopped with the teacup partway to her mouth and put it down. "Isn't that risky?"

"Not if we are careful and sensible about it. I thought I'd take it to Rundle and Bridge. They're the jewelers to the Crown, after all, not just some shady fence in St. Giles. They are very discreet."

"I suppose so," she said reluctantly. "What do you think they could tell us?"

"I'm not sure, perhaps nothing at all, but it chafes me not to know more about this fellow. Don't you want to know?"

She smiled tremulously and blinked. "Yes, I suppose—" She took a breath. "Yes, I would very much like to know who my father was."

"Good. I'll take it to the jewelers when I get a chance. Don't worry. I'll be discreet, as well."

While Annis was preoccupied with the decorator, he got the ring out of the safe and examined it. The raised and flattened top was a plain and unadorned oval, as if it should have been engraved as a signet ring or was perhaps the base upon which a setting for a large jewel could have been put but hadn't. Either way, it seemed a strange, unfinished piece.

Popping it in his waistcoat pocket, he took himself off to the jewelers. He wanted to buy Annis another piece of jewelry anyway, and it seemed to him that if anyone could tell him about this piece it was a professional jeweler. If he was very lucky, the man might even recognize the ring.

Entering the store of Rundle and Bridge in Ludgate Hill, he perused the various displays quietly until the current customer being served by Mr. Phillip Rundle left the shop.

Mr. Rundle tidied away the trays he had taken out for the previous customer and said with a welcoming smile, "How may I help you, sir?"

"Well, two things," said Emrys, stepping up to the counter. "Firstly, I'd like a necklace for my wife. Perhaps something in pearls and rubies?"

The next twenty minutes were spent reviewing what the man had for sale. Not finding exactly what Emrys had in mind, Rundle resorted to sketching out his ideas based on Emrys's imperfect description. They finally arrived at something that he wanted, and it was agreed that the piece would be ready in a month. Well pleased, Emrys then withdrew the ring from his pocket and held it out in his palm. "I wonder if you could tell me something about this?"

Rundle took it from him and, inserting his eyeglass, examined it closely. "It's a men's signet locket ring, sir." Using his thumb-nail, delicately he pushed on the side of the oval and a lid sprang up revealing a cavity beneath.

"Good heavens!" said Emrys, bending over the ring. The jeweler handed it back to him, and he noticed that there was something lining the oval cavity, *a piece of paper?* Deciding to examine that in private, he closed the lid with a tiny click and then used his thumbnail to try to open it again. Finding the tiny depression, it clicked up again, and he shut it quickly. "A signet ring, you say? But it's not carved."

"No, it would normally have been, but this one, for whatever reason, wasn't."

"Are they common?"

"Signet rings are very common sir, naturally, but ones com-bined with lockets or compartments to store relics are not, no. Where did you get it if you don't mind my asking?"

"It's an odd piece I found in my father's things," he replied, giving the man the story he'd decided upon earlier. "Do you have any idea how old it might be?"

"The style is very plain. Let me see if there is a maker's mark on it." He held his hand out and Emrys gave it back reluctantly. The jeweler examined it further with his eyeglass, turning it over and checking all angles. "No, there is nothing. However, I am confident this is solid gold by the weight of it and the soft sheen. I would estimate its value at one hundred pounds or thereabouts."

He handed it back and Emrys pocketed it. Valuable, but not overly so. Not sufficiently valuable as to provoke someone to murder, surely? But then one hundred pounds to some might be a fortune. "Thank you for your help."

"Thank you for your business, sir. To which address should I send the finished necklace?"

Emrys gave his direction and promised payment forthwith. Dropping by the bank on the way home to execute the payment for the necklace, he was itching to get home and check what was in the ring. But he really needed to show it to Annis—it was her ring.

To his frustration, she wasn't home when he got back, having gone shopping with the decorator for furnishings. Several hours later, however, Annis arrived home, coming into the nursery where he was playing Waterloo on the floor with the children and a large collection of toy soldiers. He was playing Napoleon, and Lizzie was Wellington, supported by her Cavalry Commander the Earl of Uxbridge, played by Ewen (with some help from Emrys), and Charlie as Blucher in charge of the Prussian forces.

The game was abandoned when Annis produced several swatches of colors and drawings over which the girls poured when asked their preferences as to furnishings for the nursery and schoolroom. Ewen being as uninterested in this as Emrys, continued to crawl round the floor moving horses about, and Emrys encouraged him. Mrs. Green appeared, followed rapidly by the tea tray, and Annis gathered up the swatches and drawings and repaired with Emrys to their bedchamber to wash and change her gown.

"I thought perhaps we could take the children to see the animals at the tower on Friday. What do you think?" she asked, plunging a cloth into the bowl of water and sponging her face and neck. She had removed her gown with his help and was standing in her chemise, which was highly distracting. He resisted the temptation to fondle her breasts from behind. If he started down that track, they would never get to the ring.

"I think it is a splendid notion," he said, sitting on the bed and watching her appreciatively as she bent over the bowl. He was fascinated with her breasts it was true, but her bottom held its own attraction, too. Dragging his eyes upward, he caught her looking at him looking. She smiled, flushing faintly. "Emrys, you didn't hear a word I said then, did you?"

"What? You were talking about taking the children to the tower and I said it was a splendid notion."

"After that!"

"Oh. No. Your bottom is rather distracting. Come and put it down here," he said, patting the coverlet beside him. "I went to the jeweler." He reached into the pocket of his waistcoat as she came and sat beside him.

"Oh. Did you discover anything?"

"Yes, he showed me this." He clicked the lid with his thumbnail, and she gasped in shock as it flicked open.

"How could I not have found that in all these years?" she asked, peering at it, fascinated.

He shrugged. "It's well made, and the seam is difficult to see. More to the point, there is something inside it. I haven't looked—it is your ring, and you should be the one to see what it is." He held the ring out on his palm.

She took it gingerly and, using her nail, extracted the tiny, folded slip of paper from the cavity. She unfolded it with visibly shaking fingers and Emrys had to restrain himself from seizing it from her and unfolding it himself, so anxious was he to see what was written on it.

She finally had it open and smoothed out. Written in a spidery hand were the words:

St. Michael's, Monkton Combe, 7th January 1790

Annis stared at the piece of paper her heart racing.

"This is Mama's writing." She traced it with her fingertip. *What did Mama say about the ring when she gave it to me? "This is for you; he would have wanted you to have it." Did she mean for me to find the piece of paper? Almost certainly, but she died before she could tell me it was there . . .*

"What does it mean?" asked Emrys. "Do you have any idea?"

"I might," she said cautiously. She licked her suddenly dry lips. *Could it?* "My birthday is on the 12th of August 1790," she said, looking up at him to see if he made the same connection she did.

"Could this be the date and location of your parents' marriage?"

"I don't know. It might be." She swallowed, tears stinging her eyes. She raised a hand to her mouth to try to suppress them.

He slid an arm round her waist and kissed her hair. "Don't cry. This is good news, isn't it?"

"I've been so accustomed to thinking I was—"

"Illegitimate." His voice was calm, no judgement in it.

She nodded. "You knew? And you married me anyway?"

"Given the deliberate holes in the story you told me of your past, I guessed that may have been the case, but you didn't confirm it, and I didn't ask."

"Why?"

"I didn't want to know," he said with a rueful expression. "But now it seems we may have been wrong."

"I don't know. I hardly dare to hope. But if it's true, why didn't Mama tell me?"

"You mean your aunt?"

"You guessed that, too?"

"It was sort of obvious," he said with a wry smile.

"I lied to you," she said hollowly.

"Not exactly. You thought she was your aunt for a long time, after all."

"Yes, until she was dying and she told me the truth. Or part of it, but not the whole. I can't fathom why not. Why would she let me think I was bastard-born?"

"We may never know the answer to that." He rubbed her arm comfortingly, and she leaned against him, suddenly feeling worn out. It was such a relief to tell him the whole truth as she knew it.

"But we should be able to discover the identity of your sire with this." He said holding up the precious slip of paper. "Go and pack, and we will leave at once. Unless you would rather wait until morning?"

"No. No let us go at once. But what of the children?"

"We will leave them with Mrs. Green, I think. Time is of the essence now that we have this much information. Are you equal to riding? It will be quicker than traveling by coach."

"Yes, of course."

"Good." He kissed her, grinning.

"You're excited about this!"

"Ecstatic! I've been worried sick about who might still be after you. This way I will know what to do to protect you and where the threat is coming from, and maybe even why."

She flung her arms round his neck and kissed him, just barely swallowing the words that wanted to burst out about how much she loved him. "Thank you," she choked out instead.

He rose, heading for the door. "I'll see to the horses and let Mrs. Green and the children know. You pack and then pen a note to the duchess and ask her to pop in and check on the children while we're gone."

TWO HOURS LATER they were mounted and heading out of London. Charlie had clung a bit when informed they were going to be away for a couple of days, but when Lizzie told her to buck up, she suppressed the tears and tried to be brave, which got Emrys in the chest. He gave each of his children a big hug in farewell and left them in Mrs. Green's capable hands. The woman was truly a treasure.

By his calculations, they had four hours of daylight left. With any luck, they would reach Reading tonight, which would leave them eight, perhaps ten hours of riding tomorrow. They would stay with his grandmother in Bath tomorrow night.

Chapter Twenty-Six

THEY ENTERED THE village of Monkton Combe in the late afternoon. The church was situated at the end of the village's main street in a cul-de-sac. It was a small building, rectangular with a small spire, and stained glass windows down the side. It looked surprisingly new. Leading the horses under a tree, Emrys dismounted and helped his wife down. He was tired and a little saddle sore himself. He could imagine how she must feel, but she hadn't complained once.

"All right?" he said, his hands still resting on her waist. Her riding habit of green velvet was fitted to the waist and displayed her figure to perfection.

"Terrified," she admitted with a rueful smile.

"Come on," he said, offering her his hand. "Let's go and find out who your sainted papa is before I expire of curiosity."

She took his hand and picked her way across the tussocky grass toward the little church. *Would there be anyone here at this time of day?* He looked about for a rectory building nearby but couldn't see one.

They reached the entrance to the church. The door was ajar, and it was rather gloomy inside. He poked his head in and called out. "Hallo, anyone about?"

Annis slapped his arm, embarrassed. "Emrys! It's a church.

You don't yell in church!" she hissed.

He shrugged, and a figure appeared in the aisle toward the front. He was a middle-aged man with a shock of thick partially graying hair. He was in shirt sleeves and carried a cloth in his hands as if he might have been polishing something.

"May I help you?" he said, walking toward them.

"I hope so," said Emrys, stepping over the threshold. He held out his hand. "I'm Viscount Ashford, and this is my wife, Lady Ashford. I was wondering if we might take a look at your parish records?"

The man blinked. "My lord, this is most unexpected. We don't get nobility visiting us very often. Reverend Paul Annerley at your service. Do come in!" He wrung Emrys's hand enthusiastically and waved them in. "You're lucky I was still here. I was about to shut up shop and go home for tea. This way—the records are kept in here," he said, leading them to what Emrys guessed was the vestry, a small room off the right of the altar.

"Has the church been here long?" asked Emrys. "It appears to be relatively new."

"Oh, this building is very new—only four years old! But the original church was Norman, very ancient and uncomfortable. It was demolished and this one rebuilt in its place."

"Oh, do you have all the records from the original church?" asked Annis anxiously.

"Yes, of course. The registers were transferred," said the reverend, holding the vestry door open for them. "Which year were you interested in?"

"We actually have a date" said Annis, blushing. "We—we think it might be for a marriage."

He nodded and smiled. "And the date?"

"The seventh of January 1790."

"Mm, 1790, 1790." He turned to peruse a shelf with large, bound volumes on it. There were a lot of them taking up the entirety of the inner wall of the vestry. On the very topmost shelves Emrys even spied some scrolls. "Ah, here we are—1789 to

1794. We don't get a lot of births, marriages, and deaths here you understand." He drew out the large volume and rested it on the table. Opening the parchment pages, he leafed through them until he found the correct year. "Here we are, there are three entries for January 1790. Take a look." He stepped back, and they bent over the book. Emrys peering over Annis's shoulder.

The third was what they were looking for. He heard Annis's in-drawn breath as her finger traced beneath the spidery, hard to read letters.

Notice of banns for three consecutive Sundays was followed by "Seventh of January, Mr. Nicolas Benedict Red—. . . Can you make out the rest of the name?" she asked. Emrys bent closer and shook his head. It was a scrawl. "And Miss Janet Adelaide Pringle, residents of this parish!" She clutched at his arm with excitement. The officiant was also named along with two witnesses to the marriage, listed below the participants.

He smiled and squeezed her hand. "Mr. Nicholas Benedict Red—" He squinted trying to make out the rest of the name. "Redman, Redfearn, Redford?" he guessed.

He turned to the reverend. "By any chance were you here in 1790? Would you know this gentleman's name? We can't make it out."

"No, I'm new to the parish. It would have been old Mr. Beagle back then. He's been dead for three years."

"How frustrating, but still the first part of the name is clear enough and we have the Christian names."

"Benedict!" said Annis. "My second name is Benedicta!" The tears rolled down her cheeks. "She named me for him!" He put his arm round her then and pulled her close, never mind what the other man might think.

"She did," he murmured. "We might have guessed that!" He turned to the reverend.

"Thank you very much. I should like to make a donation to the church plate."

"That would be most kind of you, your lordship."

Emrys handed over a purse and then bethought him of something else. "No one else has come asking about this, have they?"

"This record? No. In fact, I can't recall anyone asking for our records in the whole time I've been here."

Emrys nodded. "Had enough, love?" he asked quietly of Annis, and she nodded.

They declined the reverend's offer of tea and returned to the horses.

Annis was still wiping tears off her face, and he put his arms round her. "All right, love?" he asked.

"I'm overwhelmed," she admitted. "Nicolas Benedict Red . . . what do you suppose the name could be?"

"We'll find out. If he's a peer, we'll discover it. We're heading to my grandmother's house now. You will like her, and she will love you. Another half-hour's ride and we can be comfortable," he said and kissed her briefly. If he kissed her the way he wanted to, they would shock the reverend and delay their trip.

⇻⟫⟫⟩⟨⟨⟨⇷

"Good heavens, Emrys, is it true you've married a governess, or is Maria Fortnum all about in her head?" Annis's wandering gaze came back to the wizened little old lady with the pure white hair sitting in a chair by the fire.

"It's true, Grandmama. I've brought her to meet you." He put his arm round Annis's waist and shepherded her forward. "Annis, this is my grandmother, Lady Stavely."

Annis made her best curtsy. "Lady Stavely, it's an honor to meet you. Your grandson speaks very highly of you."

"Does he now?" The old lady's eyes ran over Annis speculatively. "Well, she's not a beauty like the other one, but perhaps she'll treat you better. Have you brought those beautiful children with you?"

Emrys took all this without a blink and said, "No, not this

time. We won't be staying long, I'm sorry. But we will bring them back soon, I promise."

"Hm. Come here, girl, I want to look at you, and my eyes aren't good in this light."

Annis stepped forward, suppressing a smile. She was used to obstreperous old ladies. She'd met a few in her time as a governess. She sat down on the cushion by the lady's feet and presented her face for inspection.

"Mm. A good chin and a fine complexion. She doesn't look stupid either."

"She isn't," snapped Emrys. "That's enough, Grandmama, you won't put her out of countenance, so stop trying."

"Protective, isn't he?" she said to Annis.

Annis smiled.

"Yes, I am. And if you understood what she has been though, you would understand why," he said.

His grandmother looked at him directly. "Well, I hope you mean to explain that."

"I do. But do you think we might wash and change first, and have something to eat? We've been riding all day, and I'm famished."

"There—always loved his food! Even as a little boy," this to Annis. "Of course, take her upstairs. You can have the blue room."

"Thank you," he said and held out his hand to Annis. She rose gave the old lady a second curtsy and followed him upstairs.

Annis walked straight into his arms after he shut the door to their room, her face buried in his chest. "Thank you. Thank you for supporting me, being with me. I—"

"Hush. I'm your husband. Where else would I be?"

"You're the most wonderful husband a woman ever had!" she said, lifting her face to look up at him and reprising her words of a few days ago.

His expression twisted, and a flare of unaccustomed anger flicked through her like a whipcrack. *That woman had hurt him in so many ways!*

"I'm not Caroline! You must know how much I value your support, Emrys!" she said softly. She reached up and cupped his face. His dear, adorable face. The amount she loved him took her breath away. The fact that he thought himself less, that Caroline could still hurt him so—that he must therefore still bear love for his first wife—was a knife in her chest. The knowledge continued to stop her from blurting out her own feelings, but it was hard. She wanted to tell him how wonderful he was, how kind and sweet and downright gorgeous. Instead, she kissed him.

His arms came round her and almost lifted her off her feet. His response to her kiss was devouring. He walked her backward until her legs hit the bed, and they fell on it together. He showered kisses all over her face and neck to the line of her high-cut riding habit. "Annis." His voice, deep and gravelly, told her that whatever his feelings were about his first wife, it was his second wife he wanted to fuck. *That must mean something . . .*

His hand pushed up the heavy skirts of her velvet riding habit, and she felt him scrabbling at the buttons of his falls. He freed his cock, and she felt it graze her damp flesh as he shuffled into the cradle of her hips. She shifted her legs up. He seemed in more of a hurry than usual, and the notion that she excited him that much was arousing.

"Annis, forgive me," he whispered and shoved his way inside her, hard. He held her hands under his, palm to palm, and her gaze with his as he drove into her, his thrusts hard, deep, and increasingly rapid.

She looked back at him, lifting her legs farther to take him deeper, surging up with him as he drove himself ruthlessly and rapidly to climax, panting and groaning, his body a rictus of pleasure-pain by the expression on his face. He collapsed on her with a grunt and an exhalation of something like a moan. He buried his face in her neck, and she felt dampness against it and realized it was tears. *Why?*

She wrapped her arms round him. "Emrys?" she whispered.

"I'm so sorry," he husked thickly.

"Why? What's wrong?"

"I'm a beast."

"You are not."

He lifted his head and stroked a tangle of hair off her face. The pins had come loose. "I fucked you with no preliminaries. I used you."

"It was nothing I did not want. I was happy to be useful."

He swallowed. "You're the one that has been through the emotional turmoil, and I'm behaving like an animal."

She smiled and stroked a finger over his lips. "You make me feel wanted."

"You are." His tone was raw. He shifted and slipped out of her. Lying beside her on the bed, he reached down and stroked her gently between her legs. "Let me at least make it up to you a little."

She gasped and moved under his touch, sharp tingles of pleasure radiating up from his fingers.

"I won't say no," she said panting.

"Annis." He kissed her, his fingers slipping inside her, working her to climax. He was rather good at that by now. He knew what touches worked, and she was primed after his abrupt and rapid taking. There was something so arousing about a man who couldn't resist you.

She came quickly, and he stroked her gently down the other side. "There, I don't feel quite so bad now," he said, kissing her cheek. He sat up a bit, and she thought their intimacies were over. But he put a hand on her to stop her rising. Catching her gaze he said, "I know you're not Caroline, and I'm glad of it."

She subsided back on the bed, swallowing the sudden lump in her throat. He kissed her fingers. "I'll make love to you again later, properly, but for now we had best get ready for dinner, because I'm ravenous, and even your breasts won't satisfy me right now." He grinned, pulling her up off the bed.

Chapter Twenty-Seven

"NICHOLAS BENEDICT REDMAYNE," said Lady Stavely waving away the butler's offer of buttered peas. "He was the Earl of Tavistock's son. Gerald Redmayne was one of my beaux. That was before he came into the title himself, of course."

"Tavistock?" Emrys asked. "I know that name."

"Yes, that will be Gerald's grandson, the current earl. I forget his name. I don't think I've ever met him. He would have still been in the nursery when I retired from London society." She sipped her wine and picked at the chicken on her plate.

He glanced at Annis, who had given up any pretense of eating. She was staring at Lady Stavely avidly.

"Can you tell us anything about him? Nicholas?" she prompted-ed.

The old lady frowned. "There was something. Something happened to him . . ."

Emrys squeezed Annis's hand surreptitiously under the table. He could feel her tension.

"I think there was an accident of some kind. He was never the same afterward."

"How—how did he die?" asked Annis, her voice tremulous.

"Some illness, I think. I don't recall, just that Gerald was devastated. Nicolas was his only child, and he loved that boy to distraction. Not that he was easy on him."

"When did he die?" Annis sipped her wine and set it down with a hand that shook slightly.

"Now you're asking me to remember details, and everything is a blur." Lady Stavely set down her fork and sipped her wine reflectively. "It was after Christmas, I remember that much, possibly in January. It was still wretchedly cold. I know, because Harry—that was Emrys's grandfather—took to his bed with a cough and we were afraid he was going to expire on us. He didn't, but Gerald's son *did*. You wouldn't remember that, Emrys. You were only five or so, I think. Which means it must have been '72 or '73."

"Then who was the current earl's father?" asked Emrys, puzzled.

"Nicholas, of course. He married Lady Damaris Godfrey, the Earl of Grenville's daughter. He and Gerald were thick as thieves since their school days."

Emrys glanced at Annis, trying to figure out if she had come to the same conclusion he had. She looked somewhat pale, and he was worried she was upset.

"He must have married Lady Damaris after your mother died, my dear," said Lady Stavely with a smile at Annis. Annis tried to smile back, and Emrys changed the subject.

They left the old lady soon after dinner, pleading fatigue. With the door shut, Emrys sat down on the bed to remove his boots and said, "Well, we have some of the answers we have been looking for."

"Do we?" asked Annis in a hollow voice.

"Certainly, we do," said Emrys, attacking his neckcloth. "Why, what are you thinking?"

She swallowed. "Nicholas must have had his marriage with Mama put aside."

"But did he? On what grounds? It couldn't have been annulled for lack of consummation; you're evidence the marriage *was* consummated."

"Based on the dates, my parents anticipated their vows by at least a month!" said Annis, her hands on her flaming cheeks. She blinked at the tears in her eyes. "I am a bastard after all if the marriage was set aside, Emrys!"

He rose and pulled her into his arms. "I wouldn't jump to that conclusion, my dear. It is far more likely that his second marriage is invalid. Bigamous, in fact."

"You think so?" she said, her face buried in his jacket.

"I do. So, no more tears, hm? I hate to see you crying. I'll be forced to tickle you just to make you laugh," he said, squeezing her.

She choked. "Oh Emrys!" She looked up at him and he kissed her. "Don't you care if I'm illegitimate or not?"

"Not one whit," he said, kissing her nose. "I'd not like it widely known, but mostly because it would make you uncomfortable. Since Caro, I'm a walking scandal anyway. I couldn't care less what the gossips say about me. But I'd rather they not say nasty things about you."

She sighed. "But I do care!" She chewed her lip. "I have been feeling such a fraud, and then when I thought I was legitimate it gave me such a feeling of confidence. I can't explain it, but I will feel more worthy of you if it's true."

"Annis, you are more than worthy of me, whatever your birth. In fact, it's I who feel unworthy of you, if anything." He frowned. "But this information does make me feel much better, regardless, for I now know where the threat is coming from. I can take steps to protect you."

"Emrys . . ." Her choked voice told him she was going to cry again. He needed to fix that and kissed her.

⇥⟫⟪⟵

LATER THAT NIGHT, Emrys lay awake while Annis slept beside him. As promised, he had made love to her slowly and thoroughly, only taking her at the last after she had experienced several orgasms. He was still shocked by his own behavior this afternoon and trying to puzzle out what had caused it. It was nothing new to be overcome by lust for his wife. He frequently felt it, often in inappropriate moments, but to be so overwhelmed by it that he couldn't wait—that was new.

She had said she wasn't Caroline, and there was pain in her voice when she'd said it, even as she sprang to his defense. She was so sensitive to his moods. How had she known he was thinking that he wished Caroline had thought him half as wonderful as Annis seemed to? Of course, she wouldn't like to feel she was being compared to the wife he had loved and lost. Even if that comparison was in Annis's favor. He should have told her that, but instead he'd behaved like a beast.

His uncontrolled lust came from a place he didn't recognize. A primitive part of him that wanted to own and possess. The odd thing, though, was in the aftermath he had wanted to curl up in her arms and cry. Not because he'd behaved like a beast, but because a part of him wanted comfort, like a child. He craved the comfort of her arms, of her body. It was *that* that drove him to take her so quickly—he was desperate for the comfort that she offered. It eased the hurt inside him, the empty ache of betrayal.

God, Caroline had made a mess of him, hadn't she? It went deeper than he'd thought. Annis soothed that wound, and he craved that soothing. It made him want to crawl inside her and just be—not think or feel or be responsible, just be. Learn to be whole again, learn to be himself again. But not his old self, rather the new self that was emerging like a butterfly from a chrysalis. He wanted to learn to be the husband she needed, the father his children needed.

God, I love her. The revelation was like a sunrise, warm and almost blinding in its intensity. It brought tears to his eyes, and he lay with them trickling out the corners and pooling in his ears. A giddy joy came in its wake, and he couldn't decide if he was happy or sad. He glanced down at her curled into him, her head on his chest and he wanted to squeeze her and kiss her and *tell* her . . .

But would she trust that I mean it? Do I trust that I mean it? Is this just some rebound reaction to Caroline's betrayal? He didn't know. He was so confused by his own emotions; he was a mess. And if it was one thing Annis didn't deserve, it was a mess. She deserved steadiness and dependability. He had promised her that, and here he was veering all over the map emotionally like a crazed creature.

He took a slow, steadying breath. He would wait a bit and see if these feelings consolidated. When he was sure, he would speak. But only when he was sure. Annis was worthy of that, and he cared for her too much to want to inadvertently to hurt her . . . like he'd hurt Caro. He needed to be absolutely certain before he said anything. He would take steps to protect her . . . then he would tell her that he loved her . . . when she knew she was safe with him . . .

His thoughts became muddled, and he fell asleep holding her close.

Chapter Twenty-Eight

STEPPING OVER THE threshold of the house in Cavendish Square, Annis was conscious of a sense of homecoming that surprised her. Especially when the butler Latham greeted her warmly and then a squeal of joy from the staircase heralded the stampede of children hurrying to greet them.

As Emrys caught and hugged the girls, she was pelted by Ewen throwing himself at her legs. She picked him up, her heart catching as he flung his arms round her neck and kissed her. "Mama!"

She laughed; her heart suffused with joy at the name. She had transitioned from Miss Pingle to Mama, and it made her heart sing. She looked across at Emrys, who had Charlie in one arm and Lizzie hanging off the other. They exchanged a warm smile amid the children's chatter, and her heart overflowed. She had a family, and it now seemed possible, perhaps even likely, that she was born legitimate, so her secret shame might soon be no more. *Is it possible to be any happier?*

Mrs. Green stood at the bottom of the stairs.

"I'm sorry, my lord, my lady. I couldn't stop them."

Emrys juggled Charlie on his hip. "Not a worry, Mrs. Green. We are as glad to see them as they are to see us. Latham, see to the horses and our luggage, will you? Come on, race you back to the nursery, Lizzie!"

Annis followed in his wake, Mrs. Green bringing up the rear. "How do you keep up with them?" she asked over her shoulder.

"I don't, my lady, and that's a fact. They need more exercise here in town. It's hard on them, cooped up in the house. If you'll pardon my saying so."

"You're absolutely right. We will have to do something about that. I'll speak to his lordship."

They spent an hour with the children, learning all about what they had done while she and Emrys were in Bath.

"The duchess came to see us," said Lizzie importantly.

"And she brought Miss Deborah who played dress ups with us." said Charlie, crawling into her father's lap.

Charlie's propensity to cling to Emrys every chance she got was not diminishing yet, though Annis held out hope that over time it would lessen, as the little girl's trust increased. They were doing all they could to improve that, but going away as suddenly as they had probably hadn't helped.

But if affection could make any difference, then it was simply a matter of time. Emrys loved his children so much. Annis marveled at the fact that he was as unstinting in his affection for the girls as he was with Ewen. She knew this wasn't common. Many men ignored their female offspring as being unimportant. But not her Emrys. He valued all his children equally.

She wondered if her father would have paid her any attention had things fallen out differently. She had so many unanswered questions about him and why he had apparently never lived with her mother and why their marriage was never acknowledged publicly. And she couldn't quite shake the nagging fear that he'd somehow had the marriage put aside so that he could marry Lady Damaris. *Had he loved Damaris? Was that that why he abandoned them? Shunned them?*

The notion hurt. For herself and especially for her mother. Janet hadn't deserved that. She had worked hard all her short life and taken very good care of Annis. Not that she had coddled her—Mama was strict but fair. And protective. Annis realized just how protective she had been in hindsight. Many of the restrictions Janet had placed upon her she could see now were born out of fear and desire to protect.

Janet had been afraid—every day of Annis's life, she now realized. *What had she been afraid of? Nicholas? Or the man who attacked and threatened me? Who is he?*

Emrys had promised to find out.

IT WAS THE day after their arrival home that Emrys suddenly bethought himself of *Debrett's Peerage*. He didn't possess a copy, so he went to Hatchard's to purchase one. Returning home from the bookshop with this treasure of knowledge of the English, Scottish, and Irish peerage, he retired to his study to search through its pages for the Earldom of Tavistock.

Twenty minutes later he was in possession of several facts. Nicolas Benedict Redmayne, the eldest son of Gerald Benedict Redmayne, 6th Earl of Tavistock, was born on the 20th of November 1768. He married Lady Damaris Godfrey, eldest daughter of the Earl of Grenville on the 14th of November 1791. She bore him a son, Lawrence Percival Redmayne, on the17th of November 1792. And Lawrence was the current and 7th Earl of Tavistock, Nicolas having predeceased his father Gerald, dying on the 8th of January 1793. The 6th earl had died last year on the 12th of July 1817 and was succeeded by his grandson.

Having copied out these notes on a piece of paper, Emrys contemplated what they meant. If the marriage between Nicolas Benedict Redmayne and Miss Janet Adelaide Pringle was valid and never set aside, then Annis was not only legitimate, but she was Nicolas's *only* legitimate offspring, her half-brother Lawrence being the product of a bigamous marriage.

This suggested strongly that the agent of Annis's terror was Lawrence Redmayne, since her very existence threatened his legitimacy. But how to prove it, without placing Annis in any more danger or distress? There was no doubt in his mind that he needed to share this information with her, but until he had a plan to prove the man's culpability and neutralize the threat he posed to Annis's peace and security, he was reluctant to do so.

He was trying to think what he knew of Tavistock, but it wasn't much. He wasn't even sure that he had met him. He had a vague memory of the 6th earl, a big bluff fellow with the old-fashioned, high-handed arrogance of many men of his generation. A hard rider to hounds, if he recalled, a man's man. Not one for gallantry or pretty speeches. But of the grandson, nothing.

He resolved to speak to Robert about it. As reluctant as he was to reveal Annis's secrets, if he meant to bring Lawrence Redmayne to book, assuming the man was still alive and Annis hadn't done him in on that field after all, he would need some help. But first it behooved him to confirm that he was indeed still alive. How Emrys was to do that, he wasn't sure.

One more thing occurred to him. He had been assuming that Annis's parent's marriage hadn't been set aside for some reason, but did he know that? For what reasons could a marriage be declared void or annulled apart from nonconsummation? He needed to consult the marriage act, but damned if he knew where he could get hold of a copy of that. His best bet was to see his solicitor—he would know or could find out.

Two hours later he left his solicitors office confident that Annis was legitimate. His man had listened closely to all the facts Emrys could give him and had done a bit of quick research himself. From what they could tell, it seemed Nicolas had abided by all the rules and the marriage was legal, even down to the residency requirement of living in the parish in which they were married. Not that he had revealed to his solicitor the true reason for his questions, but the fellow had been most forthcoming on the topic.

THAT EVENING THEY had yet another ball to attend, this one hosted by Countess Lieven, whose husband was the Russian ambassador to Great Britain. Annis was surprised to find that the idea that her birth may be legitimate gave her so much more confidence, even without knowing for certain yet. For the first time attending a society event, she didn't feel like a fraud and welcomed the opportunity to mingle with the *ton* as, if not precisely an equal, at least one who should not be scorned. She was proud to be Emrys's wife, and she smiled and curtsied to their hosts, the very regal and beautiful Countess and equally haughty Count Lieven, refusing to be intimidated. Entering the main ballroom on her husband's arm, she was delighted to find acquaintance among the guests and to feel herself more at ease.

Emrys was attentive as always and only left her side to fetch her refreshment or speak with his friends when she was dancing. And when it got too hot to be comfortable, he took her walking in the gardens. They were taking a rest on a seat in a pretty rose arbor when she caught the sound of a voice that instantly destroyed all her pleasure, sending chills of horror down her back.

"What is it?" asked Emrys as she clutched his arm.

She looked around wildly to try to work out where the voice was coming from. It was behind them, she fancied. Their view was obscured by a high hedge, but the voices were clear enough.

"My dearest Cecelia, you have inflamed my passions to an extraordinary degree, I cannot wait until our wedding."

"My lord, I am indeed sensible of it, yet I beg you, restrain yourself!" came the lady's reply.

"It's him!" hissed Annis, her breath coming short in panic.

"Him? The man who attacked you?" asked Emrys, keeping his voice low.

Annis nodded frantically. She was trembling, partially from fear and partially from relief. She hadn't killed him, after all. But that meant she was still in danger if he saw her and recognized her.

"We have to go! If he sees me—"

Emrys nodded and stroked her arm in a soothing manner. "Hush, stay here. We will leave in a moment, I promise."

"Emrys!" she whispered desperately as he rose and trod quietly along the hedge, peering through the foliage. Seemingly unable to see anything, he walked quietly to the gap farther up and disappeared from her view. In an agonizingly slow few minutes, he was back and slipping an arm round her. He said softly in her ear, "All is well. Come, I will take you home."

She rose on legs that shook and let him lead her away from the spot.

"Who is he? Did you see him?" she murmured.

"Yes, wait until we are in the carriage," he said quietly.

She nodded, swallowing and trying to calm her panicked nerves. It took some minutes for their carriage to be called and for him to hand her up into it. When they were settled and the carriage under way, he put his arms round her and stroked her back.

"Yes, I know who he is. Lawrence Percival Redmayne, 7th Earl of Tavistock."

"Then the girl he was with is his fiancée, Cecelia Woodrow." At Emrys startled expression, she added, "Hereward told me when we were dancing the other night. His brother Kenrick was dancing with her. She is the most extraordinarily pretty girl and quite young. Oh gosh, should we warn her?"

"Did you see Tavistock then at Sarah's ball?"

"No, he wasn't there. Hereward said he had been ill."

"No doubt." Emrys nodded and appeared to hesitate a moment.

"What is it?" she asked, clutching his arm.

"He has a scar on his right cheek."

She covered her mouth with her hand, a cold shiver running down her spine. "Then I was not mistaken in the voice, for I did score his face with my knife!" Tears started to her eyes and a sob escaped her.

Emrys drew her closer. "It's all right, you don't need to be afraid. We know who he is now and why he was trying to kill you."

"For the ring," she said, trying to swallow her sobs and not succeeding. She was shaking still. Hearing his voice had brought it all back.

"Well yes, but primarily because your existence as well as your possession of the ring are the proof of your parents' marriage which makes *him* illegitimate and calls into question his accession to the earldom. His own parents' marriage was bigamous—at least unless he can prove that Nicolas's marriage to Janet was set aside in some way. If he can't, then you are Nicolas's only legitimate offspring."

"So, he is my half-brother?"

"Yes, his father married his mother a year after he married Janet. I don't believe Lawrence can prove your parents' marriage was invalid. I checked with my solicitor this afternoon and everything seems to be aboveboard. Which means that second marriage is bigamous, and any children born of it are illegitimate."

"What do we do?" she asked, all her newfound confidence draining away.

"We find a way to eliminate the threat to you."

"But he's an earl and I stabbed him!" she said helplessly, wiping tears off her cheeks.

"He threatened to kill you, and he terrorized you!" Emrys's tone was grim. "Forgive me if I have scant sympathy for him." He hugged her close. "God, if anything happened to you—" he muttered, kissing her hair. "I won't let him hurt you, I swear it!"

The coach drew up at Cavendish Square, and he helped her down from the carriage and into the house.

While she removed her jewels and the pins from her hair, she watched him pacing the floor of their bedchamber.

"What are you thinking?"

"I have to find a way to trap him, get him to confess." He came to a stop behind her at her dressing table, resting his hands on her shoulders. Meeting her eyes in the glass he said, "Will you trust me, Annis?"

"Of course, but what are you planning?"

"I think it best if you don't know yet. But I promise, I will tell you shortly."

"Why?"

"I need you to let me protect you. Please?"

She swallowed the questions clamoring at her lips and nodded slowly.

"I also need your permission for me to share some of your story with my nearest friends. I'm going to need some help to pull this off. Will you let me tell the duke, Ravenshaw, and Pendrell? I assure you they can be trusted. The four of us have known each other since we were fifteen. I'd trust each of them with my life."

"Yes." She cleared her throat and nodded again.

"Good." He kissed her and straightened, turning toward the door.

"Where are you going?" She couldn't keep the panic from her voice.

"Out. I need to set things in motion."

She rose and ran to him. "Promise me you won't challenge him to a duel or try to kill him. He could hurt you; I couldn't bear that! Please!"

He smiled down at her. "I'm not going to do anything like that. I'm a rotten shot, for one thing, and only indifferent with a sword. I'm not the sort of heroic figure who fights duels. Besides, I have children. Getting myself killed wouldn't be responsible."

She smiled in spite of herself at this practical view of things. "Good, I'm glad." She frowned. "Though I'm still not happy that you might be putting yourself in danger."

"If I do this right, there will be no danger to anyone, including and especially you. Do you think I would do anything that might endanger you or the children?"

"No." She clung to him all the same. "Do you have to go? I'm behaving like a ninny, but I really don't want to be alone."

"You'll be safe here. If I thought you were in any danger, I wouldn't leave. I'll be back before you know it, I promise." He kissed her softly and she held him close. She loved him so, her heart felt like it would burst.

"Where's my brave warrior woman who went out alone in the night to face down her nemesis and won?" he asked, husky voiced.

She smiled wanly. "She seems to have turned into a sniveling wretch! All right, I shall try to be strong. Go forth, my brave knight, and defend my honor!"

He dropped to one knee and kissed her hand, "I accept your commission, fair lady!" he responded with a smile, a warmth and tenderness in his eyes that fairly undid her.

"Go, before I start bawling!" she said.

He rose, gave her one last lingering kiss, and went.

Chapter Twenty-Nine

DOWNSTAIRS, EMRYS REMOVED her ring from the safe where he had stashed it and set off for the house of the Russian ambassador again.

In the vestibule, he ran straight into Pendrell who was just collecting his coat preparatory to leaving.

"Thought you'd left, old man," he said.

"I took Annis home, but there is something I need to do." Emrys looked about and lowering his voice he said, "Are Troubridge and Ravenshaw still here?"

"Aye, why?"

"Is Tavistock?"

Pendrell frowned, which accentuated his hawkish features. "Tavistock? Haven't a clue. Not sure I know who he is."

Emrys sighed. If Tavistock had already left, this wasn't going to work. "Can you find the others for me and meet me in the gazebo in the garden in fifteen minutes?"

"Of course. What do I tell them?"

"I need their help, yours too."

Pendrell raised his eyebrows and opened his mouth for more questions.

"I'll explain when we meet."

Pendrell nodded and ambled off. The man seldom moved

quickly; he was just too big.

Emrys passed into the ballroom and scanned the room for his quarry. It took him a few minutes, but he finally spotted him dancing with a lady in a purple turban. His fiancée's duenna. Cecelia, he saw, was also dancing—with Kenrick! Since Kenrick was well over six feet tall and Cecelia Woodrow was quite short, they made an odd-looking couple.

Tavistock, by contrast, was a more appropriate height for such a little woman, being just under six feet, Emrys would guess from this distance, and of medium to slender build. He had dark-brown hair, fashionably cut, and his clothing was in impeccable taste.

Having satisfied himself that Tavistock was still here and showing no signs of leaving yet, he headed out to the gardens and the gazebo. His friends joined him shortly thereafter.

"What's to do, Emrys. Is Annis all right?" asked Robert.

"Yes, she is fine. Thanks for coming, chaps."

"No thanks needed," said Ravenshaw, folding his arms and widening his stance. "What do you require?"

Emrys smiled. These men would die on a hill for him. It gave him a warm feeling in his breast.

"Rob, you'll know some of this, but I'll tell the whole story for Deo and Jerome's benefit. Goes without saying that this is absolutely confidential. It concerns Annis."

All three looked grave, nodded, and murmured "Of course."

"Whatever you need, old chap," said Pendrell gruffly.

"You will all know that Annis was the Laynes' governess. What you don't know is that for a number of years she has been terrified out of her wits by a man stalking her."

Pendrell shifted, his right hand tightening into a fist. Ravenshaw tensed but said nothing. Rob, who already knew this, didn't react.

"This fellow threatened to kill her a number of years ago, soon after her mother died, in fact. She never knew who he was or why he threatened her. And for a few years she thought she had eluded him or at least that he had gone away. Then earlier this year she began to feel that someone was watching her. Turns out there was. While I was staying at The Castle, her room was ransacked by the villain—looking for this!" He held up Annis's father's ring.

"Annis, very bravely, if a trifle totty-headedly, decided to confront the miscreant and managed to stab him and give him a scar on his cheek."

"Good God—Tavistock?" asked Robert.

Emrys nodded. "Yes. Annis heard his voice tonight and recognized it. That's why I took her home. She was understandably upset." Emrys smiled wryly. "Although she was a little relieved, too. She was worried she had killed him."

"Bravo!" murmured Ravenshaw, his deep blue eyes glittering in the lamp light.

"But where's the connection to Tavistock, Emrys?" pressed Robert.

"This ring belonged to Nicolas Benedict Redmayne, son of the 6th Earl of Tavistock . . . and Annis's father." He stopped, waiting for what he had said to sink in.

"The current fellow is the 7th earl, this Nicholas's son?" asked Pendrell.

"Yes, his name is Lawrence."

Ravenshaw said delicately, "So Annis is his illegitimate daughter? And the current earl's half-sister?"

"Yes and no," said Emrys with a small smile. He was enjoying himself a bit. "Annis was born Nicolas's legitimate daughter, and it appears that it's Lawrence who is the illegitimate one. Her parents' marriage predates his, and it seems the marriage was never set aside—I checked. Instead, it was Nicolas's marriage to Lawrence's mother that was bigamous."

"You can prove this?" asked Robert.

"We've seen the marriage record and there are no grounds for the marriage being annulled. Nicolas wasn't impotent—Lawrence himself is evidence of that, even if Annis is not. And my solicitor believes no measures were taken to set the marriage aside or void it for any other reason, either."

"Hence why he wants her removed and to retrieve the ring. She is a threat to everything he has." Ravenshaw's tone was low and sent a shiver over Emrys's skin. Jerome DeVere was not a man to make an enemy of.

"But why threaten her all those years ago, and then again now? Why wait all that time?" asked Pendrell.

"I don't know—perhaps he lost track of her. She did move away from Bath to London and thence to the Laynes' employ."

"What is your plan, Emrys? You do have a plan?" asked Ravenshaw.

"I do. I plan to lay a trap for him, for which I need your help."

"Whatever you need, old man," said Pendrell, placing a big hand on his shoulder. The other two assented.

Fifteen minutes later, all four gentlemen returned to the ballroom. Emrys collected a drink from a passing waiter and watched while the Marquess of Ravenshaw very smoothly invited Tavistock to join him in the card room.

The two men left the room together, and Emrys followed slowly. Pendrell and the duke were already there. Ravenshaw led the unsuspecting Tavistock to their table and a few minutes later Emrys joined them, just as Robert, who held the bank, was about to deal.

"Room for a fifth, gentlemen?" asked Emrys, pulling out a chair.

"Of course!" The duke smiled at him. "I don't believe you've met Tavistock?"

Emrys smiled, reaching out his hand upon which he wore Annis's ring. "Pleasure. It's Lawrence Redmayne, isn't it? My grandmother knew your grandfather *quite well*, by all accounts." This provoked some laughter which covered Tavistock's color change as he caught sight of the ring. Emrys wondered if he would ask about it, but he didn't.

Close to, Lawrence Redmayne was of medium height and

athletic build. He would be accounted good looking if it weren't for the nasty scar on his right cheek. He had brown hair and grey eyes, and Emrys at least could see a faint resemblance to Annis in his coloring and the cast of his features. A little more than two years younger than Annis, this young man would be twenty-six soon.

They played for an hour and Tavistock stole many glances at the ring during that time, but he never asked about it. Eventually, the last game drew to a close, and Ravenshaw as usual had won more than his fair share. The man couldn't play without winning, he had the damnedest good luck—and skill of course. Then Emrys said casually, "Well chaps, I need to call it a night, but I'll see you on Thursday when perhaps we can all have our revenge on Ravenshaw?"

This was greeted with laughs, and Emrys added, "You're most welcome to join us, Tavistock. I will send you an invitation with my direction. You will come?"

Tavistock flushed faintly, well aware that to be feted by such a group of titled, older gentlemen was a social feather in his cap, and said politely, "I would be delighted, my lord."

"Good. See you on Thursday at eight, then."

Emrys strolled from the card room, well pleased with his stratagem.

Crawling into bed later, he cuddled Annis and murmured "Everything is in train, love. This nonsense will cease very soon, I promise."

"What have you done?" she asked anxiously.

"Nothing yet, except set a trap. We will spring it on Thursday night." He rubbed his hands over her appreciatively and gave her a squeeze. "Missed you," he murmured, kissing her neck.

And when it is all over, I will tell her how much I love her. He had no doubt of his feelings anymore. He adored this woman. He just hoped nervously that his feelings were returned. An attack of insecurity assailed him at the thought, and he squeezed her tighter which made her yelp.

"Emrys!"

"Sorry," he muttered.

She turned in his embrace and stroked his face and kissed him. "Thank you."

"What for?" he said gruffly.

"For being my knight in shining armor. I've never had one of those before."

"And you'll have no other now," he said somewhat forcefully.

"I know. I wouldn't want anyone else, Emrys. No one can compete with you."

He flushed, pleased. *Perhaps my feelings are returned. But even if they are, I can't afford to take them for granted, Caro loved me once, too, and grew out of it or got bored or . . . something. I can't afford to let that happen with Annis. If she falls out of love with me, I don't think I will ever recover.*

He kissed her, anxious to ward off such dismal thoughts, and she kissed him back. Soon he was lost to the bliss that was Annis.

Four nights later, Viscount Ashford hosted a card party at his house in Cavendish Square. Five gentlemen were invited: the Duke of Troubridge, the Marquess of Ravenshaw, the Earl of Pendrell, the Earl of Tavistock, and a gentleman by the name of Gerard Newbury, lately of Bow Street, under the sobriquet of Baron Knightsbridge.

Chapter Thirty

EMRYS WATCHED THE play of the cards with his usual lazy air of inattention. In fact, his awareness was all on the man seated opposite him at the round table big enough to seat six comfortably.

Emrys reached out to play a trick with a casual flick of the card, and the candlelight caught the gleam of gold off the plain signet ring on his right hand. Annis's ring, of course. The same one he had worn back to the Russian ambassador's party and ensured that the so-called Earl of Tavistock got a good look at when he introduced himself to the young man.

The ring was clearly inspiring a certain fascination in Tavistock. He had difficulty keeping his eyes off it, just as he had the other night. Emrys was wondering how such a callow youth could have terrified Annis for so long. She had told him the first attack occurred seven years ago. Lawrence Redmayne would have been eighteen then, and not yet come into the title. *Why had he left it so long to try again to get the ring from her? It didn't make sense.*

Annis was tucked away upstairs with Sarah to keep her company. He would send for her at the right time.

"You're having the most damnable luck, Ashford," remarked the duke.

"I am, aren't I?" said Emrys, surveying his losses with a faintly bemused look.

"What will you stake next?" said Pendrell with a harsh laugh. "That ring?"

"I may have to," said Emrys with a rueful smile.

Tavistock's eyes flashed. *Really, this is too easy.*

Tavistock cleared his throat and said, "It's an unusual ring, my lord. Where did you get it?" *The bait on the hook!*

"It belonged to my wife's father," he said, casually shuffling and cutting the cards.

Tavistock, in the act of taking a sip of brandy, changed color and choked. "Your wife?" he gasped, when he could speak.

Emrys, enjoying the tightening of his snare, said, "You wouldn't have met my new wife. We were only married recently. She's upstairs with the duchess. Why don't I have the ladies join us for tea?"

Tavistock gaped like a fish, and Emrys rose to ring the bell. When Latham appeared, he ordered tea and requested that Lady Ashford and the duchess join them.

A few minutes later, the door opened, and Annis and Sarah entered the room. Emrys tensed. This was the bit he felt most uncomfortable about, for Annis didn't know that Tavistock was here. *Would she recognize him? Would he recognize her?* It was vital for the verisimilitude of the situation that she react naturally, so he hadn't prepared her. He expected to be fully raked over the coals for that later.

"We didn't expect you to be finished so early, my dear—" she said and came to a complete stop when her eyes alighted on Tavistock. Her color changed, and Emrys was out of his seat and catching her before she could falter.

"My dear, are you perfectly well?" he asked, all solicitude. She threw him an expression that would have cut glass. At the same time his awareness was on Tavistock who, like all of the men, when the ladies entered the room, had risen from his seat. He was now looking warily from one man to the other as if trying to decide what to do. "Take a seat," he murmured to Annis and passed her to the duchess. The two women sat on the couch nearest the fire, but with a view of the table around which the gentlemen were still clustered. He noted Sarah clasping Annis's hand.

"*Have* you met my wife, Tavistock?" he asked with a certain degree of challenge in his voice.

Tavistock opened his mouth and shut it again. Before he could say anything further, the door opened to admit the servants with the tea. Absolute silence reigned while the tea was arranged on the table before the ladies. The servants left, closing the door behind them, and Emrys went on in a conversational tone, "You needn't be afraid to admit the truth. Nothing said in this room will leave it, provided you meet certain conditions."

Tavistock drew himself up with an effort and cleared his throat. "I do not take your meaning, my lord."

"I think you do. However, if you prefer plain speaking, I'm happy to oblige. You threatened my wife a number of years ago with unspeakable violence in order to obtain this!" He held up his hand with the ring on it.

Tavistock blinked and licked his lips. "Th-that wasn't me." He glanced round the room and then at Annis. "It wasn't me, I swear. It was my grandfather." He swallowed visibly. "I never knew about any of it until he was dying last year. And even then, he didn't tell me much. Just that there was a ring that belonged to my father, and if anyone found out about it, it could stop me inheriting. And he muttered something about 'the Pringle girl.' That was all he said. He was raving. I thought he was out of his head.

"I forgot about it until I found my father's old diary and read it through. Then I started making inquiries. Quite by chance I discovered the Pringle Academy for Young Ladies in Bath. Miss Woodrow, my fiancée, went there. I traced Miss Pringle to—to—" He stopped, swallowing, and nodded at the duke. "I traced her to Troubridge's employ. I broke into her room and ransacked it looking for the damned ring! But it wasn't there. So, I left her a note to bring it to me. I just meant to get the ring from her—I didn't mean to do her harm. But she stabbed me!" He threw a fulminating look at Annis. "And she scarred me!" He touched his face. "She left me for dead in the middle of that field! I'm lucky to be alive!"

Annis was white as a sheet and swaying in her seat. Emrys wanted to go to her, but the duchess had her. He needed to finish this and quickly. But before he could say anything, Annis spoke.

"Yes. I think that is probably true. The—the man who attacked me seven years ago was not this man. It must have been my grandfather. He was a bigger man with a gruffer, deeper voice. I never saw his face; he wore a mask. But I got the impression he was older." She pressed her fingers to her trembling lips, tears spilling down her cheeks. Emrys's hand clenched in distress at her anguish. *The sooner this is over the better.*

She went on, "He threatened me to keep me quiet and tried to force me to give up the ring. I don't think he was really sure I had it. He seemed to accept it when I said Mama hadn't given me anything."

"So, you really are my father's brat?" said Tavistock, staring at her in disbelief.

Annis flinched, and Emrys snapped, "She is your father's legitimate daughter. That is why your grandfather tried to obliterate all knowledge of her. Your father married her mother before he married yours."

"So? "Tavistock was breathing fast.

"Janet Pringle Redmayne didn't die until six years ago, and there is no record of the marriage ever being set aside." Emrys paused. "That makes your parents' marriage bigamous, and you a bastard."

Tavistock went white and then red. "You can't prove that!"

"I can actually. The record of the marriage is valid—I checked. And you'll have a devil of a time proving it isn't," said Emrys grimly.

Tavistock clenched his hands in frustration. "What do you expect me to do? Give up the title?"

"Not necessarily." Emrys glanced round the room. "If you provide me assurance, witnessed by each of the persons here, that you will never seek to harm anyone in this room or any member of my family or the families of any of these gentlemen, then the information disclosed in this room will remain here. You have my word as a gentleman."

"And if I don't accept your word?" Tavistock was panting.

Emrys waved to Mr. Gerard Newbury. "Then this gentleman will take you into custody and I will charge you with whatever the law will allow in regard to your attempted assault and terrorizing of my wife."

"And I will bring charges against you for attempted robbery and willful damage to property," said the duke.

The fight seemed to go out of Tavistock at this point, because he sagged and said wearily, "Very well."

"You give us your word that you will take no steps against any of us or our families?" pressed Emrys.

"Yes. Yes, I do."

"Good, because if you do, I will denounce your father as a bigamist and you as a bastard. I will see to it that you lose everything."

Tavistock bowed stiffly. "If that is all, I will bid you good evening, my lord."

Emrys bowed to him, and he left the room.

With the closing of the door, the frozen state of the room thawed, and everyone started talking at once. Emrys ignored them and went to Annis, sitting like a statue on the couch. The duchess rose and let him sit beside her.

"I'm sorry, love. I needed your reaction to be natural to force him to confess. Can you forgive me?"

"I'm not sure," she said. And then she collapsed against him. "Is it really all over?"

"Yes. I doubt that he will bother us again. He would be mad

to try it," Emrys said, wrapping his arms round her.

LATER, AFTER THEIR guests had departed and they were alone in their bed, Annis turned in Emrys's arms and said, "The only thing I don't understand is why Mama kept the secret of their marriage even to her grave. Why would she do that?"

"I doubt we will ever know that, love," he said.

She traced a finger over his chest, thinking back to her last moments with her mother, wishing she had told her—

Sitting up with a jerk she said, "The box!"

"What?" he said bewildered. She pushed back the bedclothes and padded over to the bookcase against the wall where her mother's wooden box sat. She brought it back to the bed and climbed back in.

"Emrys, is there any way there could be something hidden in this box? It was Mama's, and she gifted it to me on her death. It's where she kept the ring. I'm wondering if there might be something else in it? I can't believe she wouldn't tell me . . ."

He took the box from her and examined it, turning it this way and that, upside down. "Annis, bring that candle closer, will you?"

She picked up the beside candle and held it while he ran his fingers over the scratched and dulled surface of the box that must have once been highly polished. He unlatched the clasp and opened the box removing its contents: a collection of papers her mother had left her, things from her childhood, the papers for the school, and her will. He felt around inside the box and said, "Ah! I think—"

"What?"

"It has a false bottom, I think. See, it is much narrower and shallower on the inside than one would expect."

"Why did I never notice that?"

"You weren't looking for it. Now, how to release—" He

frowned, running his fingers all over the inside of the box. "This bit of wood here," he muttered, pointing to a square of wood flush with the inside panel, near the lip at the front. Using his nail, he prized it out and underneath revealed a catch. Lifting it, the bottom of the box popped up. Raising it up on its hinge, a space was revealed and sitting in it an envelope. He drew it out and handed it to Annis, who took it with shaking fingers.

Her name was inscribed on it in her mother's spidery writing.

She looked at him, and he smiled encouragingly, putting the box aside. "Open it."

"I'm almost afraid to," she said with a tremulous smile. "I realize now, looking back, how afraid Mama was all the time, how protective she was of me. I didn't realize it then. I just accepted that Aunt had an anxious disposition. But now I am sure it was because she was afraid. I almost don't want to know what is in this!"

"Annis! I am going to expire of curiosity if you don't open it!" he said, half joking to make her smile. "What's the worst that could happen, love? At least you might know what really happened."

She nodded and opened the envelope, spreading out the single sheet.

Her eyes scanned it briefly then she began to read out loud.

My dearest Annis,

If you are reading this, I am dead, and you have managed to figure out the box's secret. You will have found the ring, too, if I didn't give it to you. There is so much to tell you and so much you will need to forgive me for. The ring contains the information you need to know to prove the legitimacy of your birth. I put it there for you to find.

I kept it all from you for your safety, I hope you will come to understand that with time. One will do anything to protect one's child, and you, my precious baby, are my child.

You must know that I loved him, your father, and he loved me. Of that I am absolutely convinced. He left us to return home because his mother had died, but he always meant to come back to us. I discovered some time later that he had been in an accident, and I was told at the time he was dead.

He'd had a falling out with his family before we met. His father was a harsh man, and he knew he would not approve of our marriage. Your father impressed upon me the need for caution until he could make all right with his sire. I believed, for a while, he had not had that opportunity.

*It was only sometime later that I discovered my mistake. That was when his father, your grandfather, found me and threatened me. Nicolas was truly dead by then. It broke my heart all over again to learn he hadn't died in the accident, only two years later from a congestion of the lungs. But the accident had robbed him of his memories of me and of you. **That** was why he didn't come for us.*

Your main question will be why I covered up the fact that we were married. It is because his father made me. He said he would "eliminate you" if I didn't. Even now I hesitate to tell you all this, for I am afraid that with my death he may still find a way to hurt you.

I pray that the dear Lord will keep you safe, my baby girl, and I am so sorry to have kept the truth from you, but I did it to keep you safe. Please know that you were a much-loved daughter of both your parents, and you were prevented from claiming your birthright through no fault of either of us.

All my love,
Janet Adelaide Redmayne

Annis was sobbing by the end of the letter and Emrys took it gently from her and wrapped her in his arms. Kissing her hair and stroking her back. Her tears slowed and she sniffed. She reached for a handkerchief and blew her nose, wiping her eyes.

"Well, now we know the truth," he said. "Quite romantic, really."

"She must have loved him very much, I think," she said softly.

"Hm. Not as much as I love you," he said, his arms tightening round her.

Annis heart jerked and beat a rapid tattoo in her chest. "What did you say?"

He pulled back enough so he could see her face and said soberly, "I love you, Annis, so much it damned well hurts! The notion of anyone trying to do you harm tears me apart. I think I fell in love with you when I saw you sitting on your luggage in the rain by the side of the road, although I was more than halfway there before that. It's just taken me a while to sort out all my feelings. Can you forgive me for not knowing it sooner, love?"

She stared at him, blinking back tears, and then hugged him tight. "Oh, Emrys, I adore you! You're the perfect husband and father. I thought you were still in love with Caroline, and it was breaking my heart."

"I thought I was, too," he admitted. "I've suspected for a while that you cared for me, and I was worried I didn't deserve it, that I couldn't give you everything you deserve, that Caroline had wrecked me for anyone else." He traced her cheek with a finger.

"I thought I was happy with Caroline, you see," he continued. "But I wasn't. Though I didn't realize that until you showed me the difference. Caro and I were so young when we got married, and I have only recently come to understand that I never really knew her. She kept parts of herself hidden from me and I never suspected. I dare say I kept parts of myself from her, as well, without intending to. I hurt her in lots of little ways that I never appreciated until much later. When she left me, I was heartbroken and angry. Then she died, and I was sad and angry and confused." He sighed out a deep breath. "And then there was you." He smiled. "Beautiful, loving, adorable, practical you." He shook his head. "I couldn't keep my hands off you, and at the same time I was scared as hell I'd hurt you and lose you like I did Caroline. I wanted to be absolutely sure I knew what I was doing before I declared how I felt, because I couldn't bear to hurt you, love."

"Emrys!" She hugged him again. "How could I not love you when you're so wonderful? So kind and affectionate, playful and considerate, so downright adorable."

"I'm not handsome," he objected.

"You are to me."

He sighed contentedly, snuggling down the bed a bit. "I need you, you know. That was why I was so high-handed in convincing you to marry me. It wasn't because I couldn't keep my hands off you—or not only because of that. In truth, you fill up this hungry space inside me that I never knew I had. And I felt it instinctively even then." He stroked her back. "When we were in Bath and I took you so roughly, that was the neediness taking over. I couldn't get close enough to you. I wanted to curl up in your arms and shut out the world. Like a child," he admitted, looking shamefaced and embarrassed.

"Emrys, that is the most beautiful thing you've ever said to me," she whispered softly. Pulling his head down onto her bosom she cradled him. "I'll be your shield, as you are mine, my love," she murmured.

He lifted his head. "Ah Annis, you are priceless. Is there anything you don't understand?" He kissed her pressing her back into the pillows.

"Plenty of things, I'm sure, but we will figure them out together."

"Yes, love, we will." He kissed her again, and there was no more talk for a while.

Postscript

"Emrys?"

"Yes, love?" He looked up from the newspaper he was reading at the breakfast table. Annis sat across from him with a pile of letters at her elbow, as she had been working her way through their mail. But now she was holding a small book with a red cloth cover in her hands with an odd expression on her face.

"What is it?" he asked, dropping the newspaper and leaning forward, concern making his heart flip.

"Lawrence sent me this." She showed him the book. "It's Papa's diary. He said since most of what was in it concerned me, I should have it."

Emrys raised his eyebrows and came round the table to her side. "Are you going to open it?"

She bit her lip. "This is worse than Mama's letter. What if Mama was wrong and he didn't love us after all?"

Emrys crouched down by her chair and put an arm round her shoulders. "Do you want the truth or a fantasy?"

Annis swallowed visibly, and then nodded. "The truth."

"Well, then." He nodded at the book.

She pushed her plate aside and set the book down on the tablecloth and opened the first page. Emrys read over her shoulder.

14th May 1790

My name is Nicolas Benedict Redmayne, and I have lost ten months of my life . . .

Annis read the first entry and then the subsequent ones until she reached the end of the entry for the 24th of November 1792, when she stopped to wipe her eyes and blow her nose.

Emrys rubbed her arm comfortingly.

Annis flicked forward. "There are only four more entries, and they are very brief." She glanced at Emrys. "He must have died soon after this. Didn't your grandmother say it was in January of 1793?"

"Yes." Emrys rubbed his nose. "It doesn't seem as if he found you. Do you want to read the last three entries?"

"I suppose I should."

"You're afraid of what they might say?"

"Not exactly. It's more that I had hoped to have more written in his voice. It's almost as though I can hear him speaking as I read, and being inside his head like this—it gives me a glimpse of him. Although it's quite obvious he is not the man Mama fell in love with. The accident changed him, robbed him of so much . . ."

"Yes, that is true, yet the essence of him is there, I think. He loves his children. He would have adored you. Speaking as a father, I can tell you that daughters play havoc with your heart. I can't even express how much I love Lizzie and Charlie and the lengths to which I'd go to protect them."

Annis squeezed his hand with a wry smile. "Yes, he does seem as if he would have been a devoted husband and father, doesn't he?"

Emrys nodded and kissed the top of her head as she leaned it against his chest.

She sat up and turned the page to the next entry.

5th December 1792

I've exhausted my search of the county and widened it to the neighboring one. I will work outward from here. I will not rest until I have found them.

25th December 1792

It's Christmas day and we are snowbound. I am forced to remain at home until the snow eases. It is Lawrence's first Christmas; I should be paying attention.

5th of January 1793

I went to MC today. I recognized it as soon as I arrived. I even found the house where we lived and the church we were married in. I remember now. Everything. As I stared at the record of our marriage, I realized with horror that I was a bigamist. My marriage to Damaris is invalid and Lawrence is a bastard.

The poor vicar thought I was going to collapse, I went so pale. He gave me a drink and I left, my brain in a whirl. How could I forget that I was married? And where was she, my precious J.?

My questions elicited the fact that she left MC some weeks after I returned to my home, but no one here knows where she went. We had lived here under a different name, Benedict, my second name, for fear my father would find us.

And now there is an even more pressing reason that he not find my dear J. and A., for he would be horrified to discover our Lawrence, the much-needed heir to the earldom, is a bastard. I shudder to think what he might do should he find out. I must find J. with all haste and protect her and my daughter.

I shall spend the night here and continue my search in the morning. I am weary, and my throat is scratchy. The weather is beastly cold, and my feet are frozen in my wet boots.

7th January 1793

I have been forced to return home, for I am running a fever and coughing my lungs up. I feel wretched. Stay safe, my loves, until

I can find you. I will come as soon as I am recovered.

The last word was scrawled and blotched, as if the writer had lost control of the pen.

Annis thumbed through the rest of the book, but there was nothing else. She wiped her eyes and sniffed.

"Well, at least we know the whole story now," said Emrys hugging her close. He hated it when she cried.

"Yes. I wonder what would have happened had he survived his illness? Would he have found us?" She sighed. "I wish Mama could have read this. She would have known he loved her and was prevented from coming to her by his loss of memory."

"She did know. She said so in her letter. She believed in him to the last. That's devotion."

"It is, isn't it?" Annis looked up, still sniffing. "I wonder if I would be that strong?"

"You are that strong, my darling. You're your mother's daughter."

"Perhaps." Annis said softly, closing the book and hugging it to her chest. Emrys absently and inappropriately envied the book. His obsession with his wife was showing no signs of abating.

He drew her up into his arms and hugged her. "I love you," he murmured, nuzzling her neck, as she dropped the book on the table and surrendered to his attentions.

"I love you, too," she whispered, smiling up at him misty eyed.

He was the luckiest devil in the world.

Epilogue

Christmas 1818, The Castle, Leicestershire

THE HOUSE WAS full of children, not that anyone seemed to mind, least of all Emrys. His own small fry were enjoying all the delights snow and ice could provide, with snowman building, snowball fights, sledding, and ice skating on the lake, all provided by mother nature.

His memories of Ewen's fall into the lake in summer still vivid in his mind, he couldn't help but be nervous of the ice cracking and dragging his precious offspring down to a frozen death. But after he, the duke, the duke's brothers, and Ravenshaw all thoroughly tested the ice, he was grudgingly brought to agree that it was safe enough for the children.

A pity Pendrell wasn't there. If it could carry his weight, it could carry anything. However, he was at his country house in Sussex, working on some new find uncovered by a land slip on the coast. Apparently, it was a pressing matter to record and recover the artifacts before wind and weather washed them out to sea.

Emrys ventured out with Annis, Ewen securely between them. Nothing and no one was going to stop him keeping hold of his son's hand as he and Annis traversed the lake in lazy circles, while his girls and the Watsons skated past them at speed, shrieking and giggling when someone fell over.

Returned to the house and changed into dry clothes, the company assembled for Christmas Eve dinner before a roaring fire. The children packed off upstairs for their own meal and bed, the adults settled in for a convivial evening. Seated on the couch with his arm round Annis, Emrys reflected that happiness was an ephemeral thing, easily snatched away.

He watched Rob bending over Sarah with every appearance of loving concern as she placed a hand on her swollen belly. She was six months along now. She smiled up at Rob, and he sat beside her as she placed his hand where hers had been. The babe was kicking, Emrys guessed. He glanced down at Annis, talking to Deborah, Sarah's sister, and knew a moment of longing to see her like that, swollen with his child.

She hadn't caught yet, despite the amount of attention he'd lavished on her. But then she wasn't as young as Sarah, who was only twenty-three. Annis was twenty-eight. He hoped it wasn't too late for them to be blessed with a child, too. It shouldn't be— he knew of cases where women had children well into their forties. And it had only been four months. Besides, even without more children, their life was full and happy.

He allowed himself to be drawn into a conversation with Hereward and Ruth, Sarah's next sister after Deborah, on the best way to poultice a horse. All the while though, he was conscious of Annis beside him, the warmth of her leg pressed against his, the comfort of her snugged under his arm. The comfort she represented to him had not abated. If anything, it had grown even stronger with the passage of time. She was as essential to him as air and water.

After the tea tray, they retired to bed, checking on the children on their way. This was a nightly ritual unless he was away from home, in which case he did it by himself when he got in.

Standing by the girls' bed, which they shared, with his arms still securely round Annis, he smiled at their angelic faces slightly flushed in sleep, curls escaping from their plaits.

"Beautiful, aren't they?" he murmured in her ear.

She nodded bending to straighten the coverlet and ensure they were snuggly warm. "So sweet," she whispered, planting a soft kiss on each forehead. He did the same and Lizzie murmured something that he thought might be "'Night, Papa" without opening her eyes.

Finally arriving in their own room, they went through their usual routine of undressing, washing, teeth cleaning, in a companionable silence. They had grown accustomed to each other's habits by now and developed that comfortable way of being that made him realize even more starkly how different this was from his first marriage. With Annis it just felt right.

His limpet habits in his sleep hadn't abated. He still woke wrapped round her like an octopus. *Not that she seems to mind, but still . . . am I still insecure?*

She had climbed into bed with a book, and he followed, sliding under the covers, bollock naked as always. She wore a nightgown in the cooler months, but he found wearing anything, even in winter, stifling.

"You want to read?" he said, nodding at the book.

"Depends," she said with a smile. "I have a feeling you want to talk; you've been awfully quiet. Lots of thinking going on behind those eyes?" she asked, tapping his temple.

He smiled ruefully. "How do you do it? You always know."

She shrugged. put the book aside, and settled back against the pillows, holding out a hand to take one of his. "Tell me."

He sighed. "I'm not sure I can articulate it very well."

She smiled encouragingly.

"Come here," he said roughly. "I think better when you're in my arms."

She came willingly, resting her head on his chest, her legs tangling with his. "You're sounding quite growly, my love," she said.

"Am I?" he said getting comfortable with his arms round her.

"Hm," she murmured. "So, tell me what's bothering you."

"Nothing, really. In fact I'm really happy. That's rather the problem."

"Waiting for the other shoe to drop?"

He snorted. "I suppose."

She nodded, tracing a finger in his chest hairs, which he liked. His cock stirred a bit. "I know the feeling," she said. "I feel the same way. I am so happy, but I keep expecting it to get snatched away."

"Yes, that's it exactly!" he said, hugging her tight. "I get this desperate feeling sometimes and want to hang onto you, as if you're the only thing that's stopping me from drowning. It's not healthy, but I can't seem to help it."

"I like it," she confessed. "Makes me feel you need me."

"I do," he said husky voiced, nuzzling her hair. "You are happy?"

"Deliriously. Didn't I just say so?" She looked up at him.

"But if you weren't, you'd tell me?" he asked, his anxiety breaking through.

Her face softened, and she cupped his face with her hand. "Of course. I wouldn't pull the rug out from under you like Caro did."

He let out a breath and sighed. "You always understand. Better than I ever do. You're so *clever*, Annis. God, I love you!"

He kissed her and a bit later he said, "I think your growly husband wants to fuck you."

"Yes, please," she said, pressing closer and rubbing against his thigh.

Which made him groan and peel off her nightgown, throwing it over the side of the bed, and nuzzle into her breasts for a feast. "Delicious," he murmured round a mouthful of nipple and breast. With his hands all over her, he nudged her legs apart and nestled his cock against her lips rubbing slowly up and down.

She gasped, her hips jerking under him. "Emrys!"

"Good?" he growled against her throat, cupping and squeezing her breasts.

"Yes!"

"Hm." He grunted, adjusting his cock to slide down and

engage her body. With a neat thrust of his hips, he joined them and began a steady drive to completion. She kept pace with him every step, her eyes glued to his. He pressed his palms to hers beside her head and kept driving into her. It felt good. It always felt good, but there was an element of total openness in her gaze tonight, as if she was giving him not only her body, but her soul.

He made a noise in his throat that came from his gut. "I'm yours, Annis," he breathed. "All yours." His body surged, the pleasure rising with each stroke. "I love you," he whispered brokenly as the pleasure peaked, and he lost control of his body. He felt her body tighten on him as she groaned. The orgasm flowed between them like two streams mingling, his seed loosed in a flood of heat, pulses of pleasure swamping his senses.

"Annis," his voice croaked in the middle as his body gave up the last of its seed, and he collapsed on her, his heart thudding heavily in his chest. Her arms held him, her legs tucked over the back of his, as he drifted in a haze of pleasure and connection. Whatever just happened, he didn't want it to stop.

Finally, he lifted his head and said, "There are no words for that."

She stroked his face and nodded. "I love you," she said and kissed his nose.

He laughed, and a lightness filled him. Separating them gently, he flopped onto his side and drew her close.

"I love you Annis Benedicta Fitzgerald. Never leave me."

"I won't," she murmured against his chest.

"I think I believe you," he said with gentle smile over the top of her head. He closed his eyes, holding his wife close and slept, secure in the knowledge she would still be there in the morning.

ACKNOWLEDGMENTS

I must thank my friend and fellow writer, Melanie Page, again for reading the first draft of this book and, through her insight and stinging wit, making the second draft so much stronger. Thank you, Mel. You never let me down.

I would also like to thank the team at Dragonblade: Kathryn for taking a chance on me and my series; my lovely Editor Courtney Brown who is a delight to work with—you are amazing; and the rest of the team who have made this book shine.

ABOUT THE AUTHOR

Wren St. Claire lives in Brisbane with one confused Mini Schnauzer and six mad Bengal cats. She writes Steamy Historical Romance, where the heroes spoil the heroine and readers get to tag along for the ride, enjoying a roller coaster of emotions. Wren has a Masters Degree in Egyptology and used to lead tours to Egypt up until the Revolution of the Arab Spring in 2011.

www.ingramcontent.com/pod-product-compliance
Lightning Source LLC
Chambersburg PA
CBHW072111300726
48975CB00003B/776